THE UFO CASEBOOK

Captain Kevin D. Randle, USAF, Ret.

P9-CFF-851

WARNER BOOKS

A Warner Communications Company

Author's Note: The names of certain individuals have been changed herein to protect their privacy.

WARNER BOOKS EDITION

Cover photo by IMAGE BANK/Chris Alan Witt
Cover design by Rolf Erickson

Warner Books, Inc.
666 Fifth Avenue
New York, N.Y. 10103

 A Warner Communications Company

Printed in the United States of America

First Printing: September, 1989

10 9 8 7 6 5 4 3 2

Contents

THE SIGHTINGS . . .

NEW MEXICO, 1947: Two separate sites are dicovered, yielding a large disc-shaped craft, debris made of substances previously unknown on earth, inscription in unfamiliar hieroglyphics, and the remains of several alien humanoids.

LUBBOCK, TEXAS, 1951: Formations of flying objects, giving off soft, bluish lights, are seen by dozens of witnesses.

SOUTH AMERICA, 1957: A man is abducted aboard a vessel and subjected to an experiment testing human reproduction.

SOCORRO, NEW MEXICO, 1964: A police officer hears a loud roar, spies a flash of light, and encounters two small figures in white. They flee back into their ship, which rises from the earth spitting a blue flame.

. . . AND THE SUPPRESSION

WASHINGTON, D.C., The Present: These are UFO reports the government has been secretly investigating, while publicly denying their existence. But the facts are out. You'll find them in this book . . .

THE UFO CASEBOOK

October 1988: Introduction

UFO research is an ongoing activity. Each case is unique and there are no simple answers. People's memories fade and the facts become distorted. Debunkers and skeptics feed on that, spilling half-truths and half-baked notions in books and magazines until the issue is clouded and the truth is lost.

The *Casebook* is the result of twenty-five years of personal research into the phenomenon. I have, over the years, been a skeptic, a believer, a researcher, and an investigator. I have looked into hundreds of cases and traveled from one coast to the other looking for the answers. The end product is the book that you are about to read.

Although this introduction is dated October 1988, it is, in fact, February 1989. The original manuscript was delivered in October, accepted, and put into production. But then, just days ago, I had the opportunity to travel into the Roswell, New Mexico (*See July 2, 1947: Roswell, New Mexico*) area to interview people involved in this important case. I had meetings scheduled with Frank Joyce, the radio reporter in Roswell who remembers things about the crash. We met with a man who has lived in the area his entire life who provided some interesting insights to the case. I found the field where the UFO crashed in 1947 and understand, completely, why Mac Brazel took six days to alert the authorities. It took me half a day to get there, and that was with modern roads. In the summer of 1947, it had to be even worse. But, most important, I met Bill Brazel, the man whose father originally found the downed disc. Because of this, two chapters have been rewritten—again, to reflect the new information we uncovered.

Investigation of the UFO phenomena is one loaded with frustrations. It is a topic, if true, that could change life as we know it on Earth. It has the potential of destroying industries and causing us to rethink some of our sacred beliefs. Maybe that is why there is such a reluctance by so many to even enter into debates on it.

In the last few weeks, I have come across the story of a crashed saucer in Montana (see *October 1988: The Montana Crash*). I had little documentation. In fact, in the beginning, all I had was one paragraph taken from the *Cedar Rapids Gazette*. Wanting to learn more, I checked other editions of the paper, but there was no update anywhere. Since it was a *Gazette* story, I walked into the newspaper's city room with a copy of the clipping, which says that a pilot claimed to have knocked down a flying saucer.

That was all I had—just a short report that a pilot had downed a "flying disc." I wanted help in tracking the story. The reporter I talked to was very helpful. She suggested a couple of directions to go, but she wasn't interested in the story. I wasn't a crackpot making something up. The source, for the *Gazette* reporter, was unimpeachable, since it was her very own newspaper, but she didn't care to learn any more about it. She was too busy with a city council meeting to worry about the alleged crash of a flying saucer.

I left, later learning much more about the crash, but it wasn't with the help of the media. They don't seem to care about such things. It would take some work to run down the story, and why do that when they have other things to do?

The Roswell case is the same way—no interest by those outside the field. I've talked to people who tell me they don't accept the Roswell case because in an age of Watergate, Iran-Contra hearings, and a government that has more leaks than hundred-year-old plumbing, they don't believe the story could be kept hidden. I point out there have been leaks—dozens of them—but that falls on deaf ears. They didn't see anything about it in the papers back then, and they haven't seen anything about it now, so it just didn't happen.

And the papers don't print it because they aren't interested in it. We're talking about a story that is forty years old and if there was anything to it, there would have been something in the papers about it.

What's grabbed the headlines in the last decade have been the reports of cattle mutilations and UFOs (*See February 1975: The Minnesota Mutilations*). And although I spent time in Minnesota, Colorado, Wisconsin, Texas, and Arkansas, I found no evidence that linked the two. But more than ten years after the fact, there are still reports that UFOs have been mutilating cattle.

And there are the Allende letters (*see April 1956: The Allende Letters*). There have been books and dozens of articles on them, and all they are is a series of letters from one man trying to stop Morris K. Jessup from writing any more books on flying saucers. Yet they have to be examined and reexamined to the exclusion of some of the more important cases. I interviewed Sidney Sherby, who was with the Office of Naval Research when the book arrived. I wrote to Charles Berlitz about them. I talked to Jim and Coral Lorenzen, and to Brad Steiger about them. I learned that it's time to forget about them and move on to other things.

In fact, that is why the selection for the material included in here was made. Some cases that are of great importance have been overlooked, while others of dubious value have been exhaustively researched. It's time to put that all into perspective, and *The UFO Casebook* has tried to do that.

I did more than travel around looking into the well-publicized cases. I was in Brooksville, Florida to talk to John Reeves about his sighting. I've been through the Project Bluebook files, searching for answers there. I've been through the Condon Committee records at the University of Colorado, looking for information. I talked to the people at the Institute of Meteoritics at the University of New Mexico about Dr. La Paz and his work on the green fireballs.

The list of places I've gone and the people I've talked to is huge. For the El Indio crash, I spent days searching for the names of the witnesses and only recently succeeded. I talked to Delbert Newhouse about the Tremonton movie, and dozens of witnesses of the October 1973 sightings, including Charles Hickson, Pat Roach, Susan Ramstead, and Leigh Proctor. Air Force officers gave me the inside story of Kinross, and police officers helped me in the Pineville, Missouri investigations. I spent two weeks there, learning all that I could.

I could go on with this, but the purpose of *The UFO Casebook* is to examine some of the most important cases in the field. It is designed to provide the serious researcher with the best information available on the physical evidence cases, the photographic cases, and some of the more famous hoaxes, so that he or she can move on to other things. There is so much work left to be done that we can't waste time going over the same ground, again and again. Researchers waste too much time duplicating each other's work. It's time to stop that and get on to other cases, other reports.

My findings are based on over twenty-five years of investigation. I have talked to hundreds of witnesses, gone to the sites of the reports, and had the materials analyzed. To those who claim that there couldn't have been a cover-up because there would have been leaks, I say, "Here are the leaks." To those who say there is no evidence, "Here are the names of my sources. Check it yourself." And to those who say that there couldn't be flying saucers, I ask, "Why not?"

June 24, 1947: The Modern Era Begins

No account of the UFO phenomenon would be complete without a mention of the Kenneth Arnold sighting. Although it was not the first to be recorded that summer, and it certainly wasn't the most spectacular, it was the one that sparked the whole craze. Arnold got the national press, and it was in the accounts of his sighting that the term "flying saucer" was coined. It marked a definite beginning, and although Donald

H. Menzel thought he had a solution to the sighting, to most researchers, Arnold's report remains unidentified.

Arnold, a Boise, Idaho, businessman, was also a private pilot. He flew in the Northwest—Washington, Oregon, Idaho, Montana, and Wyoming. On June 24, 1947, he was returning home, with a detour into the Yakima, Washington, area to help in the aerial search for a missing troop transport.

At about three in the afternoon, as he flew at nine thousand feet, a flash of light caught his attention. He turned and saw nine cresent-shaped objects bobbing and weaving through the clear air, flying in an echelon formation. They were flat, like pie tins, with highly polished surfaces. It was the bobbing and weaving that caught the sunlight, flashing it into Arnold's eyes, alerting him.

Years later, Arnold would say that he thought they were some kind of military craft, belonging to the Army or Navy. The thing that fascinated him was the fact he could see no tails. They were disclike, flat, and moving at a high rate of speed. Even with that, they didn't seem to be hostile, and posed no threat to him or anyone on the ground. He couldn't understand the uproar when he landed.

From that point, a brief news conference held at Pendleton, a small field in Oregon, the world learned of the "saucerlike" objects that skipped through the air. The Air Force would later label the case a "mirage," but Arnold was never convinced of that.

But the damage had been done. The world had heard of flying saucers, and the debate would rage from that point on.

July 2, 1947: Roswell, New Mexico

In the years that followed Kenneth Arnold's first sighting, there were rumors of wreckage from flying discs and crashed UFOs. For the most part, the stories seemed to be little more than the ramblings of men and women who wanted to see their names in print. Secret reports, secret buildings, and secret meetings seemed to be the stuff of science fiction, not of government investigation. Those telling the stories rarely had anything to offer in the way of proof, and researchers studying the cases pronounced them hoaxes (*see 1948: The UFO Crashes Begin*).

But in 1980 came the first rumors about a crash near Roswell, New Mexico. At first, the reaction about the Roswell incident was the same as it had been with all the others—complete skepticism. It seemed that in each case of a crashed saucer, the rumors and falsehoods outweighed the few facts. No one could confirm anything. There would be an occasional report from a researcher who claimed that he had talked to someone who had been there, or who had seen the discs, or who had seen the bodies, but he couldn't reveal his source.

Roswell was different—There weren't mysterious sources and unconfirmed statements but there were hints of something going on, and there were witnesses who could be named. There were, and are, government documents that suggest something did happen there.

The story, as it has been pieced together by several researchers, and as it is currently accepted, suggests that on July 2, 1947, just eight days after Kenneth Arnold splattered flying discs all over the newspapers, the people of Roswell, New Mexico, saw a large, disc-shaped object fly over their town. They reported that the craft seemed to have stability problems. William (Mac) Brazel, a local rancher, reported that he heard a tremendous explosion later that night, but thought nothing of it. There are reports that a thunderstorm was in progress, so the sudden explosion was believed to be a thunderclap.

The next day, Brazel found a widespread debris field on his ranch. He picked up some of the metal, but thought nothing more of it, at that moment. Bill Brazel, Mac's son, told me he thought his dad had filled his Jeep pickup with the larger pieces of debris, transported them to the ranch headquarters, and stored them in a shed. Later, hearing stories of the flying discs, he alerted the authorities in Roswell, supposedly first going to the newspaper, where he was told to tell the sheriff. Word reached Major Jesse Marcel at the Roswell Army Air Field, and he went out to investigate. Marcel collected some samples and returned to the base, where Colonel William Blanchard ordered Lieutenant William Haut to release a statement confirming that the wreckage of a flying disc had been recovered in the Roswell area.

Marcel reported that he had found the debris scattered over an area nearly a mile long and several hundred feet wide. According to him, the material recovered included small beams with hieroglyphics on them; metal that looked like balsa wood and was as light, but couldn't be dented with a sledgehammer, although it was flexible, and would not burn, no matter how much heat was applied; some brown, extremely strong, parchmentlike paper; and metal that looked like tinfoil but wasn't.

Bill Brazel told me that the foil could be folded in half and then left to open itself again. There was no crease in it when it was flat. He rolled it into a tube and let it unroll itself. Brazel said that it was fun to play with and it got him interested in the rest of the pieces he'd found.

The one thing that Marcel was sure about, when interviewed later, was that there were no bodies in the wreckage. They had found part of a craft, but not the whole thing.

Marcel returned to the crash site to retrieve every scrap of metal that could be found. There was one four-foot chunk that was difficult to transport. He was ordered to take it to Carswell Air Force Base in Fort Worth, bypassing many bases that were closer. He loaded it into his "Carryall" and returned to the Roswell base, where the wreckage was loaded into a B-29 and flown to Carswell.

At Carswell, the debris was transferred, under guard, to another aircraft for transport to Wright Field in Ohio. At Carswell, Roger Ramey took charge and ordered Marcel back to Roswell.

A second news conference was held, where the official story was released. Mac Brazel had found the remains of an experimental balloon that carried a radar reflecting dish. That was why there was initial confusion about the wreckage. Brazel was held by the Army for nearly a week while the crash site was examined closely. When he returned home, he refused to talk to anyone about what had happened, saying only that they had scared the hell out of him.

Some of the story leaked to the press and went out over the teletype wires. In Albuquerque, a station KSKW had its broadcast interrupted with the warning, from the FBI, to: "Cease transmission. Repeat. Cease transmission. National security item. Do not transmit."

The story doesn't end there, however. Another crash site was reported, this one west of Socorro, New Mexico, near the small town of Magdalena. (There is some speculation that Barnett might have been closer to the Brazel crash site, and researchers are still trying to learn the truth.) The witness, Grady L. Barnett, claimed that he had found the remains of a disc-shaped craft, twenty-five to thirty feet in diameter, in the desert. While he was examining it, a small group of people arrived who said they were part of an archeological research team from the University of Pennsylvania.

Barnett recalled that they were all standing around looking at bodies that had fallen to the ground. He thought there were others in the machine, and that all the creatures were dead. He tried to get closer. He described them as humanoid with round heads, small eyes, and no hair. All were dressed in gray, one-piece suits that didn't have zippers or buttons or belts. Barnett claimed that he was close enough to touch them, but didn't. The military had arrived, taken charge, and escorted him away.

Like Barnett, Brazel kept quiet about the case. Although he refused to talk about it, his son Bill, interviewed years later, made much of the crash. He even talked about returning to the site later and finding more of the metal. When he told friends that he had it, Air Force investigators showed up and requested that he surrender the material to them. In a personal interview conducted in 1989, I was able to confirm the story, along with everything else that happened on the Brazel ranch in 1947.

(There was one other problem. It seems that many researchers have called the Brazel home to ask the same questions, over and over. They are polite to the callers, but would prefer to be left alone. The story is true as it appears here, as it has appeared on various television reports, and as it appears in *The Roswell Incident*, by Charles Berlitz and William Moore. Brazel doesn't need to confirm that again and refuses to answer questions on the phone.)

Marcel, interviewed in the mid-1980s by researchers, talked about what the material looked like. He talked about the metal being light-weight and almost indestructible. News reports released within days of the Roswell incident talk about tinfoil and balsa wood. Warrant Officer Irving Newton at Fort Worth was quoted by some sources as saying that the material found was a balloon. According to Newton, "The object looks like a six-pointed star, is silvery in appearance, and rises in the air like a kite, mounted to a one-hundred-gram balloon."

Marcel was convinced that the object he saw, and the wreckage he picked up, was not that of a balloon. He was familiar with weather balloons and certainly wouldn't have talked about metal that couldn't be dented if all he had was some aluminum and tinfoil. And, the wreckage of a balloon certainly wouldn't have filled the aircraft, as Marcel claimed it did.

During my interview with Brazel, I mentioned that many researchers had said his father had found a balloon. Brazel's answer was a quick, one-word reply that suggested those researchers were mistaken. The material he had found was nothing like anything made on Earth.

The wreckage of a balloon which, according to news accounts printed the following day, had been identified quickly by everyone involved, would not have been shipped from Carswell under guard. Someone along the way would have seen that it was a balloon and stopped the silliness, but that didn't happen. General Ramey intercepted Marcel at Carswell, sent him back to Roswell, and then sent the wreckage on to Wright Field. And, the pilot who flew the wreckage to Ohio has been located and has confirmed that that he took something unusual to Wright Field.

There is a report that Marcel was livid when he learned what was being said about Roswell. He apparently stormed into Blanchard's office demanding a court martial because the news releases made him look incompetent. He wanted the truth to come out. He had handled the material and had tested it. There was no way that it could have been a weather balloon.

Interestingly, Colonel Blanchard was sent on leave the next day. Reports are that he was in trouble for allowing the story about the debris to be released. In fact, Blanchard had ordered the news release over the objections of some of the other officers present.

Given the fact that the Air Force (Army Air Corps at that time) knew about Roswell, that the intelligence officer at Roswell was involved from the beginning, and that the material was shipped to ATIC at Wright Field, the natural place to begin a paper search for information seemed to be Project Bluebook. Bluebook didn't exist in 1947, but Project Sign, Bluebook's predecessor, did. The files go back to the summer of 1947. Arnold's sighting is filed there among dozens of other sightings, many of them being resolved as balloons. But there is no reference to Roswell.

Since the feeling among many debunkers that Roswell was a hoax at worst and a misidentification at best, there would be no reason not to file the case. It wasn't a flying disc or a flying saucer; it was a weather balloon.

I searched the Bluebook/Sign files for a reference to Roswell. I found physical evidence cases that covered small discs found in Black River Falls, Wisconsin, and Shreveport, Louisiana. Both cases were hoaxes, pure and simple, and both had files in Bluebook. But not Roswell.

One thing I did find in the Bluebook files that was interesting was a case from Circleville, Ohio. Sherman Campbell reported finding the wreckage of a flying disc on his farm. According to the report, ". . . it was in the shape of a six-pointed star, fifty inches high and forty-eight inches wide, and covered with tinfoil. It weighed about two pounds. Attached to the top were the remains of a balloon."

And interestingly, the description of the balloon found in Ohio is almost identical, in words and tone, to the news releases from Roswell and from General Ramey. They moved quickly to stop rumors from Roswell and in 1947 there were so many stories about the flying discs that it wasn't hard to bury Roswell at the time.

As it stands now, the search for proof that the Roswell incident took place is still on. Unlike most of the reports of crashes near Aztec, New Mexico, or Phoenix, Arizona, (*see 1948: The UFO Crashes Begin*) we are provided with a list of witnesses as well as other documentation that suggests the Roswell incident is real.

The significance of the Bluebook files is not in what we found, but in what we didn't. With so many military people involved, there should have been a mention. With the fact that Marcel, an intelligence officer with the 509th Bomb Group (atomic), picked up the pieces and put them into the intelligence system, there should have been a reference to it. This suggests that the reports and evidence went not to Project Sign, but somewhere else. Until all those secret government records are declassified, we'll have to stumble in the dark.

July 31, 1947: Maury Island

Only a month after Arnold's report and three weeks after the Roswell incident, two Air Force officers (in reality they were Army Air Corps officers; the Air Force wouldn't exist for another six months) heard about a UFO physical evidence case. This might be the conclusive evidence that everyone wanted and this was the sighting that would set the tone for the next several years. It should be noted that the lid had been clamped so tight on the Roswell sighting that not even Ed Ruppelt, who headed Project Bluebook at one time, was aware of the case.

It was on July 31, 1947, that the intelligence unit at Hamilton Air Force Base, California, first learned that two harbor patrolmen had recovered what they claimed to be metal from a flying saucer. Lieutenant Frank Brown got a call from a man he had met while on the Arnold investigation. Ruppelt identified the caller as an airline pilot named Simpson, but it was later learned that the caller was Kenneth Arnold himself. Because Brown knew Arnold and respected his judgment, Brown decided he would follow the lead.

Within an hour, Brown, with a Captain Davidson, left California for Maury Island, near Tacoma, Washington, the site of the UFO report. Brown and Davidson met Arnold at the airport and they all returned to Arnold's room for a quick briefing. While there, Arnold mentioned that he had received some money from a Chicago publisher for his part in the investigations. Although it was never revealed, further investigation suggests that Ray Palmer was the publisher. With the report of physical evidence, photographs, and the injury of a young boy, Arnold felt that the story was getting too big and that he should have help, so he had called Brown.

Arnold had already heard the whole report about Maury Island but he wanted the intelligence officers to hear it firsthand. He delayed telling them any more than they already knew because he didn't want to prejudice their investigations. The two harbor patrolmen were called, but they were already on their way to the hotel.

Once again, Ruppelt identified the men by using fictitious names, but their real names have been published since. The men, Dahl and Crissman, along with Dahl's son and a pet dog, claimed that they had been operating in the area of Maury Island in June 1947. It was a bleak, overcast day with a relatively low cloud cover. Everyone's attention was suddenly drawn to six doughnut-shaped objects that appeared just below the clouds. The objects dashed toward the boat, stopping only five hundred feet above it.

Dahl said that he thought one of the objects was in trouble because the other five circled it. The objects were hovering so everyone got a good look at them and described them as one hundred feet in diameter with a hole twenty-five feet in diamter in the center. The surface appeared to be bright metal and no one heard any noise or saw any type of trail behind the craft.

While the UFOs hovered, Dahl took pictures. He photographed one of the objects as it maneuvered to the disabled craft and appeared to make contact. Minutes later, when the contact was broken, there was a dull thud, and the UFO began to spit "sheets" of light metal from the hole in the center. As the metal floated down, the object began to throw off a harder, rocklike substance and this fell to the beach on Maury Island. The harbor patrolmen turned their boat toward the island and the rocklike slag fell onto the deck, damaging the boat, burning the arm of Dahl's son, and killing their dog.

On the beach, the man gathered samples of the "slag" and kept an eye on the UFOs that were leaving the area at high speed. Dahl tried to radio for help, but the reception was so bad that he couldn't make contact. After gathering the samples, the men returned to their base, obtained first aid for the burns, and reported the incident to their supervisor. The supervisor didn't believe the story until he went to the island and saw the metal. That convinced him. Both Dahl and Crissman agreed this was the whole story as it had happened. They had left out nothing.

That, however, wasn't the end of it. The next morning, Dahl claimed that a strange man dressed in a dark suit came to visit him. The man was aware of the incident, described the scene to Dahl, and suggested that he forget all about it.

Later that same day, Dahl had the pictures developed, but they were badly "fogged" and spotted. One man suggested that the film had been exposed to radiation.

Next, Arnold said that he had problems with mysterious callers and tipsters. Somehow the Tacoma newspaper was getting a great deal of information about the discussions going on in his hotel room. If none of the men in the room were leaking the story, how was the paper finding out about it? Arnold, with help, made a thorough search of the room and found no hidden microphone. He was completely baffled.

Brown and Davidson didn't stay long after hearing the story. They asked a few questions and tried to leave. Dahl, or Crissman, offered some of the metal, but Brown was reluctant to take it. Some have claimed that Brown knew the story was a hoax at that point and didn't want to become more involved. He had recognized the metal as worthless slag.

Brown and Davidson returned to McChord Air Force Base in Washington and while waiting for their plane told the intelligence officer there that they thought the story was a hoax. Quickly, they outlined why they felt that way but were reluctant to talk about it, feeling that the Air Force had already wasted too much time, effort, and money on the case. It was a good thing that they did talk to the intelligence officer at McChord because a few hours later they were both dead in a plane crash.

Newspapers hinted that the plane had been sabotaged and that it was carrying classified material. The hint was that the classified material was the case file and metal samples from Maury Island. That is not true. Classified material was on the plane but it had nothing to do with UFOs.

Later, there were reports that the harbor patrolmen disappeared. Ed Ruppelt suggested that they should have disappeared "right into Puget Sound." He said that Maury Island was possibly the dirtiest hoax in UFO history mainly because it indirectly cost the lives of two men.

The official Air Force report on Maury Island claimed that they knew it was a hoax from the very beginning. Everyone seemed to know it except Arnold and the Chicago publisher. Both Dahl and Crissman later admitted that the rock fragments had nothing to do with UFOs. They had said that the rocks were from UFOs because that was what the Chicago publisher wanted to hear. They had written to the man (Palmer), enclosing a small piece of rock. They had done it as a joke, but it had snowballed. Palmer then called Arnold and asked him to investigate.

Neither man could ever produce the photographs. That, of course, makes the case very shaky. If they had pictures of six UFOs, they would have taken care to protect them, but both men said that the pictures had been misplaced. They never said that they had been stolen, only lost.

One of the men, Dahl or Crissman, was the mysterious caller to the newspapers. That was how the Tacoma paper had found out what was happening behind closed doors. If the story had been true, Dahl and Crissman wouldn't need to leak parts of it for publicity. In a few days they would have been very famous almost immediately.

And, neither Dahl nor Crissman were harbor patrolmen. They owned a couple of beat-up salvage boats and worked the sound looking for floating lumber. That also ruled out part of their story and destroyed the little credibility they had left.

The airplane crash was just that—an aircraft accident. An engine had caught fire and a wing came off. It hadn't been "shot" down by UFOs to prevent the men from reporting. If that had been the purpose, the UFO failed. The box of fragments forced on Brown was recovered from the wreckage and was available for analysis.

Brown and Davidson had smelled the hoax from the beginning and had gotten out as fast as possible, after they confirmed it. That was the reason they didn't want the fragments. They were afraid they would inadvertently lend a note of credibility to the story. At McChord, an unidentified informer had already told the intelligence officer that the metal was worthless slag, which confirmed what Brown had believed.

Brown and Davidson didn't tell Arnold about the hoax because he had been so thoroughly taken. It is understandable and doesn't reflect on him. If anything is to be said about Arnold's handling of the investigation, it should be good. He had the sense to call in others when he found himself in over his head. It may have been a disservice on the parts of Brown and Davidson for not telling him the truth, but they didn't want to embarrass him.

The final point, the one that convinces some that Maury Island wasn't a hoax, is that neither Dahl nor Crissman were prosecuted for inventing the sighting. Air Force records show that it was considered, seriously considered. In fact, an investigation was made to determine whether or not the government had a case. The outcome was that neither man had wanted to cause trouble, but the story, which started as a harmless joke, had snowballed. The deaths of the two officers and the loss of the plane were not directly caused by the story and nothing would be accomplished by prosecuting Dahl and Crissman.

The last chapter to the Maury Island story was written months after it had begun. Air Force officers, to keep from prejudicing their case while they were considering prosecution, did not leak any information about the hoax. They withheld it. When it was finally released, it was old news, and almost no one reads old news. The public was left with the mistaken belief that the Air Force had no answers for the Maury Island story. That simply is not true and the Maury Island report should be eliminated from the files.

September 24, 1947: The Majestic Twelve

Shortly after the Roswell disc was recovered, and the wreckage moved to Wright Field, President Truman realized that he would need a panel of experts to study the wreckage and the phenomena. Code-named Majestic Twelve or MJ-12, the group was formed on September 24, 1947, by then President Truman. When Eisenhower was elected in 1952, a top-secret document was prepared for him. Portions of that document received by researchers mention the Roswell crashed disc and state that four alien bodies were recovered.

Naturally there is controversy surrounding those documents and the MJ-12. Some researchers have claimed they are faked and that the Majestic Twelve doesn't exist.

There is another twist to this bizarre incident. In 1980 one level of command in the Air Force asked another for the interpretation of a number of films and photos of UFOs. In the response, there is a mention of the MJ-12. That document, which looks to be authentic, confirms the existence of the Majestic Twelve.

There is also a side issue that should be noted. In 1948, the Air Force made an estimate of the situation (*see September 1948: Estimate of the Situation*) concerning the flying disc problem, which concluded that the flying discs were extra-terrestrial in origin. The top-secret report went all the way to General Hoyt S. Vandenburg who read it, said that the conclusions were not warranted by the evidence presented, and ordered all copies of the report destroyed.

Vandenburg is listed as a member of the Majestic Twelve.

In 1953, concerned about the large public interest in flying saucers and the cry for a complete, objective investigation of the UFOs, the CIA sponsored a panel of experts to review the situation. *(See January 1953: The Robertson Panel)*. Again, after examining the best evidence available in the Project Bluebook files at the time, which included the Great Falls movie and the Tremonton, Utah film *(See August 1950: Great Falls, Montana*, and *July 2, 1952: Tremonton, Utah)*, the Robertson Panel determined that there was no threat to national security and no evidence that the flying saucers were anything real.

One member of the panel, Lloyd Berkner, is listed as a member of the Majestic Twelve.

During the 1950s, as the various evidences of UFO sightings were ridiculed, one of the most famous of the debunkers was Donald Menzel. He wrote books pointing out how rational, intelligent observers could be fooled by the usual seen under unusual circumstances. He reported in one of his books that the Tremonton film had been proven, conclusively, to be birds seen at the very limit of the visual range.

J. Allen Hynek, while watching the film twenty years later, was heard to exclaim incredulously, "Birds! Birds?" Hynek didn't except that answer. In fact, anyone who has seen the film would wonder how a scientist of Menzel's stature could accept an explanation that is so obviously a label slapped on to identify the film rather than let it linger in the public mind.

Menzel is listed as a member of the Majestic Twelve.

According to my information, the original members of the panel were Admiral Roscoe H. Hillenkoetter (also a board member of NICAP), Dr. Vannevar Bush, Secretary of Defense James V. Forrestal (replaced 1 August 1950 by General Walter B. Smith), General Nathan F. Twining, General Hoyt S. Vandenberg, Dr. Detlev Bronk, Dr. Jerome Hunsaker, Sidney W. Souers, Gordon Gray, Dr. Donald H. Menzel, General Robert M. Montague, and Dr. Lloyd V. Berkner.

It is interesting to note that every time we've run into a roadblock in the search for information about the UFO phenomenon, whether it's about the Roswell Incident, the Robertson Panel, or any of the many other UFO cases, there is a link to the MJ-12.

The final question has to be: "Does the MJ-12 exist?"

The information is that it does. And it is interesting to note that the names of the people are those who were in the position to inhibit the early years of research into the UFO phenomenon. Hillenkoettter was a director in the National Investigations Committee on Aerial Phenomena—a perfect place from which to gauge public reaction to UFO sightings, and a perfect place from which to find good UFO cases. He could watch what was going on without arousing public suspicion because NICAP was a civilian organization.

The argument about the MJ-12 is just beginning to rage. Philip Klass claims it's all a hoax, and there are a few reasons to accept his assessment. Although Klass claims that the style, the dating system, and the adding of a zero in front of the single digit dates prove the document is a hoax, researcher Stan Friedman had produced other documents from the time frame written by Admiral Hillenkoetter, which match the MJ-12 briefing. The style suggests it is authentic.

But there is a major flaw. The document is constructed as a briefing paper for President-elect Eisenhower, suggesting that Eisenhower had no knowledge of the Roswell crash. The problem is that Eisenhower, as the Army Chief of Staff in July 1947, would have been completely aware of the Roswell crash. That fact makes me suspicious.

Others who believe that UFOs are extraterrestrial are not convinced of the validity of the MJ-12 documents. Researchers are, however, doing everything they can think of to prove their case, including analyzing the style of the writing, the paper, and the format of the documents. Although that research has not been completed, research in other areas may have already given us the answers (*See December 6, 1950: El Indio, Mexico*, and *September 4, 1964: Glassboro, New Jersey*).

January 7, 1948: The Mantell Case

Just after 5:00 P.M. on January 7, 1948, searchers found the wreckage of Captain Thomas Mantell's F-51 Mustang. He had crashed two hours earlier while chasing a UFO near Fort Knox, Kentucky. In the forty years since his death, hundreds of articles and books have been written trying to explain the incident. The controversy about the case still rages with many of the facts distorted, missing, and overlooked. No one is sure what happened, although the Air Force now claims that Mantell was chasing a Skyhook Balloon launched a few hours earlier.

It was at 1:20 P.M. that the Godman Air Field tower crew "sighted a bright, disc-shaped object," according to official Air Force records. Some writers have claimed that the Kentucky Highway Patrol first reported the UFO, but whoever or however it was sighted, it was quickly brought to the attention of the base operations officer, the intelligence officer, and finally, the base commander, Colonel Guy F. Hix.

For an hour and twenty-five minutes, dozens of people, including Colonel Hix, watched the UFO as it hung almost motionless in the southwestern sky. In towns separated by more than 175 miles, people saw the UFO. Some claimed it drifted silently and slowly to the south and others watched as it hovered for minutes before it resumed its slow flight.

Conventional aircraft and helicopters were quickly ruled out. The object moved too slowly or quietly and was too bright. For the same reason, most other explanations were, at first, eliminated. The UFO was too large for any known balloons. All the witnesses were puzzled by it.

At 2:45 P.M., the situation changed when a flight of F-51s flew over Godman Field. The UFO was still visible and the flight commander, Thomas Mantell, was asked if he could investigate. He replied that he was on a ferry flight but that he would attempt an intercept. He began a spiraling, climbing turn to 220 degrees and 15,000 feet.

As the flight passed through 15,000 feet, two of the wingmen turned back. At that altitude, they were supposed to be on oxygen, but not all the aircraft were equipped with it and none had a full supply. The Air Force records show that "the wingmen attempted to contact Captain Mantell but were unsuccessful."

In the tower, they heard Mantell make a call at 15,000 feet. Records of that transmission differ. Mantell did say that the UFO was "above and ahead of me and appears to be moving about half my speed." Later he said that it was "metallic and it is tremendous in size." Finally, he said that the UFO was just above him and he would continue to climb.

At 22,000 feet, the remaining two wingmen, Lieutenant A.W. Clements and Lieutenant B.A. Hammond, were forced to turn back. The oxygen supply of one of the fighters wasn't working right and military regulations require oxygen above 14,000 feet. Mantell had no such equipment on his plane. Hammond radioed that they were forced to abandon the intercept. Mantell continued to climb. He didn't acknowledge the call.

For thirty minutes, the flight chased the UFO. Each of the wingmen broke off the intercept and turned back. At 3:10 P.M., Captain Mantell was alone at 23,000 feet, still climbing and closing on the UFO. He made no further radio calls to either the tower or his wingmen. By 3:15, everyone had lost both visual and radio contact with him. Within minutes a search was launched.

Just after 5:00 P.M., on a farm near Franklin, Kentucky, the remains of the F-51 were found splattered over half a mile. Contrary to some writers, Mantell's body was inside the shattered cockpit. His watch had stopped at 3:18 P.M. and it was believed that the plane had impacted at that time. There were no mystery wounds. Mantell had died in the crash.

The Air Force began a thorough investigation of the accident. First, they explained the UFO as the planet Venus, then as a huge balloon, and finally, as two balloons and Venus. They leaked word that Mantell had chased a weather balloon and let the matter drop. They believed that if something was "explained," no further investigation was needed.

In late 1948 and into 1949, the Air Force became disgusted with UFOs. They explained as many as they could and ignored the rest. It wasn't until early 1952 that the UFO project was reorganized and renamed the Bluebook. A new attitude took over and they began to seriously investigate all UFO sightings. One of the first things they did was reopen some of the older cases and examine the answers. The Mantell incident was studied again.

The Bluebook file of the Mantell case grew fatter. Ed Ruppelt asked for the "microfilm" copy and found that "someone had inadvertently spilled something on the film. Part of it was impossible to read."

Ruppelt knew about the Navy's high altitude research using the huge Skyhook balloons. They were classified in 1948 and not many people were aware of the project. Ruppelt applied his knowledge to the case and thought that Mantell might have chased a Skyhook. He tried to pin down a launching, but in 1952 could find no records that put a balloon over Godman Field at the right time. A few people thought there might have been one up, but no one could be completely sure. Ruppelt left the case that way, "as a probable balloon."

Others weren't content with a probable answer. At some time, someone inside the Air Force spent a great deal of extra time on the Mantell case because its sensational aspects were just what the public wanted: a World War II pilot killed while chasing a UFO, a closed-casket funeral (probably because he had been killed in an aircraft accident), and a secret investigation. The case had to be solved, at least, on the surface.

The investigators asked all who had seen the UFO to give a description of it. They said, "It was huge, fluid. It had a metallic sheen and looked like an upside-down ice cream cone." Estimates of the speed varied from a few miles an hour to several hundred miles an hour. That gave the impression that the UFO would hover and then move.

The Air Force investigators finally settled on the planet Venus for an explanation. Reports showed that Venus would have been visible as a pinpoint of light at that time when the UFO was over Godman. In the official file, one of the reports goes into depth about Venus. "However, under exceptionally good atmospheric conditions and the eye shielded from the direct rays of the sun, Venus might be seen as an exceedingly tiny bright point of light. It can be shown that it was definitely brighter than the surrounding sky, for on the date in question, Venus had a semidiameter of six seconds of arc. Assuming that a square second of sky would be a trifle brighter than the fourth magnitude, the planet was six times brighter than the equivalent area of sky. While it is thus physically possible to see Venus at such times, usually its pinpoint character and the large expanse of sky makes its casual detection very unlikely." They were saying, in essence, that Venus was brighter than the surrounding sky and could, therefore, be seen.

The report, however, was not finished. The writer had provided an out for the Air Force, but now he took it away. "The chances, of course, of looking at just the right spot are very few. Once done, however, it is usually fairly easy to relocate the object and to call the attention of others to it. However [and here is a very important part of the report], atmospheric conditions must be exceptionally good. It is improbable, for example, that Venus would be seen under these circumstances in a large city."

What all this suggests is that an Air Force officer, after studying the Mantell case, concluded that it wasn't Venus. Although he shows that Venus was almost in the right position and was bright enough to be seen, he doesn't believe that it was Venus. Saying that atmospheric conditions must be "exceptionally good" effectively rules out Venus. Weather reports show that the sky was clear but that there was considerable haze. The atmospheric conditions were anything but good.

Venus, however, is not the "preferred explanation." The official report says, "It had been unofficially reported that the object was a Navy cosmic ray balloon (Skyhook). If this can be established, it is to be preferred as an explanation."

This suggests that the Air Force knew in the beginning that the Venus answer was weak. It made no difference because they tried to use it. When they began to receive flack about it, they changed their minds. Maybe it wasn't Venus. The Navy Skyhook project provided the source for an answer.

The report now shifts gears and launches into the reasons that it might not have been a balloon. "If one accepts the assumption that reports from various locations in the state refer to the same object, any such device must have been a good many miles high . . . 25 to 50 . . . in order to have been seen clearly, almost simultaneously, from places 175 miles apart."

Now that the Air Force investigator had shown why the object could have been Venus, was not Venus, could have been a balloon, and wasn't a balloon, he puts it all into perspective and says, "It is entirely possible, of course, that the first sightings were of some sort of balloon or aircraft and that when the reports came to Godman Field, a careful scrutiny of the sky revealed Venus, and it could be that Lieutenant (sic) Mantell [I wonder how good the investigator was if he couldn't even get Mantell's rank right] did actually give chase to Venus."

He then tells why he believes that Mantell was chasing Venus. It did not move or appear to move away from him. Of course, if the object didn't want Mantell to get too close, it would have been trying to avoid him and it would have been moving away. That is, if you accept the idea that it was an extraterrestrial spacecraft. That didn't seem to cross the mind of the Air Force investigator.

The final conclusions of this report are a masterpiece of double talk. If the first two thousand words sounded as if the writer was using everything in every way—unsure what to say—the conclusions prove it. Now that he has again said that it was Venus, he explains that for the explanation to work he needs not only the balloon and Venus, but also another object. Given these three items, he feels that he can satisfactorily explain the case. He says, "Such a hypothesis [Mantell chasing Venus] does still necessitate the inclusion of at least two objects other than Venus."

In other words, the Air Force officer didn't know what Mantell had chased. He finishes by saying that the information about Venus should be given wide circulation so that tragic mistakes will not occur in the future. The report is an unfortunate example of a low-ranking officer given a report to write that will be read by higher-ranking officers. No matter what they say about it, he can point to some other part of it and claim that the point was covered. It is an inept attempt to explain something without an explanation.

In 1952, a major magazine wanted to run an article about many of the spectacular UFO sightings and how they had been solved. Because the thrust of the article was that UFOs did not exist, the magazine was receiving information from the Pentagon. They provided the answer to the Mantell case. High-ranking Air Force officers assured the magazine editors that the official explanation was Venus. A week after the magazine was published, the Air Force released a new answer. Mantell had chased a balloon.

Captain Ruppelt and others, after reviewing the case, failed to find evidence proving the balloon answer. Wind charts showed that if a balloon had been released from Clinton Air Force Base, Ohio, on January 7, 1948, it might have been in the right position. Ruppelt could not confirm it and none of the others have been able to prove it either.

Then a funny thing happened. After the CIA sponsored the Robertson Panel of 1953 (*See January 1953: The Robertson Panel*), the probable was left off the balloon answer. One of the recommendations of the Panel had been to remove the aura of mystery around UFOs and the Air Force attempted to do that. In the cases where there was a possible answer, they began to say it was a definite answer.

In 1956, Captain Ruppelt wrote a book about his experiences as the head of Project Bluebook. Because he had been an "insider" to the UFO investigations, what he said about a case carried weight. When he claimed that he could not find records determining that a Skyhook was in the area, people listened.

Later, others who were still with the Air Force project claimed that they found proof that it was a balloon. In a report to Project Bluebook, Dr. J. Allen Hynek said that he didn't believe Mantell was chasing Venus. "It is possible that Venus was also a cause to this sighting, and was observed by some of the witnesses on the ground. However, the prime culprit is believed to have been the Skyhook balloon released by the Navy. Captain [at least Hynek got the rank right] Mantell was attempting to close in on this balloon which was still more than 40,000 feet above him.''

The only problem with Dr. Hynek's answer is that the balloon isn't high enough for all the other sightings. Air Force calculations showed that it would have to be twenty-five to fifty miles high. Hynek's balloon had only half the altitude needed.

When the Air Force quit writing, talking, explaining, and investigating the Mantell case, dozens of civilians were only too happy to take over. In the years that followed, dozens of rumors, half-truths, and out-and-out lies have been published about the incident. Most of the spectacular information about the case is not true.

For example, many writers have said that the UFO was spotted on radar and that is how the tower crew learned of it. That is not true. There are no accounts of radar being used in the official records of the Mantell case. Ruppelt makes no mention of it. In fact, the earliest reference to radar is from a book published in 1956. After that book, dozens of authors picked up the radar idea and have continued to perpetuate it. Millions now have that idea that the UFO that killed Mantell was tracked on radar.

Other writers have claimed that Mantell was a World War II ace. That is apparently not true either. Military records show that Mantell was a transport pilot during the war and didn't shoot down the five enemy planes needed to become an ace. It doesn't mean that Mantell was a poor pilot or prove that he was careless, but shows instead how some writers will try to make a story better. To have an "ace" killed chasing a UFO makes a good story.

Others have created a number of rumors to make the story more interesting. Some have said that Mantell's last words were about seeing men inside the UFO, but there doesn't seem to be any verification of that. Some have said that the body was never found, but that idea seems to be the ramblings of the deluded and not supported by the facts. One or two have even claimed that Mantell's F-51 was disintegrated by some type of ray from the UFO. In other words, the number of rumors created by the public almost exceeds the number that were started by the Air Force.

The question that everyone asked is, "What really happened to Mantell?" Is there any way that the facts can be dragged from the mud at the bottom of the mess? And, can we ever be sure that we are right about a case that should have been closed by the summer of 1948?

As near as can be determined, the real story of the chase is correct as presented here. The times and dates are from the official records and there has been no controversy about them. Everyone accepts the fact that Mantell was chasing a UFO, meaning an unidentified flying object, but not necessarily an extraterrestrial spacecraft. The real conflict revolves around what Mantell chased and why he died.

There seems to be no good answer to the question of what he chased. The Air Force and Dr. Hynek provided a series of different explanations, none of which was satisfactory. The more complicated a solution becomes, the less likely it is the proper solution. The description of the object, that it was large and had a metallic sheen, rules out Venus. By taking Venus out of the solution, the Air Force answer, by its own admission, falls apart. They can no longer explain the widely separated locations of the sightings.

The fact that no one has yet shown the records of a balloon launching that would put a Skyhook in the right place at the right time is further proof that the Air Force reached for the answer. If the records existed, they would have been presented by now. With all the problems that the Air Force had with this case, if they had found proof that a balloon was launched from Clinton Air Force Base at the right time, they would have made sure that the public saw it. A further complication is the description of the object. An upside-down ice cream cone is not right for a balloon because it puts the large part at the bottom and not at the top where it should be. Coupled with the lack of records, it suggests that the Air Force has no answer to the case. It is in essence, and in fact, unidentified.

The bigger and more important question, now that it is

fairly certain that Mantell was chasing something unusual, is "How was he killed?" Did the aliens shoot down his plane or did he get too close to the UFO and was accidentally disintegrated? The Air Force answer here seems to be the correct one. All the information in the files, from private research and from physical evidence at the crash site, points to it.

Mantell's fighter was not equipped with oxygen. Air Force records show that part of the flight had the equipment but none had a full supply. Mantell went too high, blacked out from a lack of oxygen, the plane went into a dive and crashed before he regained consciousness.

Before this is laughed off, or read as another attempt to cover up, a few points should be made. Air Force pilots are shown the effects of oxygen starvation in an altitude chamber. Anyone who has been through the experience will tell you that it is quite illuminating. Many are given a simple task to complete, such as separating the suits in a deck of cards, but by the time the altitude reaches 25,000 feet for more than a few seconds, the task is impossible. The people can't even separate the reds from the blacks. Many studies indicate that over 25,000 feet the average length of consciousness is ten seconds. Mantell's wingmen said that they left him at 23,000 feet. As they broke formation, Mantell must have been on the verge of losing consciousness. The plane was trimmed for a climb and probably continued to climb at an ever-increasing angle, until it stalled and entered a power dive. As the stress increased during the dive, the wings separated and Mantell was killed.

But a mystery remains. What did Mantell see? What made an experienced pilot continue to an altitude that he knew would kill quickly? It must have been something so important that Mantell felt he had to take the risk. We may never know what he saw, but it is almost certain that it wasn't a balloon or Venus. He was too experienced to be killed trying to fly to Venus.

August 1948: The Estimate of the Situation

The UFO phenomenon took an unexpected turn in 1948 when officers assigned to ATIC prepared a top-secret briefing about the state of UFO research. Their conclusions were that UFOs were extraterrestrial spacecraft. The report, which contained the best of the UFO information at the time, went all the way to the top of the Air Force chain of command. General Hoyt S. Vandenberg got the report in the Pentagon, looked at it, and returned it, saying that the conclusions drawn were not supported by the evidence.

Ed Ruppelt, writing about the incident years later, claimed that a group of officers traveled from Wright Field to the Pentagon to try to change Vandenberg's mind, but they had no luck. Vandenberg just wouldn't accept the conclusions that UFOs were spaceships without some kind of physical evidence to support the claim.

Ruppelt claims that the report was declassified and then burned. A few copies, according to Ruppelt, were kept as mementos and he was lucky enough to see one four or five years later. Unfortunately Ruppelt doesn't tell us what was in the report or which cases had been used by the officers preparing it.

The effects of Vandenberg's refusal to accept the document, again according to Ruppelt, weren't felt immediately. Project Sign, however, lost its momentum. Those assigned to it knew they didn't have top level support and they gave up. Sightings were treated as routine and no effort was made to investigate them. It was a haphazard, hit or miss proposition.

That was an interesting turn of events. UFOs went from

an unknown that threatened the existence of the world to the workings of sick minds. There was nothing to UFOs except in the overactive imaginations of the unenlightened. To investigate UFOs was a waste of time.

That was where the story hung for me, until an Intel Conference I attended in the early 1980s. These were biannual events with the officers from various units all over the United States in attendance. We discussed the ways our shops ran, things we did that would improve the efficiency of our operations, and the latest advances in technology or terrorism. In the evenings we all trooped out to dinner.

During one of those outings, the topic turned to UFOs. One of the officers there mentioned a couple of magazine articles he'd read, not realizing that I had written them. From that moment on, I was talking about UFOs to everyone at almost every break during the conference. I didn't mind because I could pick up interesting items that way.

One of those interesting items came from a full colonel who had been a newly minted second lieutenant in the early days of the UFO phenomenon. He'd been at ATIC during the heady days when they were talking about UFOs as spaceships. They had talked about dogfights with them and if our weapons would be effective if it turned out they were hostile. The discussions turned to where they came from with the opinion being they were from outside the solar system. Speculation ran wild, especially when the rumors of a crashed saucer reached them.

My source didn't know much about it and I had always been of the opinion that the crash stories were little more than rumors, and bad ones at that (*see 1948: The Crashes Begin*). But then, here was a man who had been there at the time.

I asked him about the crashes and he didn't remember much about them. "It was so long ago," he said. "And after General Vandenberg refused our report, I thought nothing more about it."

That made sense to me. If there had been a crash, Vandenberg would have been one of the few men to know about it.

Then the colonel told me that the Estimate of the Situation hadn't been rejected out of hand by Vandenberg. The first document, more of a working paper than a finished report, had been sent up the chain of command.

I remember he grinned when he said that because a top-secret report isn't just dropped in the mail. Someone hand carried it to Washington and the Pentagon, sat outside Vandenberg's office, and then let the general read it when he had time. It wasn't required that they do it that way, but a courier did have to take the documents to Washington and a courier had to bring them back. Having it coordinated with Vandenberg in advance allowed them to get back to work quickly.

The document returned with a couple of paragraphs removed under Vandenberg's instructions. At that time, it sounded as if they were removed because they didn't have a foundation in fact. Those paragraphs referred to physical evidence recovered in New Mexico. Vandenberg had made it clear that no mention of that physical evidence would be tolerated in the final document.

The men finished writing their report knowing that without the physical evidence, it was nearly impossible to prove their case. But then, they knew the evidence existed and were confident that sighting reports of extraordinary maneuvers, craft that looked like no conventional aircraft, and a few photographs of disc-shaped objects would be enough. The physical evidence was the icing on the cake, but without it, they still had the cake.

Vandenberg saw the final document, dated 5 August 1948. After reading it, he said that the conclusions weren't warranted without physical evidence. But the paragraphs that had contained information about the physical evidence had been eliminated by Vandenberg's orders.

Ruppelt claimed that the document was ordered declassified and burned. But that makes no sense. If the document was declassified, then there was no reason to burn it. If it remained classified, then the only way to get rid of it was to burn it. Each intelligence office that received a copy would then be required to certify that the document had been destroyed.

Naturally I asked my source more about the subject, trying to learn as much as I could about it. He went over it again, explaining that all he could remember was that the physical evidence case came from New Mexico and he talked about pieces of metal. He had no other details and hadn't been privy to them in 1948. Later he could find out nothing more about them. When he asked, the answer was always the same. "I don't know what in hell you're talking about."

At the time I talked with the colonel, I didn't realize the significance of the information. Learning a little more about the famous Estimate of the Situation was one thing. Finding out that Vandenberg wanted physical evidence to make the case and taking out the evidence to ruin it was interesting. But I hadn't heard of the Roswell incident (*See July 2, 1947: Roswell, New Mexico*), so I didn't realize I was getting some confirmation of it. The colonel just said New Mexico and nothing about Roswell.

Now, looking back, I see why Vandenberg wanted the report destroyed if it mentioned Roswell. Of all the UFO cases, this was the one that they couldn't allow to be discovered. This one case handed them the answers, gave Vandenberg the physical evidence he wanted, and proved that UFOs were extraterrestrial. The Estimate had to be destroyed and Vandenberg took it upon himself to assure that it was.

Unlike what Ruppelt claimed in his book, I don't think it was declassified. If it had been, then copies would have gotten out. A declassified document does not have to be protected. It wasn't declassified. It was destroyed.

And it was destroyed for one reason. Someone had put in data about Roswell in the rough draft. Although Vandenberg made sure that information was not circulated, he also wanted to made sure that no one believed UFOs to be from outer space. Such a conclusion could evidently lead back to Roswell and he was taking no chances.

It's only now, five or six years after that conference, that I realized the significance of the data I was given. Unfortunately, there is no longer any way for me to verify it. My source, like so many of the people involved with the Roswell incident, has died.

November 1948: Project Twinkle

Not all UFO sightings are of glowing disc-shaped objects or bright points of light shooting across the sky. Anything that cannot be easily explained or identified is a UFO. Some sightings remind the witnesses of a well-known, natural phenomenon but will differ enough to cause questions about its true identity. Some have been explained, but there was one group of reports that caused a special project to be created and that stumped some of the best scientific minds in the country.

The official Air Force UFO project was only a few months old when a complication in the investigation arose. The officers at the project had been worried about "flying discs" when the green fireballs flashed into the picture. At first, many believed meteors were responsible for the brilliant displays but continued sightings and thousands of witnesses caused a change in the explanation.

The first of the green fireballs were only streaks of bright light seen over Albuquerque, New Mexico, in late 1948. None of the sightings lasted long and the intelligence officers on the scene thought that someone was shooting flares. The descriptions of bright, brief, green lights fit thousands of flare guns that had been stolen after World War II. But the reports continued and got much better. As more people saw the lights, the descriptions no longer sounded like flares and intelligence officers were left with no explanations.

On December 5, 1948, the flare idea was completely and utterly destroyed, as a brilliant green object flashed by a C-47 and a commercial airliner. The crewmen on the C-47, a military plane, were startled when they saw the bright green object appear slightly below them, arc upward, level, and then streak by them. At first, they thought that it might have been a meteor but dismissed the idea because the object had been too green and traveling too straight. In fact, the crew believed that they had seen it climb toward them and they had never seen a meteor do that.

After a brief discussion, they decided that they should report the incident to someone, especially since it was the second such object that they had seen that night. About 9:30 P.M., the crew of the C-47 called the control tower at Kirtland Air Force Base to describe the green UFO.

A few minutes later, the crew of a commercial airliner called Kirkland to report that they had just seen the mysterious green object. They were just east of the Las Vegas, New Mexico, radio range when the fireball flashed by them. They were on their way to Albuquerque and said that they would make a full report when they landed.

They had no problem finding someone to talk to about the sighting. When the Pioneer Airlines DC-3 rolled to a stop in Albuquerque, intelligence officers were waiting for the crew. Inside the flight operations office, the intelligence men asked dozens of questions. The whole story, according to the airline captain, was that they were near Las Vegas, at 9:35 P.M., when the copilot spotted the "meteor." It took them only seconds to realize that it was too low and too slow to be a meteor. The red-orange color changed to a brilliant green and the captain watched as the object headed straight for his plane. As it became bigger and brighter, the captain was afraid that it would hit them and he forced the DC-3 into a tight, spiraling turn. When the object was abreast of the plane, it began to fall away, growing dimmer until it finally disappeared.

For almost an hour, the Air Force intelligence officers interviewed the plane crew. When the officers returned to their office, later that night, they found dozens of other reports waiting for them. By morning there would be a full-scale investigation of the green fireballs.

Although the fledgling Air Force was involved with UFOs, they weren't concerned at first with the green fireballs as UFOs. The real problem was the locations of the sightings. New Mexico is loaded with top-secret installations of one type or another. There are, of course, the Los Alamos Laboratories, the secret Sandia Base, Holloman Air Force Base, the White Sands Missile Range, as well as several other unnamed but vital bases. For that reason, the Air Force decided that an investigation was needed.

Because the fireballs acted like meteors and looked like meteors, the intelligence officers at Kirtland called Dr. Lincoln La Paz, one of the country's experts in the study of meteors. He agreed that the fireballs sounded like meteors except for a few minor points.

The easiest way to find out if the fireballs were meteors was to see if there were any fragments. If Dr. La Paz could find the pieces, they would have the answer and the December 5, 1948 fireball was made to order. Using the method that had been so successful on so many other occasions, Dr. La Paz set to work.

Using a detailed map of the area and interviewing the witnesses of the fireball, he determined the flight path of the object. By drawing the observer's line of sight to the fireball, he could eventually tell where they had converged, and then find the fragments of the meteor. He knew it would work because he had done it before. Rarely had he failed to find remains of the meteors (or meteorites if you want to get technical) using this method.

By checking the times, locations, and heights above the horizon, it was discovered that eight separate fireballs had been seen on December 5. One was obviously more spectacular than the others, so La Paz and his assistants concentrated on it. The witnesses reported that the green fireballs had been traveling west to east and the scientists followed the trajectory the best they could. They worked their way across New Mexico and into west Texas, finally determining where it should have come down. They searched the area and found nothing. They retraced their steps and re-searched the area. Still they found nothing. In fact, they went over the ground several times and found no trace of the fireball.

Dr. La Paz was so sure that he was right about the location and had been so successful in locating meteor fragments in the past that he began to seriously doubt that the fireballs were meteors. However, good science is not built on one case, so La Paz continued to investigate the fireballs and continued to try to locate fragments. He was sure that if there was anything to be found, he would be able to find it.

Reports of the fireballs were becoming quite numerous and two intelligence officers at Kirtland Air Force Base decided that they should try to see one. On December 8, 1948, they took off just before dark and began to circle north of Albuquerque. They had worked out who would observe what if they saw one of the fireballs. At 6:33 P.M. they put their plan into effect.

They were flying at 11,500 feet, twenty miles east of the Las Vegas, New Mexico, radio range station, when the object was sighted. The copilot saw it first and the pilot spotted it a split second later. They estimated that it was two thousand feet above them and was approaching them at a high rate of speed from thirty degrees to the left of their course. The color was the same as the green flares used by the Air Force but a great deal brighter. The trajectory was flat as the object approached the plane and it continued that way as the fireball shot past. A few seconds later, the glow faded and the object began to lose altitude, dropping rapidly before it disappeared.

Throughout December and January, the fireballs continued to flash through the New Mexico skies. By the end of January, most of the intelligence officers at Kirkland, dozens of scientists, including Dr. La Paz and quite a few of the Air Force defense people, had seen at least one fireball. Opinion about them was divided among meteors, another natural phenomenon, and some type of manufactured objects.

In mid-February, 1949, a conference about the fireballs was called at Los Alamos. There were quite a few high-power scientists involved including Dr. Edward Teller, Dr. Joseph Kapland, and Dr. La Paz. Unlike other conferences about UFOs, there was no need to decide whether or not the phenomenon was real because they already knew that it was. The question was what they were.

One group was still sure that the green fireballs were meteors. They claimed that meteors do have a green color and cited dozens of examples. They claimed that the trajectory of some meteors appeared flat, and that fit with the description of the fireballs. The reports were localized because the air had been extremely clear over that part of the country and with all the publicity, thousands were looking. The case of the intelligence officers proved their point. If the officers hadn't been looking for a fireball, they wouldn't have seen the December 8 display.

Dr. La Paz disagreed. He said that the color was too green, the trajectory was too flat, and he hadn't found any fragments. He produced a well-worn color chart and pointed to a sickly yellow-green, saying that it was the color reported by witnesses of normal meteors. Then he pointed to a bright, intense green and said that it was the color reported by the witnesses of the green fireballs. There was quite a difference in the colors and no one disputed Dr. La Paz's claims.

For two days, those at the conference argued about the fireballs, but in the end, and agreeing that Dr. La Paz's idea was interesting, they decided that the fireballs were a natural phenomenon. They recommended that a project be established to identify the fireballs. This was the beginning of Project Twinkle.

Project Twinkle called for the establishment of three camera-type tracking stations in New Mexico. Each would be equipped with a 35mm movie camera that would photograph the object, as well as dials giving the time, azimuth, and elevation angles of the camera. If the object was photographed by two of the stations, then a wide variety of information could be obtained, including the speed and height of the fireball.

Project Twinkle failed. Only one of the cameras could be obtained, there were never enough men to man the project, and the Air Force would not provide the funds needed to finance the operation. Even the backing from the Air Force's Cambridge Research Laboratory didn't help. Nothing was photographed or triangulated or even seen by the one camera team.

One of the major problems was that the team did not remain in one place. Each time there was a series of sightings, the team would move to the new location, always arriving too late to see anything. When another series broke out, the team would move again. However, anyone who has fished or hunted or searched for a lost person will know what was wrong with that approach. The team should have picked a good spot and waited for the green fireballs to come to them.

The beginning of the Korean War marked the end of Project Twinkle. The war became the most important project and all others took a second or third seat. Project Twinkle was allowed to quietly die. With the end of the project, most think that it was the end of the green fireballs, but that doesn't seem to be the case. During the next several years, there were a number of sightings, most of them in the southwest desert, but a few were observed over parts of mid-America, some as far east as Pennsylvania.

Interest in the green fireballs was again stirred in 1952 when *Life* published a story about the UFO phenomenon. One of the areas covered was the fireballs. They reported that there had never been a real solution to the problem, meaning no one could say definitely whether they were natural or manufactured. The article did uncover several new reports, including one from Korea.

On January 29, 1952, a B-29 flying near Wonson, Korea, was at an altitude of twenty thousand feet. The crew saw what they thought was an orange fireball approaching at a high rate of speed. As it closed, the fireball apparently slowed and then paced the aircraft for five minutes. The pilots reported that the object had a blue-green flame from the rear and as it streaked away, the green glow drowned out the other colors. Sometime later that evening, another B-29 reported a similar incident.

On November 2, 1951, a gigantic green fireball blazed over Arizona. Unlike some of its counterparts, where there were only a few witnesses, over 165 people reported that they had seen this one. Some claimed that it flew parallel to the ground and some were lucky enough to see it explode. All the witnesses reported that there was no sound, either during flight or during the explosion. The fireball seemed to fly apart and disintegrate.

Astronomers were interested in this last aspect of the green fireballs. When normal fireballs are seen, it is often reported that there is a loud roaring sound and explosions. This was just one more reason to believe that the green fireballs were something more than ordinary meteors.

Professor C.C. Wylie, a professor of astronomy at the University of Iowa during the early 1950s, disagreed with the others. He claimed that he had seen several green fireballs, had photographed at least one, and believed that they had plotted ten others. All orginated in a small area around the constellation Taurus, and were possibly related to a well-known meteor shower.

Dr. La Paz again disagreed. He claimed that almost all the fireballs were observed over the desert southwest during a three-year period. "They came from points thirty-five to as much as 105 degrees from the Taurid fireball radiant and therefore, were not related to this radiant."

By the end of 1952, there were almost no reports of green fireballs. They had disappeared as mysteriously as they arrived. Then, for a brief period in September 1954, they reappeared. However, they didn't stay long and no one was able to discover what they were, where they came from, or where they went.

Air Force files on the green fireballs begin in the late 1940s. All the documents were originally stamped either "confidential" or "secret." With the end of Project Bluebook, all the Project Twinkle material was declassified and the first glimpse at the information was allowed.

On November 7, 1949, a report on the mid-February conference was sent to the commanding general, Air Material Command, at Wright Field in Dayton, Ohio. The first paragraph outlines the problem quickly, saying, "The phenomenon has the appearance of a green fireball and because of the fact that it has been observed only . . . in the northern New Mexico area and only since the year 1947—it has caused a high degree of apprehension among security agencies." It ends, saying, "In view of the fact that the phenomenon has been observed by independent and trained observers, there is little doubt that something has been observed."

The report suggests an investigation of the phenomenon should be attempted by the Geophysical Research Directorate and the Cambridge Labs. It does give the impression that the phenomenon is atmospheric in nature so those assignments seemed appropriate. That was the beginning of Twinkle.

A report dated September 15, 1950, has several interesting

sentences. Again, the letter was directed to the commanding general of the Air Material Command. Paragraph four lays it all out, plainly and boldly: "There is considerable doubt in the minds of some of the project personnel that this is a natural phenomenon. As long as a reasonable doubt exists, it is not wise to discontinue the observations . . . that fireballs have been observed in the past cannot be discounted due to the reliability of several witnesses (most notably, Dr. La Paz). It may be considered significant that fireballs have ceased abruptly as soon as a systematic watch was set up."

That final line, when read again, is a blockbuster. Think about it for a minute. "It may be significant that fireballs have ceased abruptly as soon as a systematic watch was set up." It suggests that some of the Project people believed that there was an intelligence behind the fireballs.

However, others, who attended the conference, had said the same thing. They speculated that the fireballs were some type of observation craft that were "fired" from a high altitude, orbiting ship. There was no proof that it was the right answer, but it was one that came up often.

The study of the green fireballs apparently didn't advance very fast. On February 19, 1952, the same problems mentioned in 1948 were outlined in a letter to the Directorate of Intelligence. "The Scientific Advisory Board Secretariat has suggested that this project not be declassified for a variety of reasons. Chiefly, that *NO SCIENTIFIC EXPLANATION* for any of the 'fireballs' and other phenomena was revealed by the report, and that some reputable scientists still believe that the observed phenomena are *MAN-MADE*." (Emphasis added.)

That is where the green fireball phenomenon stands today. Over thirty-five years after that letter was written, we still do not know what the green fireballs were. The Air Force had a chance to find out, but they blew it. They had the people in the area but wouldn't provide the equipment and money to finish the project. Now we can only guess. Were they some kind of research vehicle launched by extraterrestrials, or were they some kind of other manufactured object built on another planet, or just a brilliant type of natural meteor?

The fireballs might have provided the clue needed to solve

a portion of the UFO problem. The fireballs had one attribute that other parts of the UFO problem didn't have: They were assumed to be real from the very beginning. No one had to waste time establishing that fact. Scientists could begin trying to determine what they were. In the end, the fireballs were left where the rest of the UFOs can be found. Not enough energy was spent where it would have done the most good.

Just what were the green fireballs?

1948: The UFO Crashes Begin

There are stories circulating, many of them having been told almost from the day Kenneth Arnold made the first report of flying saucers, that tell of mystery craft being found crashed, usually in the southwest desert. There are stories of dead Venusians, dressed in the garb of the late nineteenth century, of dead pilots, their skin burned to a dark brown, and of secret studies of wreckage taking place on American Air Force bases. There are stories of empty discs and exploding discs, and stories of sunken saucers. And nearly every one of them was rejected, out of hand, until we learned of Roswell (see July 2, 1947: Roswell, New Mexico and December 6, 1950: El Indio, Mexico). Then, because of Roswell, we began to look at some of the stories again, wondering if there might not have been a kernel of truth hidden in them.

Roswell was so brilliantly covered up that no one thought of it as a UFO crash until the late 1970s. But it was in 1950 that the first story of a downed disc got a big play. A book, written by Frank Scully, whose other books included Fun in Bed, about games to play while sick, was published containing the entire inside story of a crashed saucer that he had gotten from Silas Newton. According to Scully, Newton was a government man and a millionaire who had rediscovered the Rangely oil fields. The story, according to Scully, according to Newton, came from a scientist named Dr. Gee who was on the inside track from the very beginning.

It was 1948 and three radar sites tracked a UFO as it streaked across the New Mexican sky. Something apparently happened to it and it struck the ground. Using the information from the three radar sites to triangulate the position of the crash, soldiers, scientists, and police officers began a systematic search that led them to the downed craft. They spent two days observing the disc-shaped UFO before they ventured close to it. Through portholes in the craft, they could see the bodies of sixteen alien beings. Probing through a broken porthole with a long rod, they accidentally hit a knob or button that opened the hatch.

Scientists entered the craft then and carefully removed the bodies, laying them out on the ground. They were between three and three and a half feet tall, human-looking except for the size, and wearing old-fashioned clothes made of cloth that was nearly indestructable. The skin was dark brown— charred actually—and that led Dr. Gee to believe that they had been burned.

From studying the bodies outside the craft, Dr. Gee was able to draw a series of conclusions about them. Because they were tiny, he believed they came from Venus. Studying their features, he determined they were between thirty-five and forty, and he noticed that every one of them had perfect teeth.

This wasn't the only crash that Dr. Gee was privileged to examine. A second ship, slightly damaged, was found in the deserts of Arizona and there were another sixteen dead aliens on it. A third, much smaller ship was found crashed near Phoenix, its two pilots dead. According to Scully, the government claimed all three ships and took them away for study.

Although all information about the crashes was classified higher than Top Secret, Dr. Gee told his friend, Silas Newton, about them. Naturally Newton wanted to see the ships and the bodies, but Dr. Gee told him that government regulations prohibited that. Those regulations did not prevent Dr. Gee from giving Newton a number of small, disc-shaped samples of metal, and a few tiny gears taken from one of the ships.

Newton, knowing all about the government regulations,

knowing that it was a secret that needed to be kept, immediately scheduled a lecture to speak about it. In March, he talked with students at the University of Denver in Colorado. At first, he had refused to tell anyone his real name. There were articles in the *Denver Post* about the mystery lecture on March 12, and again on March 17, 1950. Newton's identity was then established and any hope that Dr. Gee had about keeping the information secret was gone.

J.P. Cahn, a reporter for the *San Francisco Chronicle*, was interested in the story of the crashed saucers and did a series of articles about them. He learned that Scully knew Newton and that it was Newton who was the mystery source for Scully's book. Cahn decided that he wanted to meet Newton and Dr. Gee, and to learn just exactly how much of the story was true.

Cahn's investigation showed that Newton's background was anything but sterling. He had boasted of his rediscovery of the Rangely oil fields, but other oilmen said that it wasn't true. There was no evidence of his discovery or rediscovery.

Cahn finally arranged a meeting with Newton and told the man that he was authorized to pay up to 35,000 dollars for the story, providing that Newton could provide some verification of his claims. Newton showed Cahn some photographs and the small discs. Cahn wanted one of the discs so that he could submit it to independent analysis, but Newton was reluctant. He would provide the documentation to show that they were one hundred percent pure aluminum, but Cahn couldn't have one.

Cahn, undaunted, had several small discs of his own made, figuring that he might have the chance to make a switch. During one of their meetings, Cahn made the switch, sweating as he pocketed the real one, and watched as Newton put the fake one away. As soon as possible, Cahn had the metal analyzed at the Stanford laboratories. It turned out to be rather poor-grade aluminum that contained no traces of anything they couldn't identify, and instead of resisting temperatures of more than ten thousand degrees as Newton had claimed, it melted at 650 degrees.

Through further investigations, Cahn was able to identify the mysterious Dr. Gee. He turned out to be Leo Gebauer, an electrician who lived in Arizona. Gebauer finally admitted that he was Dr. Gee but later tried to retract the statement.

With that, Cahn was satisfied that the story was a hoax, concocted by Newton and Gebauer. Scully hadn't been involved in the hoax. His role was that of a writer taking the information given him and turning it into a book. He was upset when he learned that he had been lied to.

In 1974, the Scully stories of crashed saucers and the tales of little bodies were back. This time it was Robert Carr and he had new information about the crash that Scully had claimed happened near Aztec, New Mexico.

Carr was very secretive about his sources, refusing to reveal them. He did say, however, that there had been more than one crash and that President Eisenhower had been taken to Muroc Air Force Base (later Edwards Air Force Base) to view the craft and the aliens. Later all the material was transferred to Wright Field for safekeeping and further study.

Carr also talked of other crashes in the same time frame. He suggested a number of different sites but thought that Aztec was the most likely. He even talked about the radar stations tracking the object as it fell to Earth.

Researchers then went to work trying to learn if Carr was right or if he was merely telling the same tales. Was it Frank Scully again? One man went to Aztec, talked to local residents, read the newspaper files, and spent days trying to locate the crash site. He concluded that Carr's information about Aztec was wrong. Carr agreed, saying that it didn't mean all the information was wrong, only that Aztec might not be the site of the crash.

Again, researchers wrote off the Aztec and the Scully stories as being unsubstantial. No one came forward to say that he or she had seen anything to suggest that the stories were true.

This was, of course, in the days before the data about Roswell had gotten out and stories of crashed saucers were rejected outright. Then came Roswell, and the attitude changed.

Others began to look at the Scully and Carr stories again. Some felt there might have been a kernel of truth in them. Both Carr and Scully might have missed the boat on the overall picture, but there might be something to their rumors of the crashed discs.

According to sources that have now come forward, scientists, including Dr. Carl Heiland, who was a geophysicist and magnetic expert and head of the Colorado School of Mines, and Dr. Horace van Valkenberg, who was an inorganic chemist associated with the University of Colorado, were assembled at the Durango, Colorado, airfield for transport to a suspected crash site near Aztec.

Suddenly the kernel of truth to Scully's story is apparent. Silas Newton claimed to have rediscovered the Rangely oil fields. Even if the claim was false, he would have been working with scientists at the School of Mines. He would have been talking to them on a daily basis. We suddenly have a thread that leads from Scully to Newton to the School of Mines and that brings us right up against the story of a crashed disc. Newton and Gebauer might have added details to dress up their story, but it suddenly looks better.

Now we begin to encounter other details that seemed to have been manufactured by the Scully team, but might have a basis in fact. One former Air Force officer claimed that he saw a message, classifed Top Secret, that described the crash of a saucer-shaped craft one hundred feet in diameter and thirty feet high. One porthole was broken and the five occupants had suffocated. The creatures were described as being small, under four feet tall, and all had big heads. The skin of the ship was very thin but very strong. The officer thought the object had come down near White Sands, New Mexico.

The parallels to the Aztec case are startling. There are almost too many for it to be a coincidence.

There were reports of other saucer crashes in the area. Scully talked of a crash in the Paradise Valley area in 1947. The report is that a small craft, about thirty feet in diameter, had come down and the pilot had been killed. The military moved in, sealed the site, and then carried off everything. The source wasn't Scully or Newton, but a third party who was unfamiliar with Scully's work.

Again, we have a story that has been reported as a hoax over and over, until everyone accepts it as a hoax. Now it seems that there was some truth to the Scully stories. Like so many of the researchers who followed him, I found that Scully's information wasn't perfect and he made mistakes. It might be that he was a victim of the old intelligence gambit. When a leak is found, it is flooded with bad information to discredit all the information from it. When the government found that Scully had the data on crashed discs, the intelligence officers flooded it with bad information to discredit Scully. Given that, there seems to be enough there for another investigation to be made.

Coming on the heels of all this new information is the story of another crash in the Kingman, Arizona, area. One witness claimed that while working on another project for the government, he and fifteen or twenty others were driven to an Air Force base, put on a plane, and flown to Arizona.

On arrival, they were escorted to a field where they saw a disc-shaped object that had crashed with some force into the desert. It was about thirty feet in diameter, and was stuck in the sand without any sign of structural damage.

Nearby was a tent where the single occupant of the craft lay. According to the sources, he was about four feet tall, had two eyes, two ears, and a round mouth.

Once everyone had finished his task, all of them were put on the plane and flown back to their original duties, with instructions to forget what they had seen.

There are few additional details from here. It seems to fit the pattern of all the other stories that have begun to surface.

The remote regions of New Mexico, where no one except a select few have seen anything, aren't the only places where UFO crashes have been reported. On April 18, 1962, an object was reported to have exploded over the deserts of Nevada (*see September 12, 1957: Ubatuba, Brazil*). The roar was heard for miles and the flash of light was so bright that it lit the streets of Reno like the noonday sun. A report of the incident was carried in the *Las Vegas Sun* and Frank Edwards wrote about it in one of his UFO books.

The story actually began near Oneida, New York. Lieutenant Colonel Herbert Rolph, a spokesman for the North American Air Defense Command in Colorado Springs, Colorado, told reporters that the first observers had seen a glowing red object, heading to the west, over the Oneida area. It was at a great altitude.

Radar picked up the object. Operators watched as it streaked into the Midwest, and the Air Defense Command alerted a number of bases, including Nellis in Las Vegas. Interceptors were scrambled from Phoenix.

In Nephi, Utah, witnesses reported the glowing red object flew overhead. When it was gone, there was a rumbling like that from jet engines. That might have been the interceptors as they chased the UFO.

The UFO came down near Eureka, Utah, and interrupted the electrical service from a power plant close to the landing site. It took off a few minutes later, continuing on toward the west.

The object suddenly disappeared from the radar screens seventy miles northeast of Las Vegas. That coincided with reports of a brilliant explosion.

So many of Frank Edwards's stories are impossible to check. Edwards wrote from memory and sometimes his memory let him down. The Las Vegas crash was one of the stories that I worried about because most of the major researchers knew nothing about the case. My worries evaporated, however, when I interviewed a man who was in Eureka, Utah, the night the object landed.

According to the source, he was traveling south when he saw the object coming down. It wasn't just a bright light but an oval-shaped, orange object that was making a quiet whirring sound. The ground around it was lighted as if the sun was coming up. The man said that the UFO came from the east, landed, then took off and continued on to the west, disappearing in the distance.

Edwards claimed that some people heard a roar that he attributed to fighters in the air giving chase. My source didn't hear or see the jets.

He continued on to his destination, stopping in the larger cities, buying newspapers and searching for stories of the saucer sighting. He found nothing though he continued to look. Only Frank Edwards mentioned the case.

Reports of the story were missing from most newspapers just as the source said. Only the *Las Vegas Sun* reported it. The whole story was pieced together from various sources and seems to be just one more example of how fast the public relations machinery can be put into motion. With the exception of the one story in the *Sun*, the majority of the country heard nothing about it.

That confirmed part of the case, but I still wasn't completely convinced. I had read in one book where all the information about a case was written down in the local police department for anyone who cared to check. I cared to check and found the statement to be wrong. Police records did not support the author's claim, so I decided to read the *Las Vegas Sun*. The date was April 18 and I asked to see that paper. Naturally there was nothing about the story in the paper for that date.

The next day, however, April 19, had a banner headline with giant type that proclaimed "Brilliant Red Explosion Flares in Las Vegas Sky." There was a front page story, confirming what Edwards had said. There were also the names of a few Las Vegas people who had witnessed the explosion, and the name of a police officer who had taken a search party into the mountains to look for possible wreckage.

I looked the names up in the Las Vegas phone book but couldn't find them. I called the newspaper and spoke to one of the reporters there. When I told her I was researching a story on UFOs carried by them, she turned suddenly cold. She told me that she'd never seen anything to suggest that UFOs were real, but if I wanted to believe that was my business. I mentioned the story had been carried in the *Las Vegas Sun*, the very paper she worked for.

"It's all hearsay," she said.

"But it was in your paper."

"All hearsay. The first thing I learned in Journalism 101 was that you couldn't believe anything you read."

I thought that was a strange attitude for a reporter. She was telling me that I couldn't believe anything I read in her newspaper, but I ignored that. Instead I asked her about the *Sun* staff photographer who was quoted as seeing the explosion. She told me that he no longer worked there and she didn't know what happened to him. I asked about the police officer and was told he was probably dead.

Realizing that she was too caught up in her own opinions to worry about facts, I got off the phone as quickly as possible. Frank Maggio, the staff photographer, wasn't mentioned in the phone book, but there was a Maggio Photo Lab. It had to be the same guy.

It was. He confirmed that he had seen the object over Las Vegas, but it was so long ago that he remembered almost nothing about it. A bright light, orange, and that was it.

The police officer was harder to find. Two phone calls, but I found him too. He confirmed that he had taken a search party out into the area between Mesquite, Nevada, and Spring Mountain. They searched through the night on foot and in Jeeps and the next morning they used aircraft. They found nothing.

Both Maggio and the police officer confirmed something had exploded over Las Vegas. There was enough of a doubt about it to send out search parties, but when no aircraft were reported missing, the search was halted.

The Project Bluebook files do contain some information on the case. According to them, the Las Vegas incident was a radar case, confirming the object was tracked by radar, and was listed as insufficient data for a scientific analysis. The Eureka case was listed as a meteor and was dated April 19, 1962.

The only thing wrong is that meteors can't be tracked by radar, it was seen to race across the country, and to have lit up the streets of Reno and explode over Las Vegas it would have to make a turn of at least 120 degrees. And, it was seen to touch down in Eureka and take off again—not the actions of a meteor.

So once again, like Roswell, we are left with a series of questions that have no answers. Did Scully, reporting what Newton and Gebauer told him, tell us a little truth? Maybe not three saucers, and maybe not with bodies of perfect little humans, but something that they, Newton and Gebauer, had heard, embellished to make it more exciting.

And what about this exploding object over Las Vegas? If

the Air Force wouldn't label it as a meteor, and there were no reports of missing aircraft, what could it have been? Does the Air Force know and refuse to talk, or are they as puzzled as the rest of us?

August 5, 1950: The Great Falls Movie

One of the early criticisms of the official, public UFO project was that it had little to offer in the way of proof. There were a few out of focus pictures, one or two pieces of junk that was claimed to be part of a flying saucer and labeled as hoaxes, and hundreds of reports but nothing solid. That changed in August of 1950. A short film was taken in Montana that has withstood the best efforts of debunkers to discredit it or of the skeptics to explain it. As it stands now, the case is unidentified and unless someone can offer new evidence about it, it will remain that way.

Nick Mariana was the manager of the Great Falls, Montana, baseball team and he was inspecting the ball field before the game. With him was his secretary, Virginia Raunig. It wasn't quite noon when a bright flash of light caught his eye. Over Great Falls, Mariana could see two bright, silver objects. He called to Raunig as he ran for the car to get his 16mm movie camera.

Mariana was able to film the two circular UFOs as they passed over a building and behind a water tower. In the short film, the objects seemed to flash brightly, then move away from the camera. In less than twenty seconds, the UFOs disappeared. Raunig saw the UFOs as Mariana filmed them, but she said that she watched them for only five to ten seconds.

Mariana was understandably excited about the film and called the local newspaper to report the incident. That is important. Hoaxsters usually wait for the film to be returned before they will tell anyone about the pictures. They want to be sure that there is an image on the film. Processing of film took over a week in 1950 and it was probably late August or early September before Mariana saw it.

During September and October, Mariana showed the film to various civic groups. At one of the meetings, one man suggested that Mariana send the film to the Air Force for analysis. The man wrote to Wright Field, saying that Mariana was willing to loan the film to them. Debunkers have commented that it was odd that Mariana didn't write the letter. He explained that it never occurred to him.

In October 1950, the Air Force entered the case. They sent an officer from Malstrom Air Force Base (formerly Great Falls AFB) to interview Mariana and obtain the film. During the interview, Mariana claimed that the UFOs were in sight for twenty seconds. Tests run at the ballpark, with Mariana restaging his activities, showed that it would take thirty seconds for Mariana to run down the steps and reach his car. If he watched the UFOs for only twenty seconds, or rather filmed them for twenty seconds, it would mean that they were in sight for a minimum of fifty seconds. The times become important in this case.

Early analysis of the film proved nothing. Air Force officers said that two jet interceptors were in the area when the film was taken and they caused the images. Sunlight reflecting from the fuselages washed out the other detail and that was why Mariana hadn't been able to identify them. The Air Force returned the film.

After the Air Force interest in the film was published, in early October 1950, Mariana was approached by several magazines and one movie company, who wanted to use the film. That added a note of credibility to Mariana's story, from a public standpoint, but it didn't help the Air Force or other investigators study the case.

In 1952, the Air Force UFO project was revitalized and many of the old cases were reexamined. Officers at Wright asked Mariana if they could again look at the film. He agreed and it was sent back to the Air Force.

The Air Force made another analysis of it, trying to find a possible explanation. They found records that showed two F-94 jets had landed at Malstrom Air Force Base about the time the UFOs were being seen. Bright sunlight from them could cause the images, but only if Mariana's estimate of the time was right. If it was wrong, and the tests showed that it was, it meant that the jets would have passed through enough arc that sunlight would have faded, and the jets would have been identified.

One other problem arose concerning that explanation. Mariana claimed that both he and Raunig saw some jets in another part of the sky. That should rule them out as an explanation if neither of the witnesses were lying. In fact, it may have been the Air Force that manufactured the explanation so that they could write off the case. In 1952, the Air Force put "possible aircraft" on the file, and closed it again.

When he got the film back, Mariana was mad. The Air Force, he claimed, had removed over thirty frames from the beginning of it. Those frames showed that the objects were elliptically shaped. They had turned slightly, reflecting the sun, giving them the bright, light look. Mariana demanded that the Air Force return the rest of the movie.

Air Force officers, however, denied that they had removed any of the film. Project Bluebook records show that they had asked permission to remove one frame because the sprockets were damaged, but that was all. They didn't remove any frames other than that in 1950 or in 1952, when they reexamined the film. Mariana, however, said that he had a letter about the removal of the thirty frames, although he was unable to produce it.

In 1953, the Air Force and the CIA ran a panel discussion of UFOs and possible solutions to cases. The panel looked at the Mariana film dozens of times and concluded that it could show aircraft, irrespective of Mariana's claims. Because they wanted UFOs to lose their cloak of mystery, the "possible" was dropped from the file. It was marked "aircraft."

The file was not closed. In 1955, Dr. Robert M.L. Baker made an exhaustive analysis while he was at Douglas Aircraft Corporation. He concluded, based on the evidence available from the film, that the images could not be explained by any presently known natural phenomena.

Baker went further than just looking at the films. He ran

a series of tests, the results of which appear in the Project Bluebook files. He filmed aircraft at varying distances. At twelve miles, using a camera similar to the one used by Mariana, Baker filmed a DC-3 so that it duplicated the Montana film. However, Baker wasn't impressed with those results.

Studying the Mariana film, Baker had determined that the objects were two miles from the camera. At that range, the interceptors would have been identifiable as planes. As the range increased, so did the rate of speed, until at ten miles, the objects had to be moving at six hundred miles an hour and at twelve, they were going faster than the interceptors could fly. Baker's duplicate needed a DC-3 at twelve miles and a DC-3 didn't have half the necessary speed. Another reason that Baker was unimpressed was the short time that the DC-3 duplicated the objects on Mariana's film. The plane was only masked by the reflections for a short time.

The film remained locked in that limbo until the Condon Committee was organized in 1966. Again, the films were studied, Baker's files were examined, Mariana was reinterviewed, and the complete Air Force file was seen. The Condon Committee added a new problem to the case. They weren't sure whether the date the film was taken was August 5 or August 15. If it was August 5, the aircraft explanation doesn't work.

In researching this case, the Condon Committee discovered that the August 15 date doesn't work if Mariana was in the ballpark to inspect the field before a game. Newspaper records show that there were no home games for the Great Falls team between August 9 and August 18. Air Force acceptance of the August 15 date probably stems from their desire to identify the objects on the film. If they accept the August 5 date, no easy explanation is suggested.

In the end, the Condon Committee said that if the August 15 date was correct, then the F-94 fuselage reflection answer made a lot of sense. However, they failed to make a fine distinction when writing the report and they probably hoped that their reaffirmation of the early conclusions of aircraft would destroy the case. It does not. Their investigation made that answer weaker than ever.

At the end of their study, they claimed that the Air Force was right. Mariana had filmed two jet aircraft. They mentioned the date problem but said that they found nothing unusual about the case.

Analysis of the film showed a variety of things. Possibly the most important fact came from the Condon Committee study. They found that the objects photographed had a constant shape and that was elliptical. Baker had thought that the shape had been due to irregular panning by the photographer, but it was shown that such panning had not occurred. Evidence of panning was found in one or two frames, but a complete study showed the shape of the objects had caused the images. Hard data available on the film did not provide enough definite information for a firm hypothesis to be made.

Although a complete frame-by-frame analysis has not been done, probably because a few of the frames are obscured by the water tower, long sequences of the film have been closely examined. All the studies failed to produce any data that showed the film had been faked. Data indicated, as mentioned earlier, that the objects were disc-shaped and the images on the film are consistent with high-polished metal surfaces on discs. Time becomes important. If Mariana estimated wrong and the objects were in sight for fifty seconds, the aircraft are effectively ruled out. If they were in sight for only twenty seconds, then it is possible for the jets to have caused the images.

The film did not resolve images well enough for those studying it to look for evidence of vapor trails or other types of atmospheric disturbance. At the altitude the jets would have been flying, vapor trails would not have been visible, but the motions of the air might have been. Unfortunately, cameras don't see as well as the eye so such studies are, today, impossible. It means that no evidence on the film can be used to demonstrate jets or disc-shaped objects. All the evidence suggests paths to follow, but none of it is conclusive and that is exactly what the scientists and UFO researchers want: conclusive evidence.

Baker, in 1969, reaffirmed his position on the film. He said that the physical evidence available on the film shows that it is not birds or balloons, mirages or meteors, and he doesn't think that it was reflections from jets. In that respect, he is at odds with the Air Force and Condon.

It finally boils down to the point where no one can be sure if Mariana filmed two spacecraft, or two aircraft, or something else. The hard data on the film indicates that the aircraft explanation doesn't work, but it doesn't prove that the objects are spacecraft. It leaves the film as unidentified.

The scientific data, although not completely reproduced here, can be found in a variety of places. Dr. Baker published papers on the film in at least two places. Philip Klass outlined the sighting in his book *UFOs Explained*. Although Klass feels that UFOs have explanations other than extraterrestrial, he treated the sighting fairly.

December 6, 1950: El Indio, Mexico

For me, the story of a second crashed disc came not from the briefing paper prepared for President-elect Eisenhower (*see September 24, 1947: The MJ-12*), but from a friend (*see October 1988: Warren Smith*). He was a young man in 1950 and was working with a manufacturer, installing new linotype machines at newspapers. He traveled around the country doing it and in December 1950 found himself in Lorain, Ohio.

The crew that ran the print shop and set the type ate lunch about the same time and in the same place. Smith wasn't that interested in eating lunch with middle-aged men when there were young, unattached women around, but he found himself in that situation more often than not.

One of those men had a wife who was on a dude ranch in Texas for a brief vacation. Every day she wrote her husband and every day he read the letters to anyone who would listen. The first weren't that interesting, but then one day she wrote they had seen something unusual in the sky. It appeared to be an airplane in trouble and the next day several of the "cowboys" were going to ride out to see what they could find.

The next day there was another letter. The cowboys had ridden out and located the wreckage. The only problem was that they didn't think it was an aircraft. There were bodies found, but they were so badly burned that no one could be sure what they had been. The only comment made was that it looked as if the ship had been piloted by children.

Now everyone was interested in the story. Unlike the Roswell incident where almost no one had heard of flying saucers, everyone in 1950 had. The conclusion drawn by the men in the lunchroom was that the cowboys had stumbled onto the remains of a flying disc, complete with crew.

Naturally, there was a great deal of speculation about the nature of the craft and where it came from. There were a couple of men who wanted to believe that it was an experimental aircraft that had gone down. Others argued as strongly that it was something that had been built on another world. The problem was that no one knew enough about the current technology of the aviation industry to know if the lightweight metals were something that couldn't have been manufactured on Earth.

The final installment in the story was a report that it indeed had been an aircraft accident. The cowboys, having returned to the crash site, found it crawling with Mexican and American government officials and military officers. There seemed to be some kind of fight going on between the two official groups as they argued jurisdiction. No one seemed to know if it was an American plane or a Mexican plane. The cowboys were chased off before they could get too close.

That was the end of it and Smith forgot about it. He wasn't interested in UFOs at the time. He couldn't have cared whether the cowboys had found a flying saucer or the remains of a downed airplane.

It wasn't until I saw a copy of the briefing paper prepared for Eisenhower that I thought about the story again. Like so many other pieces of the UFO puzzle, I didn't know the significance of the story when I first heard it. After all, I had heard the stories of crashed saucers almost from the day I expressed interest in them. And I hadn't believed them. Frank

Scully and his little men had soured me on the notion (*see 1948: The UFO* Crashes Begin).

But then I saw the briefing paper and there is a story of a possible crash on the Texas-Mexican border, about the time the woman was writing letters to her husband. She would have no reason to make up the story and no reason to assume that it would ever be heard. For all she knew, her letters were read in privacy. A hoax on her part made no sense.

Now there is the briefing paper. It tells of a crash in the same area at the same time. If the briefing paper was a hoax, the man or woman writing it would have no knowledge of the woman who wrote her husband. If it is a hoax, there is an extraordinary coincidence there. Two unrelated people, separated by thousands of miles and thirty years, make up a story of a crashed saucer in the same area. It's especially interesting when it's remembered that almost all the stories of crashed saucers put them into Arizona or New Mexico.

For me, it was the final nail in the coffin. Couple it to the information from the Air Force sergeant who told me about faking UFO sighting solutions (*see September 4, 1964: Glassboro, New Jersey*), and it makes a solid package. His information confirms that something unusual happened in Roswell, and this new story confirms something happened near El Indio. And both of those tend to prove that the briefing paper is not a hoax. More research is needed, and there are pieces of the briefing paper that have not been released, but we're getting closer to the answers that the government has had for over forty years.

August 1951: The Lubbock Lights

Although the case was called the Lubbock Lights and the majority of the sightings took place in or around Lubbock, Texas, the first sighting was made in Albuquerque, New

Mexico, about 250 miles away. Before the lights disappeared for good weeks later, hundreds had seen them, one man had photographed them, and they had been tracked on radar. In fact, the original set of sightings, scattered over a large part of the country, blended so nicely that they could easily be called the best series of UFO sightings ever reported.

The Air Force spent a great deal of time, manpower, and money checking the sightings and came up with nothing. They wrote the radar cases off just to get rid of them and tried to explain the Lubbock Lights by saying that they were a natural phenomenon but did not explain the how or why.

It was on the evening of August 25, 1951, that a man and his wife watched a huge, "wing-shaped" UFO, with blue lights on the trailing edge, pass over the outskirts of Albuquerque and start the Lubbock Lights case. The man, an employee of the Atomic Energy Commission, said that they had gotten a good look at the UFO because it had been quite low, only eight hundred or a thousand feet above them. The "wing" was sharply swept back and was about one and a half times the size of a B-36. Dark bands ran from the front to the back and the lights were a softly glowing blue-green. The object disappeared in the south seconds after it had first been seen.

Air Force officers from Kirtland Air Force Base in Albuquerque investigated. They found that a commercial airliner was in that area as was a B-25, but neither plane was in a position to be seen by the couple. To further complicate matters, the man was employed at a secret installation and had a high security clearance. It made it unlikely that he was involved with a hoax.

Not long after the Albuquerque sighting, several college professors, while sitting on a porch in Lubbock, Texas, saw a "formation" of lights sweep overhead. The lights were only in sight for two or three seconds and none of the men managed to get a very good look. It happened too fast.

The professors discussed what they had just seen, and were upset that they had not been able to observe more. If the objects would reappear, the professors knew what they would do. Several hours later they got their chance. Each man made a series of quick and well-coordinated observations.

The lights were softly glowing—bluish objects that were in a loose formation. The first group, the professors believed, had been more rigid and more structured. During the next two weeks, the professors saw the lights on several occasions but were unable to obtain any other useful data.

However, after seeing the lights twice in one evening, they felt that chances were good that they would see them again. They equipped two teams with two-way radios, measured a base line from the location of the original sighting, and sent out the teams on several different nights. They hoped to make sightings so that triangulation could be used to determine altitude, speed, and size.

At the home of one of the professors, Dr. W.I. Robinson, a professor of geology, the group made several interesting observations. Several of the flights traveled through ninety degrees of sky in just over three seconds. The lights would always appear forty-five degrees above the northern horizon and disappear forty-five degrees above the southern horizon. Other than the first sighting, when the UFOs had been in a roughly semicircular formation, no regular pattern was noticed.

None of the teams ever saw the lights. On the nights that they were out, the lights were not. On one or two of the occasions, the wives of the men involved said that they had seen the lights while the men were out at the bases.

During the nights, the professors had plenty of time to discuss the lights and tried several explanations. If the lights were very high, they would have to be traveling very fast, but if they were low they would be traveling much slower. With a low altitude, a natural phenomenon would fit the description. But one of the professors, Dr. George, a professor of physics, had made extensive atmosphere studies and said that he had never seen anything like it. After all their studies, they were at a loss to explain the lights.

Early on the morning of August 26, 1951, two radar stations in Washington state picked up a target traveling at over nine hundred miles an hour. An F-86 interceptor was scrambled, but the UFO was gone before the jet arrived on station. The main point, however, was that two radar stations had picked up the UFO independently. Officers at the radar installations didn't believe the targets had been caused by weather because the targets on both scopes looked the same. If it had been weather, the targets would have appeared differently.

Five days later, an amateur photographer in Lubbock managed to take five pictures of the lights as they flew over his house. Carl Hart, Jr., a freshman at Texas Tech, had pushed his bed against the window because the night was so hot. He hadn't been in bed very long when he saw the Lubbock Lights flash through a clear sky.

The lights had returned on several occasions, so Hart grabbed his Kodak 35mm camera, set the shutter at f-3.5, and went outside. Minutes later, the lights reappeared and Hart managed to take two pictures. Another formation flew over after a few more minutes and Hart took three more photographs.

The next morning, Hart took the pictures to a friend who ran a photo-processing shop for developing. Hart often used the darkroom there for his work. When Air Force investigators asked Hart why he hadn't had the film developed immediately, he replied that he was afraid that nothing was on the film. The objects hadn't been all that bright. If he had known definitely that there was something on the film, he would have called his friend that night.

The negative did have an image and Hart's friend suggested that they call the local paper. At first, even though Hart had what may have been the "biggest news story in years," the paper wasn't interested. Reporters wanted to do some checking of their own before running the photos, but later they called Hart for the permission to use them.

Hart wasn't the only Texan to make a spectacular sighting on August 31. Two women, a mother and her daughter named Telsom, reported that they had seen a low-flying UFO about 12:30 A.M. They were near Matador, Texas, about seventy miles north of Lubbock, when a "pear-shaped" object appeared about 150 yards ahead of them and only a hundred feet above the highway. They drove on slowly but then stopped and got out of the car. The UFO was about the size of a B-29 and was drifting slowly away from them. There was no sign of an exhaust or flame and there was no noise, but there was a porthole on one side. The UFO, after giving the women a good look at it, began to pick up speed and entered a rapid, spiraling climb and disappeared in seconds.

Air Force investigators spent an entire day with the women. They found out that the daughter was quite familiar with aircraft because her husband was an Air Force officer. The women had said that the object was drifting with the wind, but it was found that they were mistaken. The investigators could find nothing else wrong with the report and could not find a reason why the women would make up the story. They worked all day but still didn't have the slightest idea what the women had seen.

The investigations continued with the Air Force getting nowhere. One officer, while talking to a man from Lubbock, discovered that the man's wife had seen a UFO on the same night that the college professors had seen the lights the first time. The man said that his wife was not crazy nor was she given to carrying tales. She had been outside, taking down the wash, while he had been reading the paper. His wife, he said, came running into the house, white as a ghost, shouting about the giant, "winglike" craft that had just flown over the house. It moved silently and had several bluish lights on the back of it.

The Air Force officer was stunned by the sighting. It was a duplicate of the Albuquerque sighting, it happened only minutes after the Albuquerque sighting, and there was no way that the woman could have known about that report. Only a few Air Force officers knew about it and they hadn't given the case to the press. If the woman had been making up a story, which was unlikely, she had picked a combination of facts that showed that she knew what was happening inside the Air Force UFO project. The chances that two people would, or could, make up a story that matched so closely, yet do it independently, was considered impossible.

In September 1951, the Air Force investigation of the Lubbock Lights and the related sightings officially began. The Albuquerque sighting was checked by the intelligence officer at Kirtland Air Force Base. He made several visits to the witnesses' house and asked hundreds of questions. The women gave him a drawing of the object and it was forwarded to Project Bluebook at Wright Field. After several weeks, and because of the witnesses' reliability, the sighting was listed as unidentified. That is the way it was carried in the Bluebook files until the end of the project.

The second sighting of the lighted, "flying wing" was never officially investigated. However, because none of the witnesses could have known of one another and because the reports were made independently within a few weeks of one another, the sightings should be considered related. The Lubbock woman's description of the UFO matched that seen in Albuquerque and must, because no explanation was found in the first report, be considered as unidentified. The second sighting adds a bit of credibility to the first and also suggests a question. How many others saw the UFO but failed to report it in official channels? It was just "dumb" luck that the second sighting was "reported" at all.

The Albuquerque and related Lubbock sightings stole the show. The main thrust of the Air Force investigation was at the Lubbock Lights and they pressed for an explanation. The college professors had found none.

Dozens of witnesses reported that they had seen the lights and the Air Force chased down quite a few of them. Most of the descriptions told of soft, bluish lights, zipping from one horizon to the other. The size of the formation varied from two or three objects to several dozen and from ragtag conglomerations of lights to the precise V-formations shown in the Hart photographs.

Air Force investigators found one man who had lived in West Texas for decades. He lived on the outskirts of Lubbock and had looked for the lights. One night, he saw two or three of them fly over. At first, he was scared, having never seen anything like the soft lights silently crossing the sky in seconds. Then, minutes later a few more appeared. This time he heard a quiet cry from one of the objects and immediately identified the lights as "plover," a West Texas bird. He told investigators that he thought the birds, with their oily, white breasts, were reflecting lights from the city and that was what everyone was seeing.

The idea sounded good and the Air Force checked it out. A local game warden, a man who had lived for many years in the area, was asked about the plover. They found that the birds rarely "flocked" and it was quite unnatural to see them in groups larger that two or three. The explanation might work where the man thought he had seen plover, but it could not be applied to all the sightings.

Air Force officers did find one other important fact. Parts of Lubbock had only recently been switched from one type of street lighting to the more modern mercury-vapor lights. The lights gave off a bluish light, and that could be what was reflected from the objects. One officer said that he thought they should plot the locations of all the witnesses and all the streets using the mercury-vapor lights to see if there was any correlation. It wasn't done.

That left, of course, the Hart pictures. It didn't seem likely that Hart had photographed plover reflecting light for a variety of reasons. First, the plover don't flock. Second, they don't fly in V-formations, and last, it didn't seem likely that Hart would be able to photograph them because there wouldn't be enough light. That was finally proven in a series of tests run by a photographer for a local paper. He tried everything from super-fast film to long exposures but failed to get the plover reflecting the lights.

Air Force investigators spent a lot of time with Hart. They asked for the negatives and Hart went for them. Unfortunately, he could find only four; the fifth was lost. The four negatives were dirty, scratched, and bent, but they were sent to the photo interpretation labs at Wright. They analyzed the negatives from every angle but could find no indication that they had been faked. Unfortunately, they could not prove that they weren't, so the Air Force really got nowhere.

Air Force officers had Hart show them where he had taken the pictures and asked how long the objects had been in sight. They asked him to show them the camera and how it worked. They spent days trying to break his story but couldn't.

At Wright, with a Kodak 35mm camera just like Hart's, they ran a series of tests. They had a professional photographer try to take pictures of a moving light as Hart had done. He couldn't come close to duplicating Hart's success and that convinced some that Hart had faked the pictures. They were all acting pretty smug until one of the professional photographers said that if Hart was familiar with his camera and with panning techniques, his pictures should be better than Air Force attempts to duplicate them. Hart was familiar with his camera and photographed sports events for the local newspaper; therefore he was familiar with panning techniques.

In the end, the Air Force was left with no explanation. They didn't want to call the pictures fake because they couldn't support that, but they didn't want to classify them as unidentified either. Finally, they left a question mark on the sighting and attempted no explanation.

The professors' sightings were attacked next. After careful investigation, the officers decided that they could not really identify the UFOs. However, since the professors never heard a sound and since the two teams never saw the objects, it was assumed that they were quite low and therefore, quite small. Some of the officers believed that birds were the answer to the Lubbock Lights.

One other problem remained and that was the radar sightings that happened on the same night as the Albuquerque sighting and the first Lubbock Lights sighting. Several Air Force technicians decided that the object seen on the radar was a weather phenomenon. That it was tracked at nine hundred miles an hour was a trick played by the weather. The sighting was written off in the official records as a weather problem and not a UFO.

Weeks after the sighting, the radar unit commander called Project Bluebook to find out what had been done with his sighting. The Project officer told him the official conclusion. The radar officer wanted to know what kind of slipshod, no-good, and worthless kind of answer that represented. He told them that he was completely familiar with weather effects on radar and had checked closely. The image on both scopes was the same and because they had been operating on different frequencies, it made the chance of weather even more remote. If the object hadn't been on both scopes and if it hadn't been the same, he wouldn't have filed the report.

About two weeks after the episode started it ended. The Lubbock Lights went out, no one else reported the strange, flying wing, and no other photographs were taken. No other witnesses came forward and there seemed to be nowhere to go. All the sightings, except for the radar cases, were carried as unidentified by the Air Force.

However, several years after the Lubbock Lights were reported, a scientist working with the Air Force came up with a natural phenomenon that "explained" the Lubbock Lights. Reports of the explanation were made but none of the details were given to the public. A "secret" explanation is no explanation at all. The Air Force could say that they had an explanation if they wanted to use it, but they had sworn that they wouldn't reveal any information that might identify the man who found it. It seems to be another attempt by the Air Force to discredit a good, solid sighting.

What were the Lubbock Lights? Probably some of them were birds just as the old Texan suggested. In the sightings that involved only a couple of objects and no formation, the plover is the logical answer. However, many of the other sightings do not fit there.

Some cases were probably a form of mass hysteria. Any time that one person sees something strange, others begin to look. Many times, the new sightings aren't of the UFOs but of something ordinary that the witnesses had not noticed before. In Lubbock, however, the Air Force wasn't too concerned with this problem.

Many of the sightings, including the first by the college professors, were never satisfactorily explained. Some UFO debunkers "ripped holes" in the sightings, but the original Lubbock Lights sighting, the Albuquerque case, and the Hart pictures withstood the onslaught. They have never been explained.

One final point about the August 25, 1951, sightings must be made. The Albuquerque sighting came about fifteen minutes before the first of the Lubbock sightings. An object, traveling nine hundred miles an hour, could have easily flown the 250 miles to Lubbock. The last Lubbock sighting on August 25 came about 11:30 P.M. and the radar sightings came sometime just after midnight. A quick calculation showed that a speed of about 780 miles an hour would be required for the UFO to move from Lubbock to the Washington radar stations. That is fairly close to the nine hundred miles an hour they were tracked at as they passed the station. It turns out that the UFO sightings for August 25–26 are an amazing string of closely related and closely investigated cases.

The Lubbock Lights remain as one of the classics of the UFO era. More research on the case is almost impossible because many of the witnesses have died since 1951. Other sightings, more recent sightings, carry as much weight, but the Lubbock Lights case remains as one of the series of reports that has convinced some of the worst nonbelievers that something is, in fact, out there. More than one person has decided that UFOs must be real because of the Lubbock sightings.

July 2, 1952: The Tremonton, Utah Film

Like all other types of physical evidence, the Tremonton, Utah, film is surrounded in controversy. One group claims that the objects shown on the film are the result of sunlight on the white breasts of seagulls seen at the extreme range of human vision while others claim that the UFOs are just that, unidentified flying objects.

On July 2, 1952, Navy Warrant Officer Delbert C. Newhouse was driving across Utah with his wife on the way to a new duty station. It was just after eleven in the morning when his wife noticed a group of bright objects. She pointed them out and when Newhouse couldn't easily identify them, he stopped the car for a better look.

Newhouse was a trained Navy photographer and had a 16mm movie camera in the trunk. He got the camera and managed to film the objects before they finally vanished. Newhouse later said that he wanted to give analysts something to work with so that when one of the objects broke formation, he singled it out, letting it fly across the field of view. He didn't move the camera, hoping that it would provide a speed estimate. He let the object do that two or three times and when he turned back, the whole formation was gone.

The details of the story vary, depending on the source. Air Force files, based on information provided by others, show that Newhouse and his wife may have seen the objects at close range. By the time he got the car stopped and the camera out, the objects had moved to the long range shown in the film. In an interview I conducted in 1976, Newhouse confirmed that he did see the objects closer to the car. He said they were large, disc-shaped, and brightly lighted. If that is all true, then the explanation offered for the case by the Air Force and later the Condon Committee has to be ruled out.

Newhouse, after filming the UFOs, got back into the car and continued on to his duty station where he had the film processed. He sent a copy to the Air Force explaining that they might find it interesting. Project Bluebook investigators watched the film and the investigation began.

During the following weeks, Newhouse and his family were interviewed several times by Air Force officers. Each report was forwarded to Bluebook Headquarters and a list of questions would be sent to the investigators to clarify specific points.

Analysis of the film continued for months. They tried everything they could think of to identify the objects on the film, but failed. Together with the report and the reliability of the photographer, the Air Force was stuck. They had no explanation and said that the film contained objects they couldn't identify.

When the Air Force finished with the film, the Navy asked for it. Since a Navy officer had taken it, the Navy felt they should be provided with an opportunity to examine it. And that's exactly what they did. Navy film experts made a frame-by-frame analysis that took over a thousand man hours. They studied the motion of the objects, their relation to one another in the formation, the lighting of the UFOs, and every other piece of data they could find on the film. In the end, like their Air Force counterparts, they were left with no explanations.

But unlike their Air Force counterparts, the Navy experts were not restricted in their praise of the film. Their report said that the objects were internally lighted spheres that were not reflecting sunlight. They also suggested that the velocity of the objects was 3,780 miles an hour if the spheres were five miles away. At twice the distance, they would have been moving twice as fast and at half the distance, they would have been flying at half the speed. If the glowing spheres were just under a mile distant, they would have been traveling at 472 miles an hour. Those figures may prove valuable when the final hypothesis presented by the Air Force and confirmed by both the CIA-sponsored Robertson Panel and the Condon Committee are examined.

At the end of 1952, no one had been able to determine what the Tremonton film showed. The Air Force was saying that they were sure the UFOs were not planes or balloons and pretty sure that they weren't birds. The Navy, less conservative, did everything but say the film showed spacecraft.

In January 1953, all the data about the Tremonton film was presented to the Robertson Panel (*See January 1953: The Robertson Panel*) by the officers of Bluebook. One of the men suggested that an error in the measurements had been made by the Navy experts using a densitometer and that their calculations were, therefore, wrong. Another panel member wanted to know if Newhouse had held the camera steady as he filmed the single object, pointing out that any camera motion would throw off the speed calculations. A third said he had seen soaring seagulls in California and the motion of the objects on the film reminded him of seagulls soaring on thermals.

By the time the conference had ended, the suggestion that the film showed birds was accepted by the panel members. Later, Donald H. Menzel would claim that it had been definitely proven that the film showed birds.

In 1955, Doctor R.M.L. Baker made another study of the film, saying that he didn't think they were planes or balloons for the reasons outlined by the Air Force, and that he didn't think they were bits of airborne debris or radar chaff because they didn't twinkle. Ballooning spiders were ruled out because the UFOs were seen from a moving car, and there was no evidence of silk tails. And, he said, he found the bird hypothesis to be rather unsatisfactory.

He also attacked several of the criticisms of the Robertson Panel. The suggestion was that unconscious panning action by the photographer would reduce the speed estimates. Baker said that any unconscious panning action would be with the object. If the speed estimates were wrong, then they were too low. That compounded the difficulty with the bird idea. The objects might have been traveling faster than the Navy's estimated 3,780 miles an hour.

The Condon Committee, of course, took their shot at the films. They spent a great deal of time examining the history of the case and who had said what about it. Finally, they devoted little more than a page in their final report to their analysis of the angular size, distance, and velocity. They tried to present, using a variety of measurements and estimates, a case for birds. They rejected the Navy contention that the objects can't be birds because they are too bright but provided no supporting evidence. They did admit that there were no periodic variations suggesting wing flapping. In other words, they rejected information that did not conform to their ideas by saying that there was no proof but then turned around and accepted other information without proof. It was hardly an unbiased and objective position.

The Condon Committee ended their investigation by saying that they, too, believed the film showed seagulls. They don't say it is possible they are birds, but that they are birds, probably seagulls. They do it by making no mention of Newhouse's testimony that he had seen the objects at closer range.

In the end, and like the Montana film taken two years earlier, we are left with one explanation that is not very good. Again, the probable has been left off the file and several well-known, well-respected scientists have said that birds adequately solve the question of what the film shows. The Air Force, however, had done its job as outlined by the Robertson Panel. They had injected enough controversy into the case that its value was ruined for the serious researcher and that was their only concern.

July 1952: The Washington Nationals

The wave of sightings really began in early April of the year. Air Force officers at Project Bluebook didn't notice the increase because it came slowly. By June 1952, however, they had realized that they were receiving reports in unprecedented numbers. The general public was unaware of the sightings, and with all the other things that were happening that summer it is not surprising.

Sometimes, a study of the mood of the public or an understanding of the period can be helpful in understanding a wave of sightings. In 1952, the United States, or rather the United Nations, was fighting the Korean War. In July, the Democrats were holding their convention to nominate a candidate for president and the Olympic Games were in full swing. In other words, there were enough activities to occupy the time, but on July 29, newspapers all over the country carried banner headlines saying, "Saucers Swarm Over Capital." The flying saucers seen on radar over Washington D.C.'s National Airport had stolen the headlines from everything else.

The first press reports were made in most of the country on July 22, with stories about sightings and radar reports made on the previous Saturday night, July 19. Unlike most of the reports of the past, these were all multiple witness cases, and multiple radar cases. Returns were seen on scopes at Washington National Airport, Andrews Air Force Base, and Bolling Air Force Base.

Newspapers were quoting Air Force officials about the sightings, saying that it was the first time that saucers had been picked up on radar. (That, of course, wasn't true, but it was what the Air Force was telling the public.) There had been many of them, some flying in formations while others looped across the sky alone. Speeds ranged from one hundred miles an hour to over eight thousand miles an hour, and others hovered briefly and then shot away.

The interesting thing about the sightings was that no intercepts were attempted. According to an Associated Press story, only the preliminary report had been released so there was no reason given for the lack of an intercept.

Radar and airport employees weren't the only ones seeing UFOs. Captain Casey Pierman on Capital Airlines Flight 807 said that he was between Washington and Martinsburg, West Virginia, at 1:15 A.M., when he and the rest of his crew saw seven objects flash across the sky. Pierman said, "They were like falling stars without the trails."

Capital officials said that the airport radar picked up the objects and asked Pierman to keep an eye on them. Shortly after that, Pierman called back saying that he had the objects in sight. He was flying at 180 to 200 mph and reported that the objects were traveling at tremendous speed. They would move rapidly up and down and then suddenly change pace until they seemed to hang motionless in the sky.

Another Capital plane, Flight 610, reported that a single light followed it from Herndon, Virginia, to within four miles of National Airport. About the same time, an Air Force radar installation was tracking eight objects as they flew over Washington, D.C.

The papers again carried brief accounts of flying saucers over National Airport on Saturday, July 26, just one week after the first sightings. This time, the Air Force alerted its interceptors and sent several F-94 jets after the saucers. Although the planes have a speed of 600 mph, they were unable to catch any of the saucers.

On Monday, July 28, an Air Force spokesman said that they "had no concrete evidence that they are flying saucers. Conversely, we have no concrete evidence that they are not saucers." He went on to point out that the Air Force was taking all the steps necessary to evaluate the reports.

They were mystified by the large number of reports coming from CAA (forerunner of the FAA) radars, airport employees, National Airlines pilots, and even civilians on the ground.

Dozens had seen the lights and even watched a few of the Air Force attempts to catch the saucers.

On July 29, 1952, Drew Pearson wrote that the Air Force was becoming "less skeptical" about flying saucers. The Air Force had, according to Pearson, made several important admissions. They admitted that they had "finally" detected something on radar that looked like a flying saucer. Secondly, they admitted that "flying saucers could be craft from another planet because we could now reach the moon if we wanted to spend the money necessary for the research."

Pearson also indicated that a number of scientific watch stations were being set up in the southwest. After all, there were already scientifically trained people in the area, so they might as well look for flying saucers and "track them scientifically."

As all this was breaking in the press, the Air Force announced a plan to photograph the flying saucers. Special cameras were going to be given to members of the Ground Observer's Corps so that they might be able to provide an insight into the mystery. In fact, that plan was mentioned by several reports in several different articles, but no one seems to know if the plan was ever carried out and if it was, whether any pictures were taken.

On the evening of July 29, the UFOs returned to Washington. Air Force officers had just released their findings, hoping to break the wave, and later in the evening, the saucers were swarming all over Washington. Radar picked up dozens of UFOs, as many as twelve at one time. Because there were no visual sightings, the CAA didn't make a report to the Air Force. They did, however, watch the UFOs from about 1:30 A.M., to about 5:30 A.M.

About 3:00 A.M., an Eastern Airlines southbound flight was directed to the area of the sightings. The altitude of the saucers was not known, so they could only direct the plane to the area. The pilot was unable to find the saucers and quickly turned back to his regular course.

This was the third set of sightings in two weeks at the airport. The first two had been on consecutive Saturday nights. Those other sightings included visual confirmation and a few attempted intercepts. The Air Force, however, had the answers immediately.

On Tuesday, July 29, the Air Force called a conference to discuss the flurry of sightings made during the last ten days. The first thing they said was that there had been nothing hostile about the saucers so that no one need worry.

General John A. Samford said that of the one-fifth (20 percent) of the sightings that have no explanation (a somewhat higher figure than their 3 to 7 percent claimed in later years), "no pattern has ever been found that reveals anything remotely like a purpose."

Samford went on to explain that the hot weather "of recent weeks well might be related to the current outbreak of saucer reports." He said that a temperature inversion had been over Washington for the last several weeks and that it was enough to give the false radar returns. "During World War II, fighters had been scrambled dozens of times because of temperature inversions showing on the radar scopes."

Samford said that 60 percent of the sightings came from civilians, about 25 percent from military pilots, and around 8 percent from airline pilots. He noted that there was an absence of reports from astronomers and because they observed the sky regularly, you would expect more reports from them. (It is interesting to note that Project Bluebook files contained a survey of fifty astronomers by Dr. J. Allen Hynek. He found that astronomers report UFOs at a rate slightly above the national average.)

Samford went on to outline the use of special cameras for taking pictures of UFOs. At the time, Samford was suggesting that two hundred such cameras be distributed in the hopes that good pictures would be made.

In the paper, next to Samford's account, the *Cedar Rapids Gazette* carried a story about a veteran Air Force pilot who claimed that he had been attacked by a saucer. Lieutenant George Kinman of Birmingham, Alabama, said that he was on a flight near Augusta, Georgia, in 1951 and it was a clear day. Charles Tracy, of the *Cleveland Press*, said that Kinman had told him about the sighting.

On Thursday, July 31, 1952, "radar experts and weather

scientists'' replied to the Air Force claims of temperatures inversion. ''Radar crews at Washington National Airport, where the mysterious 'blips' have been tracked three times in the last two weeks, maintained they have recorded 'unknown objects' twisting in a weird pattern, and not light reflections, as the Air Force suggested.''

Weather bureau officials said that an inversion had existed over Washington but that it would have appeared as a steady line rather than as single objects. Later, officials would claim that the inversions were too weak to cause the sightings and radar returns.

The article started to report the happenings of the last few days but then mentioned that the Coast Guard was going to let the Air Force inspect the picture of the five ''egg-shaped'' objects flying in formation taken by a seaman in Salem, Massachusetts, on July 16 at 9:35 A.M. (EDT).

Others began to get into the picture. Dr. Harlow Shapley, of the Harvard Observatory in Cambridge, Massachusetts, said that he believed that all saucer sightings could be explained by hallucinations, meteorites, high altitude balloons, and planes. He said that all the recent sightings were due to the items that he had listed, and quickly pointed out that all of them would register on the radarscope with the exception of the hallucination.

But even with scientists saying that people were making mistakes, the reports of saucers continued. One scientist said that the sightings would peak on August 12 because a big meteor shower was scheduled, but his prediction didn't come true. In August, there were twenty sightings that were unidentified, but there were at least 150 reports made. In September, there were twenty-one unidentifieds, but the pace finally had begun to slacken. In October and November, there were an additional sixteen reports listed as ''unexplained.''

In the years that followed, the Washington Nationals became one of the classics in UFO literature. The Air Force explanations were so weak that the Air Force carried the sightings officially as unidentified. The whole case involved several sightings, both visual and radar.

The Condon Committee, naturally, looked into the Wash-

ington Nationals. They did little with them. They reaffirmed
the Air Force claim that temperature inversions were in the
area at the time of the sightings and that those inversions
could be the cause of some of the sightings. They also mentioned the meteor showers that were in progress and that the
"stars were very bright" on those nights. They believed that
astronomical phenomena may account for some of the sightings. However, they admitted that there were a number of
sightings that couldn't be explained by temperature inversions, the meteors, and stars. Basically, they said that they
couldn't identify every sighting because the time lapse was
too great and there wasn't enough data to enable them to
make positive identifications.

In the end, we are stuck with several sightings, confirmed
on radar, and made by pilots. Weather and radar experts are
at odds over the causes of the objects. From the biased Air
Force position, we heard that the temperature inversions
caused the problems. Others, supposedly unbiased, attacked
the Air Force, and others still, equally unbiased, defended
the Air Force. It all came down to what you wanted to believe.
There are a dozen explanations, none of which are satisfactory. Like so much of the UFO field, the Washington Nationals are wrapped in controversy and the real answer may
never be found.

January 1953: The Robertson Panel

By the end of 1952, the whole country was talking about
flying saucers. Objects had buzzed Washington's National
Airport twice. There were new movies and dozens of new
photographs. In September, the first occupant report to receive any kind of publicity had been made, and there were
literally dozens of books, articles, and films about UFOs that

came out around that time. Anything that dealt with flying saucers was sure to make money.

Because of the intense public interest, the CIA sponsored a panel in January 1953, to study the phenomenon. The Office of Scientific Intelligence held a series of secret meetings in the Pentagon from the thirteenth to the seventeenth of January 1953, chaired by Dr. H.P. Robertson. Sanitized copies of the report have been available to the public since the Condon Report in 1969, but it wasn't until 1975 that researchers were able to name all members of the panel. Most notable of the names was Dr. Lloyd V. Berkner (*see September 1947: The Majestic Twelve*).

During the five-day conference, the panel members looked at the best of the UFO cases that were in the Project Bluebook files, including the Tremonton, Utah, film (*see July 2, 1952: The Tremonton, Utah Film*). These were discussed at length with a final determination that UFOs posed no threat to the security of the United States and that they weren't dangerous.

The final part of the conference was devoted to what should be done about the phenomenon. Panel members recommended that a policy of debunking of UFO reports be started. It said:

> The "debunking" aim would result in reduction of public interest in "flying saucers," which today evokes a strong psychological reaction. This education could be accomplished by mass media such as television, motion pictures, and popular articles . . . Such a program should tend to reduce the current gullibility of the public and consequently their susceptibility to clever hostile propaganda.

The Condon Committee report suggested the program of education had never gotten off the ground. The economics of the time and the perception that books explaining the phenomenon didn't sell as well as those that supported the extraterrestrial hypothesis were cited as reasons that the program never started (of course, that was so much specious argument). A governmental official explaining that a sighting had been identified, no matter how ridiculous that explanation might be, always received attention in the media. Donald Menzel wrote debunking books and Philip Klass has sold several.

After the panel ended, the controversy began. J. Allen Hynek, who was invited to attend but not participate, suggested that the explanations given for some sightings flew in the face of the facts. Tremonton, for example, was not the result of birds.

Ed Ruppelt claimed that after the Robertson Panel, he was ordered to debunk sightings and ridicule witnesses. The Air Force, the government, was no longer interested in collecting data about UFOs; they were interested in explaining them. Destroy the public's belief that something strange was going on and the interest in it would be gone.

Such an attitude makes almost no sense. If the CIA and the government wanted to learn all it could about the phenomenon, especially if they were worried that it was a threat to the security of the country, a policy to debunk and ridicule would inhibit that research. Witnesses would not be willing to come forward with their reports.

That is, it makes no sense until the Roswell incident is plugged into the formula. Then, with all the answers at hand, the CIA would be interested in protecting what they preceived as valuable defense information. Any UFO sighting was a leak that could lead back to Roswell. It is standard intelligence technique to flood a leak with disinformation so that the enemy, in this case the American public, wouldn't know how much was good and how much was bad. The hope of the CIA was that all information about UFOs would be discredited.

The Robertson Panel and its recommendations to debunk UFO sightings was just one of a series of steps designed to destroy public faith in UFO sightings and investigations.

November 23, 1953: The Kinross Disappearance

The Air Force file on this case, believe it or not, contains two sheets of paper. Considering the implications of the loss of a jet interceptor while chasing a UFO, the lack of concern is appalling. Official records, the reports of other UFO investigators, and the story, as told by an Air Force colonel who was there at the time, can provide a clue about the disappearance.

On the evening of November 23, 1953, radar at Truax Air Force Base picked up an unidentified blip over Soo Locks and in restricted airspace. Because it was in a restricted area and couldn't be easily identified, an F-89 jet interceptor was scrambled from Kinross Field. No one was too upset yet, and only one plane was sent.

Ground radar vectored the jet, flown by Lieutenant Felix Moncla, Jr., toward the UFO. Those on the ground asked if R.R. Wilson, the radar officer on the F-89, had the object on his scope and when he answered "no," they continued to track it.

The UFO, which had been hovering, now accelerated as it headed out over Lake Superior. With ground controllers vectoring him, Moncla raced after it, at over five hundred miles an hour. For nine minutes, the chase continued with Moncla gaining slightly on the UFO and Wilson finally able to get a fix on the target with the on-board radar. The gap narrowed and the jet closed in until suddenly Moncla caught the UFO.

No one is sure what happened. The two blips seemed to merge, at first, not alarming those on the ground. They had no height-finding radar and thought that the jet had flown under the UFO. But the blips didn't separate. They hung there together, for a moment, and then the single blip flashed off the screen.

Attempts to reach Moncla on the radio failed. It appeared that the jet had not survived the collision—if a collision had, in fact, happened. They called out the Search and Rescue Unit, giving them the last known position of the jet, and through the night, they continued to search, later joined by the Canadians. Everyone was hopeful that they would find Moncla and Wilson because they had carried enough equipment to survive a crash into the lake.

An early edition of the *Chicago Tribune* carried a story about the crash and the radar operator's claim that the plane had hit something. The search was continuing, but the longer it took the less likely that the men would be found alive. The Air Force moved quickly to kill the story, denying that the plane had hit anything.

Although a well-coordinated search was conducted, and although everyone knew about where the plane should have gone down, they never found anything. There was no wreckage, no oil slick, no bodies. The last trace of the F-89 was seen just as the two radar blips merged.

In the years that followed, the Air Force tried a wide variety of answers. They claimed that the radar operators had misread the scope and that Moncla had been attempting to catch a Canadian DC-3. After it had been identified, Moncla, on the return trip, must have had something go wrong and the plane crashed. It was strange that he never radioed his report to the radar men who had been watching the chase on radar.

The Canadians quickly denied the report. They said that they had no aircraft over the lake at any time during the chase. Air Force officers were also catching flak for saying that Moncla had gotten vertigo, causing the crash. Pilots said that all Moncla had to do was put the plane on automatic pilot until the vertigo passed or let Wilson fly it for a while.

For a year, the Air Force stuck to the DC-3 story before changing it to an RCAF jet. Moncla had intercepted that. However, the Canadians again denied that they had a plane in the area. Whatever Moncla had been chasing, it certainly wasn't a Canadian aircraft, either military or civilian.

Later, the Air Force said that Moncla's plane had exploded at high altitude and that caused the disappearance. It overlooked the fact that an explosion would have left wreckage spread all over the surface of the lake, and none was ever found.

When I was at Maxwell Air Force Base in 1976, I asked to see the file about the disappearance. I was surprised to find that it contained two sheets of paper. One sheet said that the crash was an aircraft accident and not a UFO report, but because of all the letters that they had received about the case project officers had opened the file. However, it had nothing to do with UFOs. That, of course, overlooked the original mission of Moncla—intercept an unidentified object over Soo Locks.

The other sheet was a galley proof from a book written by Donald Menzel, a UFO debunker. He said that many writers had seized the case to prove that UFOs were extraterrestrial and possibly hostile. He accepted the Air Force answer about the loss of the jet—all varieties of the answer.

Air Force officers who were at Truax when Moncla disappeared had their own ideas. According to a lieutenant colonel who was there, the chase, disappearance, and search were carried out just as claimed here. No trace of the plane was found. He said that there were two schools of thought about the disappearance. "One group thought that the plane had gone straight into the lake. If it didn't break up, there would have been no oil slick or wreckage. It is entirely possible. However, the other school, supported by the majority of the pilots, was that Moncla had been 'taken' by the UFO."

He said that a large group of Air Force officers, pilots, radar operators, navigators, administration people, etc., believe that an Air Force jet had been captured or destroyed by a UFO. This was contrary to Air Force policy and conclusions about the case.

There are, however, other questions that should be asked. While at Maxwell, I searched the index for a UFO report from that area for the months of November and December 1953, and January 1954. I looked for any case involving Air Force personnel from Michigan, Wisconsin, or Illinois, trying to find some kind of confirmation of the case. I didn't find it.

I didn't find it because it had been removed. It had been there once because the lieutenant colonel had told me about it. Moncla's disappearance wasn't the only report from that area at that time. It was some of the other reports that convinced many that Moncla had been involved with something from space.

After Moncla disappeared, two fighter pilots reported that they were paced by a large bright UFO. They had been on a routine mission when the UFO had joined the formation. They radioed their base, telling them about the craft that was following them. Before making the call, they had gone through a series of turns to make sure that the UFO was there and that it wasn't a reflection on the canopy. The UFO maintained the same position, indicating that it was following them in the turns.

For several minutes the UFO remained near them. They discussed the possibility of turning into the object, but they remembered what had happened to Moncla and were reluctant to do it. Finally, as they neared the airfield, they decided that something had to be done and they made the turn. The UFO hesitated for a split second and then flashed away. When the pilots landed, they made a complete report to the intelligence officer who, according to regulations, should have forwarded it to Project Bluebook.

The lieutenant colonel knew the pilots involved and knew that they had forwarded a report. He was mildly surprised when I told him that the report was not in the Bluebook Files. He knew that it had been made and wondered what had happened to it.

The final questions are what really happened to Moncla and Wilson and why has the Air Force tried to hide the answers? We know that something did happen. The plane did disappear. And, there were UFO reports in the area that have never been satisfactorily explained. Did a UFO cause the disappearance or was it another tragic coincidence like that of Thomas Mantell?

July 2, 1954: The Walesville, New York Disaster

By contrast with Kinross, Walesville is a good example of the sloppy research in the UFO field. It is the report that an F-94 was "shot" down by a flying saucer in July 1954. UFO researchers and writers have been bouncing the case around for years, using it to prove that UFOs are hostile or, at the very least, dangerous. Like so many other UFO horror stories, good research shows that it is something quite different from what those writers claim.

Donald Keyhoe in *Aliens from Space* and Otto Binder in *What We Really Know About Flying Saucers* tell the story of an F-94 crash near Griffiss Air Force Base. Both men report the incident in a similar fashion.

According to them, an unidentified object was spotted on radar on July 1, 1954, flying near Griffiss (Binder misspells the name of the base, calling it Griffis). An interceptor was scrambled and given a heading so that it could find the UFO. It caught the strange, disc-shaped object near Utica, New York. The radar officer in the plane then saw the object and pointed it out to the pilot. They closed in so that they could see it better.

Before they could get too close, the cockpit filled with an unbearable heat. None of the warning lights glowed and yet the heat continued to build until the pilot could stand it no longer. He gave the order and both men bailed out.

As the two men watched, the plane flew straight and level for a distance and then began a gradual descent toward Walesville, New York. It crashed near an intersection close to the center of town as it burst into flames, hit a house, and skidded into an intersection, smashing a car. Four people died, three in the car and one in the house.

According to Keyhoe, the pilot blacked out soon after he bailed out and a psychologist suggested that the reaction was attributed to the aircraft diving into a city, but Keyhoe doubted it. He suspected that the blackout was one more side effect of the heat-ray used by the UFO. Keyhoe had talked to an Air Force officer who gave him the "real" story.

Binder claimed that both airmen were interrogated at length by Air Force investigators and that they were not responsible for the disaster. They had followed Air Force regulations and had been driven from the cockpit by the heat. Binder claimed that there was only one source for the heat and that was the UFO. He also claimed that his account was based on official Air Force records.

Keyhoe took it further. Keyhoe's mysterious Pentagon source said that the pilot and the radar officer from the F-94 were taken from the Walesville area in an Air Force staff car and they weren't allowed to make statements. Keyhoe attached some significance to that and claims that the file on the Walesville incident is still classified.

To further perpetuate the myth of Walesville, Jacques Vallee and J. Allen Hynek mention it in *The Edge of Reality*. Vallee claims that two planes were scrambled to intercept a UFO on July 2, 1954. Hynek mentions that it isn't a documented case, but Vallee insists that it is documented and that there was even a picture in *The New York Times*. Somehow, having a picture in the *Times* proved that a UFO knocked the plane out of the sky. Vallee later claimed that he saw it as the test of the Condon Committee. If they were really studying UFOs, they would have searched out more information about the case. Both Hynek and Vallee leave the impression that the Walesville case is a solid one. Both overlook the fact that Keyhoe dates the case as July 1.

Contrary to Keyhoe, the Air Force records are not classified. Contrary to Vallee, the Condon Committee did investigate the crash. According to the information available from *The New York Times*, the Air Force, and the Condon Committee, Keyhoe and Binder combined two incidents into one super space spectacular.

Official sources show that on July 1, 1954, a partially deflated balloon (at no time did anyone think that the balloon was anything extraterrestrial) was seen over Rome, New York. The officer in charge of the Air Force depot there said that he would have it investigated if it was still there the next day. It wasn't, but it explains where the discrepancy of the date and where Binder's description of a disc-shaped object come from.

According to official Air Force records, the crash took place on July 2. "The F-94 took off at 11:05 A.M. EST, for an operational training mission . . . The aircraft was only a few miles out when the Griffiss AFB control tower operator called the pilot to advise that he was being diverted to an active air defense mission. A vector of 60 degrees and 10,000 feet altitude was given to intercept an unidentified aircraft. The pilot experienced some difficulty finding this aircraft and the controller then informed him of a second unidentified aircraft in the area. This aircraft was (subsequently) identified (by the F-94 pilot) as an Air Force C-47, tail number 6099."

With that aircraft identified, the controller turned the jet and sent him back after the first unidentified. "The F-94 was at 8,000 feet, flying above the tops of broken clouds. The unidentified aircraft was not found above the clouds so the pilot started to descend. It was evident that the unidentified aircraft was going to land at Griffiss Air Force Base."

In other words, the intercept was broken because they had discovered that the UFO was in the traffic pattern to Griffiss where it landed safely. It was an Air Force plane and not a flying saucer.

"During the descent," the Air Force report continues, "there was intense heat in the cockpit and the engine plenum chamber fire warning light came on. The pilot shut down the engine and the light remained on. Due to the critical low altitude and the fire warning, the pilot and the radar observer ejected and were recovered without injury."

The brief report from the Air Force concludes, saying, "The aircraft traveled about four miles from the point of ejection and while on a heading of 199 degrees, crashed into the Walesville intersection at 11:27 A.M. EST. The aircraft struck a dwelling, killing a housewife and injuring her daughter, then struck an auto at an intersection, killing all three occupants."

The New York Times article about the story mentions nothing about disc-shaped UFOs, heat-rays, or any of the other items that the UFO researchers have thrown into the case. It's a straightforward news report of a tragedy in Walesville, New York. In fact, without the reports from Binder, Keyhoe, and all the others, there would be no reason to suspect anything different. That is Vallee's documentation. It proves that a plane crashed and that is all it proves.

It may do no good to belabor the obvious. How accurate is the rest of Keyhoe's work, or Binder's work, if they can't even get the spelling of the Air Force Base right? Binder consistently spells it without one "s." They have the date wrong, and they conveniently leave out the references to the fire warning light. They scramble the jet for an unidentified rather than have it already airborne, and say nothing about one UFO being identified and the other landing at Griffiss.

It may also be interesting to note that Air Force behavior on the incident was no different from it is after any aircraft accident. They always button it up so that they can get the facts before the pilots and witnesses have a chance to discuss the case. Any time there are witnesses, the proper procedure is to isolate them and question them separately so that their testimony won't be colored by talking to others.

The Walesville disaster is just one more example of how the facts of a case become so distorted that it is sometimes impossible to separate reality from fiction. And, it points to another important problem with all this type of research. Many of the people conducting it are biased. They want to believe, so when the facts presented are what they want to believe they stop searching, often overlooking the explanations.

Walesville has nothing to do with flying saucers or hostility of aliens. It is an unfortunate accident that should never have appeared in any UFO material. The flying saucers were both identified as Air Force planes. It is one more case that can be removed from the files.

1955: The Gun Camera Films

There have been rumors of gun camera films almost from the moment that UFOs first appeared. During my chance to read the Project Bluebook files in 1975, I spent time trying to find information about the gun camera films. There wasn't much available because an attempt had been made to eliminate all references to gun camera films. That is, with a few notable exceptions.

In his book Ed Ruppelt talked about an intercepter that had chased two glowing balls but could not get close to them. Failing to catch them, he took gun camera films of them and then broke off the intercept. When the film was processed, it showed the two glowing balls that the pilot had reported.

Investigations showed that two small weather balloons had been launched prior to the intercept, and according to the experts, the balloons would have appeared to be the same size as the objects on the gun camera films, if that was what the pilots had filmed. Ruppelt and the investigators were satisfied that the objects on the film were the weather balloons.

There were other examples. Another pilot made a short film that experts labeled as a smoke trail from a meteorite. The pilot reported that the head of the object didn't seem to be moving faster than three hundred miles an hour. The pilot wasn't convinced it was a meteorite, but the Air Force wrote it off as that anyway.

But all that isn't important. Those gun camera films were hit and miss (pilots on routine missions who saw something unusual in the distance and ones who were in a position to photograph them). There are indications that the Air Force had an official project to intercept and photograph UFOs.

Ruppelt mentioned that there had been a plan to outfit a squadron of the latest planes with gun cameras and then station them around the country with orders to scramble when there was a UFO sighting in order to get pictures of the objects. Ruppelt claimed that the plan was never put into effect because it was too expensive. The Air Force would not commit their best planes to the project so it died.

Or did it?

I have talked to a couple of pilots who told me that they were assigned to that special squadron. They did make intercepts and they did get gun camera films (those very films mentioned in the Bluebook Files but no longer hiding in them).

My source told me that their first attempt to photograph the UFOs failed. The gun cameras were set to automatically film the UFOs at thirteen hundred feet, but the pilots could never close to that range. The UFOs had managed to stay at least that far in front of the fighters.

Within two weeks, they had the chance again. Five objects were sighted and the jets took off after them. Thousands of frames of film were exposed, but the pilots never got to see it. Like the wreckage from Roswell, the film was collected and taken to Wright Field. It probably fell under the auspices of the Majestic Twelve.

According to the pilots, that wasn't the only opportunity either. There were several intercepts. The pilots began to wear down, becoming as jumpy as combat pilots. The difference was that combat pilots knew the dangers they faced; those chasing the UFOs did not. They worried about radiation, they worried about side effects, and they had heard about the disappearance of an Air Force jet chasing a UFO over Lake Superior in 1953 (*see November 23, 1953: The Kinross Disappearance*). In fact, during their initial briefings, they had been told that the UFOs generated fields that could affect the aircraft instruments. The pilots began to ask for other assignments.

The stories told by the men were very interesting and very frightening. They provided details of UFO intercepts: glowing objects that they chased across the sky while filming away with six gun cameras each. But they never saw the films and there is almost no record that the films exist.

Except for one minor comment in the Bluebook files.

On one of the pages of a project report there is a notation about a gun camera spectroscopic film furnished for analysis. It implies that the cameras were fitted with special filters for the purpose of making spectroscopic films. Someone was planning ahead.

And then we learn from the pilots on the special mission to photograph UFOs that they had some special films, that is, infrared, for example, and that there were special filters on the cameras. It seems that the Bluebook reports confirm, at least in part, the stories told by the pilots.

It is just one more indication that the government was trying to learn more about UFOs while telling the public that there was nothing going on.

April 1956: The Allende Letters

The story of the Allende Letters, as it is usually told, begins when a copy of the book *The Case for the UFO*, by Morris K. Jessup, arrived at the Office of Naval Research. UFO buffs claim that the Navy read all the notations scribbled in the margins of the book, became interested in them, and contacted Jessup. By the time the Navy called, Jessup had already received all three letters from Carlos Allende.

The Navy then, according to many authors, requested and received permission to reproduce the book in a limited edition of twenty-five copies. Each copy contained the notations in red and the original text in black. All the letters sent by Allende, including one that he signed as Carl Allen, were included in an appendix.

During the next several years, the Navy is reported to have

spent time, money, and effort in researching the whole mess. Navy investigators supposedly looked for Allende but couldn't find him. The postmarks on the book showed that it had been mailed from Seminole, Texas, and the letters from Gainesville, Texas, and Du Bois, Pennsylvania. Although the Navy checked all the return addresses and followed dozens of leads, Allende eluded them.

According to the researchers, the Navy found the letters interesting because they told of a Navy experiment with Einstein's Unified Field Theory. During the Second World War, according to the letters, the Navy succeeded in teleporting a ship from one shipyard to another. The teleportation was instantaneous, was witnessed by Allende, and there was a brief article about it in a Philadelphia newspaper. Allende, unfortunately, couldn't remember the issue or the date of the article.

Although the experiment was a success, Allende claimed that the men were failures. Half the crew was lost during the experiment and the rest manifested a variety of weird side effects. Some went mad as hatters while others would go blank or get stuck. Allende explained that they would seem to disappear or freeze on the spot. Their position had to be marked and the other members of the crew had to step around the mark.

Fellow crew members, when they saw a sailor freeze, would rush forward to "lay their hands" on the stricken man. Allende said, "Possibly because of the metal on him, he began to smolder. Both men burned for eighteen days."

Notations in the book were no less confusing. Terms like mothership, great war, force cutters, magnetic and gravity fields, and sheets of diamonds were used. The men, including Allende, who made the notations, explained how, why, and what happens to the men, ships, and planes that have disappeared. In fact, they explained a great number of mysteries.

And, according to the researchers, the Navy went on to draw a series of conclusions about the notation writers. There were three distinct colors of ink used and the differences in handwriting led to the conclusion that there were three men. The writers were referred to as Mister A, Mister B, and Jemi.

More than once one of the writers was called Jemi by the others.

The search for a solution to the riddle of the Allende Letters by Morris Jessup came to an end on April 29, 1959, when he was found dead in a Dade County, Florida, park. Writers have speculated about his death, an apparent suicide. Some have claimed that he had gotten too close to the answers and was murdered by the opposition.

But others have continued the search for him. They have claimed that the Allende Letters could provide the solution to the UFO problem. If a long study was made, they claimed, the answers would surface. Some went even further and claimed that the study has already been made by the Navy and is so highly classified that it will never be released.

Because this was reported to be the find of the century and others were getting everything they asked for, I decided that I should have one too. I wrote to the chief of naval operations to learn more.

The Navy replied quickly, saying that no copies of the book were available but that it had been reproduced by Varo Manufacturing in Garland, Texas. The Navy thought that Varo might still have some copies available.

At that time I was living near Fort Worth not far from Garland. I called Varo and asked about the Allende Letters. The secretary who answered knew what I was talking about and transferred the call to Sidney Sherby.

Sherby told me that he had been at the Office of Naval Research during the Allende era. There had been copies made and he still had one of them. He said that if I wanted to see it and could come to Garland, he would be happy to help me out. I made an appointment for the next week.

At the offices of Varo, Sherby showed me the book. It had a blue cover and was about the size of regular typing paper. As I thumbed through it and wondered what answers it could provide, Sherby told me about the activities of the Office of Naval Research when the book arrived.

Sherby said that no one there was overly excited about it. One researcher pointed out that sending the book to the Navy was ridiculous because the Navy would either throw it out or classify it. Apparently, and according to Sherby, they threw it out.

That was, of course, the first departure from the traditional lore of the Allende Letters. Writers and researchers had claimed that there must have been something to the mystery because the Navy took an interest in the book. Now, Sherby, who was there and a member of ONR, was saying, "No, the Navy was never interested and was going to throw it out."

Because that one statement about throwing away the book shot so many holes in so many theories, I decided to pursue it. The key was that the members of the ONR, acting on their own, were interested. If they wanted to go to the trouble and expense of reproducing the book, the Navy had no objections. The only stipulation was that it couldn't take up Navy time and couldn't involve Navy funds. It was the fact that they were in the Navy that led some to believe that the Navy was responsible for the reproduction of the book. "If we had all been in the FBI or in the Army, the rumor would have started that the FBI or the Army reproduced it. Actually, it was reproduced by Navy officers on their own time as private citizens," said Sherby.

For nearly three hours, Sherby and I discussed the book. Sherby said that a friend of his tried to find Allende at one of the various addresses but couldn't locate him. Again, this was not done by the Navy but by a private citizen. Sherby said that they called Dr. Jessup and asked what he had thought of the letters and the notations. According to Sherby, Jessup was unimpressed in 1956. He didn't become excited about the possibility of finding the whole answer to the UFO situation in the notations but actually agreed with the Navy. It was all a load of manure.

Other UFO researchers have taken an interest in the Allende Letters and a large part of Allende's credibility hinges on the item he claimed was printed in the Philadelphia newspaper. Many researchers have tried to find it and finally one man came forward with a copy. But he only had a copy of the article itself and couldn't show anyone the whole newspaper.

Other parts of the Allende Letters myths fell to objective

research. On page 124 of the original text of the Jessup book, the all-knowing, far advanced Allende trio makes a mistake. Jessup had been wondering if the Incas built the "fortifications" at Sacsa huaman or whether they had inherited it from an unidentified, earlier civilization. This caused quite a discussion between Mister A, Mister B, and Jemi. Jemi then claims that "Inca & Mayan peoples Did NOT know the use of the Wheel in any form or size, at all (sic)."

Anthropologists do not agree with Jemi. Wheeled "toys" have been found in many sites of ancient American civilizations. The problem wasn't the lack of the wheel but the lack of a sufficient draft animal. The closest thing found in the New World is the llama, a beast that did not live will in captivity and was extremely difficult to domesticate. Wheels existed; an animal to pull wheeled vehicles didn't.

There are other references that are as inaccurate. Einstein's theory, $E = mc^2$, is inaccurately reported in the text. Several biological facts are overlooked. Astronomical observations, made after our own spacecraft passed the outer planets, are overlooked. They were unable to predict those discoveries although they were always talking about "statis fields," antigravity, and space travel.

Mister B announces in one of his notations that our Air Force will develop saucers in 1956 or 1957. They will then feel safe to announce that UFOs are from space. Mister B claims that the Air Force craft will be jet powered. Of course, none of Mister B's predictions came true.

Some UFO researchers have pursued the Allende Letters, not because there was good information in them, but because they knew Jessup and could see that he eventually thought there was something to them. At least, toward the end of his life, Jessup began to accept the letters as something valuable and important. But then others reported that Jessup may have had other reasons for his belief in Allende.

One man reported that Jessup was upset by his career. He had been trained as an astronomer and although successful for a while, he eventually became entangled in a number of other affairs and his pursuit of astronomy suffered. This was a big disappointment for Jessup.

Jessup was also involved in a business in Washington and

that is where he became interested in UFOs. His job did not require a great deal of time and Jessup started taking books to read to occupy his time. Later, he began to write. The result was *The Case for the UFO*.

That book was relatively successful. Jessup made some money but not enough to warrant his quitting his job to write. Other books followed, but they did not have the success of his first and this was another disappointment.

Later, in 1958, Jessup decided to go into the publishing business himself. He planned an expedition to Mexico to search for proof that UFOs were real and planned a book to follow the expedition. But the expedition and then the book deal fell through. All this added to his growing sense of disappointment.

Finally, almost in desperation, Jessup began to talk about and to study the annotated book and the Allende Letters. There were a number of people interested in them and Jessup may have seen them as a way to revitalize his faltering career. He didn't believe because there was anything to them, but because he had to.

Ivan T. Sanderson, a world-famous naturalist and a writer about UFOs, placed some emphasis on the Allende Letter mess because he had known Jessup. Sanderson told others about Jessup's belief in them and even included a section about them in one of his UFO books. Now, Sanderson's claims, based solely on his friendship with Jessup, have become another support of the Allende Letters.

There was also some limited speculation in certain military circles about the Allende Letters. It wasn't because they were accurate but because they were close to a secret experiment: not the teleportation of a ship, but an experiment that was somewhat less dramatic. However, there was a slight resemblance, and a few officers, afraid there had been a leak, looked into the story. When they learned the letters were a hoax, they lost interest.

In the years that followed, more researchers began to write the Allende Letters off as a hoax. Others continued their research. One man maintained that he had finally obtained a copy of the annotated book as if it was some kind of puzzle to be worked out. I had no problems. Sherby mentioned that the copy he had was the last of the five that he had been given, but if I wanted to reproduce it or wanted to borrow it to make notes, Sherby had no objections.

After talking to Sherby, I decided to contact APRO and see if they had anything on Allende. Jim Lorenzen, the International Director, wrote back, saying that Allende had been to Tucson and confessed his part in the hoax. "He [Allende] was on his way to Denver, Colorado, with what he believed to be a terminal illness. He stopped by APRO Headquarters here in Tucson and after talking to us for hours, admitted that he had made up the whole thing. We even obtained a signed statement by him saying that it was a hoax." Lorenzen said that it was interesting to note that Allende had a copy of the Varo reproduction of the annotated book.

Lorenzen asked Allende why he had faked the letters. "Because Jessup's writings scared me. I didn't want him to write anymore and this was the only thing that I could think of."

Before Allende left he asked the Lorenzens if he could leave some of his personal belongings at APRO. In Denver, they managed to cure him and he returned to Tucson, picked up his baggage, and went home. He forgot one of the suitcases, leaving it in Tucson.

One researcher, trying to shoot down the proof of a hoax, claimed that dozens of Allendes have come forward, trying to cash in on the original's fame. The real Allende lived in Mexico and the researcher has seen various documents proving his Allende is the real one. He didn't have to go to all that trouble. His Allende and the one who visited Tucson are the same Allende. In Tucson Allende admitted his hoax. Then, several years later, having recovered from his illness, he was trying to take it all back.

However, even with Allende's confession, Sherby's story, the lack of the Philadelphia newspaper article, and the failure by anyone to confirm anything that Allende said, the controversy still rages. Writers maintain that it is the key to the UFO problem and researchers continue to track down the books.

In fact, some have taken the Allende Letters too far. In a telephone interview with a man about a different, UFO-related matter, the man kept mentioning the Allende Letters. He spoke as if he had inside knowledge but knew no more than anyone who has read the various books and articles about UFOs and Allende. He took it to the extreme when he mentioned the old Tom Snyder "Tomorrow" show and Lloyd M. Bucher, the former skipper of the USS *Pueblo*. During the show, Bucher was supposed to have "turned green and seemed to have faded from the screen while the background and Snyder remained intact." The man wondered if Bucher, because he had been involved in secret operations, might have been a victim of Navy attempts to teleport a ship. The whole idea of Bucher disappearing and later reappearing while on national television is ridiculous.

Later I found out that one of the men involved in the telephone interview about the other UFO matter knew all about Sherby and Allende's admission of a hoax but chose to ignore it. Finding that it was a hoax did not fit into his concept of the UFO picture so he preferred to think that Sherby had lied, the CIA was covering up, and Allende had been bought off.

After I wrote the original article (disposing of the Allende mess once and for all, I thought) an annotated copy of my article arrived at the magazine's editorial offices. The editor sent me a copy and I was added to the ranks of those "damn liars" that Allende had attacked in the past. None of what I wrote about the visit to Tucson was true, according to Allende. He claimed that I had made the whole story up, though he didn't know why.

Figuring that Jim Lorenzen might have been duped by one of the false Allendes, I called him. He told me that there was no doubt that the man who had visited Tucson and the one who was responsible for the Allende Letters were the same. APRO had written the episode off as a hoax.

The whole point is that the Allende Letters were not the key to anything. All they have done is confuse the UFO issue with clouds of lies and fables. Serious researchers have wasted a great deal of time and effort studying them. It was a part of the UFO phenomenon that should have died with Allende's confession. It is unfortunate that it didn't.

September 12, 1957: Ubatuba, Brazil

It was early in September 1957, when a Rio de Janeiro columnist received a strange letter from several fishermen claiming they had seen a flying disc approaching them at high speed. They had been on the beach near Ubatuba, as the disc-shaped object dived at them, made a tight turn, and then began a rapid climb. Moments later it exploded, showering the beach and the ocean with thousands of fragments. The men picked up dozens of the smaller pieces and enclosed a couple of them in the letter.

The columnist wrote his story and Dr. Olavo Fontes, APRO's Brazilian representative, saw it. At first, he believed the story to be a hoax . . . but there was something there that he couldn't forget. Here was the possibility of getting his hands on metal that had come from a flying saucer. He had to learn whether or not it was a hoax. He contacted the columnist and asked to see the fragments.

Fontes had the metal examined by a local chemist. The preliminary study showed that it wasn't from a meteorite because it was too light. But it obviously was metal and it had been burned. Also, obviously, it was not aluminum. They made several additional tests.

Spectroscopic analysis revealed the sample was magnesium, of a purity that was unobtainable. That, and a lack of evidence that the columnist had invented the story to fill space in the paper, suggested that the story as told was true. A few of the fragments, along with a complete report, was forwarded to APRO headquarters.

APRO tried to interest the Air Force in analyzing the metal. A small piece of one of the fragments was sent to an Air Force laboratory, but the spectrograph operator destroyed the sample without getting an exposed plate. The Air Force requested another sample, but APRO declined.

Next, APRO tried the Atomic Energy Commission. A density test was made and the Ubatuba metal was found to be slightly more dense than would be expected of normal samples—an interesting result that could be accounted for by oxide on the magnesium.

While the sample was at the AEC labs, another spectroscopic analysis was run. The presence of minute quantities of several trace elements were found, but the technician said that they could have been the result of contamination of the electrodes and not impurities in the sample. Another wasted test.

Lab analysis also showed that the metal came from an object that had broken up rapidly. There was no evidence of melting, so it was believed that an explosion had torn a larger object apart. They didn't say that it was a UFO because the sample did not show it to be a spacecraft. They just said that whatever it was, it had blown up.

With the new results, APRO decided to try to interest the Air Force in a joint analysis of the samples. It was thought that both APRO consultants and Air Force scientists could participate in the program. A letter sent to ATIC suggesting the project was met with a standard form letter asking that the sample be forwarded for testing.

Meanwhile, Fontes was trying to track down the witnesses to the explosion. There were things that he wanted to ask them; things that weren't covered in their letter to the newspaper. Fontes failed to find them, and APRO believed that Brazilian intelligence officials had asked them to forget about the sighting. The chain of evidence was intact from the columnist to the United States, but there was no way of getting it from the beach to the columnist. That link was gone.

Later, during the Condon Colorado UFO Study (*see 1969: The* Condon Committee), the samples were loaned to that project for further analysis. The report released at the termination of the study did not agree with all of APRO's findings. According to the Condon report, magnesium of an equal purity did exist in 1957 and was available in Dow Laboratories. It did not explain how fishermen in Brazil could obtain samples of the Dow metal, but then, they weren't required to explain it.

Doctor R.S. Busk of the Condon Committee did report that there was a high content of strontium in the sample. Strontium was not an expected impurity found in magnesium made under normal methods. The report also said that the metal probably did not come from a large, manufactured object. In other words, it was not part of an exploding UFO.

Because of the Condon Committee's negative results, APRO decided to have the remaining samples subjected to nondestructive analysis. Again, working for APRO and in conjunction with Dr. Robert W. Johnson, Dr. Walter W. Walker made several additional tests. They concluded that the fragments were directionally solidified castings. Directional solidification was not being studied as early as the Ubatuba sighting in 1957. Walker said, "This might be interpreted as meaning that the samples are from a more advanced culture." He didn't think that the object originated in space, but left that conclusion to others.

The Condon Committee had also dismissed the Ubatuba sample by saying that the general low hardness of the Dow material is equivalent to the Ubatuba metal. However, the Ubatuba sample had better high temperature properties than the Dow metal. The conclusion was that Dow had produced samples of equal purity, but that Dow probably didn't produce the Ubatuba sample.

The APRO scientists were also surprised by the Condon Committee statement that the Ubatuba sample did not come from a fabricated metal object. Their conclusions appeared in the APRO *Bulletin*, where they say that apparently the Condon Committee did not accept castings as fabricated metal objects.

The story of the Ubatuba sample ends there. Some claim that the sample is unique and others claim that it is not the proof positive that the skeptics want. Unfortunately, we'll probably never have a definitive answer now. After all these years, the last pieces of the sample have been lost.

October 1957: Antonio Villas-Boas

When the story of Antonio Villas-Boas broke, there weren't many who believed him. Unlike the other reports of 1957 that talked of flying saucers in the sky, a few close to the ground stalling car engines and dimming lights, he talked about a craft that landed and the creatures coming from inside it. Because he was taken on board, his story was rejected by some researchers out of hand. Now, years later, as we're buried in reports of abductions, some of them suggesting biological and reproductive experiments, we must take another look at this case. It might have been the first of a kind, and because of that, we, as researchers, weren't interested in it.

Imagine then how a young South American farmer felt in October 1957, when he stepped forward with a story of abduction. Not only did he see the craft, but also he was confronted by a naked woman who had an obvious interest in him.

Antonio Villas-Boas told his story to outsiders the first time in February 1958 (Barney and Betty Hill wouldn't have their experience for another three years and it would be another couple of years before it was reported by UFO researchers). Villas-Boas certainly couldn't have read about them, so their case provided no guidance and no incentive. His was the first of its kind.

According to him, "It all began on the night of October 5, 1957." Villas-Boas was in his room after a party and for some reason, he looked out at the horse corral. In the middle of it he could see a bright, fluorescent light. It seemed to sweep upward, into the sky, but there was no object over it. Jaoa, Villas-Boas's brother, also saw the light. Neither of them had an explanation for it.

A few days later, Villas-Boas was working in a field when he saw another bright light. This one was about three hundred feet in the air, shaped like a wheel, and was intensely bright. Villas-Boas called to another brother who didn't care to see it. For twenty minutes, Villas-Boas chased the light from one end of the field to the other, but he finally grew tired. As he left the area, he glanced back to it several times and saw it throwing off rays like the setting sun. It finally just disappeared.

The next night, it came back for the second time. Villas-Boas was plowing the field late because it was too hot to work in the sunlight. At one in the morning, he noticed an extremely bright red star overhead. He watched it and realized that it was moving, growing larger as it approached. Villas-Boas hesitated, wondering what to do, and in those few seconds, the light changed into an egg-shaped craft descending toward his freshly plowed field. It stopped to hover over him, its light so bright that Villas-Boas could no longer see his own headlights.

For two minutes, the UFO hovered and Villas-Boas stared. He thought of driving away from it, but he knew it could easily catch the tractor. The ground was too soft for him to run very fast. The UFO moved again, diving toward the ground, and for the first time Villas-Boas could see the details on it.

The bright red light seemed to come from the front of the craft that looked like an elongated egg. There were purple lights near the large red one, and there was a small red light on a flattened cupola that spun rapidly. As the UFO approached the ground, three telescoping legs slid from under the machine.

The legs, like those of a camera tripod, were for landing, and as Villas-Boas realized that, he turned the tractor and stepped on the accelerator, trying to escape. He made it only a few feet before the engine sputtered and died and the headlights went out. He tried to start it, but the ignition didn't seem to work. When it failed to start, he opened the door on the side of the tractor opposite the UFO and jumped out. He had only taken a few steps when something touched his arm. Villas-Boas spun, looking at the short creature that had grabbed him. Struggling to escape, he put a hand on the creature's chest and pushed. The creature released him, staggered backward, and then fell. As Villas-Boas turned to run, three other creatures grabbed him and lifted him from the ground. He twisted, trying to jerk his arms free so that he could fight the aliens who held him tightly. He shouted for help and the sound of his voice seemed to fascinate the creatures, but they didn't relax their grips on him.

A door had opened in the craft and there was a narrow metal ladder extending from it to the ground. The aliens tried to lift Villas-Boas into the machine, but he grabbed the narrow railing on the ladder. One of the creatures peeled his hand from the flexible metal, and he was forced through the door.

The new room was larger than the first. There was a metal rod running from the floor to the ceiling and Villas-Boas thought that it held up the roof. To one side there was an oddly shaped table surrounded by backless chairs.

For several minutes, Villas-Boas and the aliens stood in the room. The creatures talked among themselves in a series of low, growling sounds while they held Villas-Boas. Finally they began to strip his clothes from him carefully so that they didn't tear anything. When he was naked, one of the aliens began to "wash" him with an oily-looking liquid that made him shiver as it dried.

As the aliens worked around him, Villas-Boas studied them. They wore tight-fitting jumpsuits made of soft, unevenly striped cloth. The cloth reached up their necks and over their heads almost like the hoods of wet suits worn by skin divers. Villas-Boas had the impression that the hood was some kind of helmet because it hid everything except the alien's eyes. There didn't seem to be any tanks for an air supply and Villas-Boas was unable to explain this. He did say that the helmets seemed to be almost twice as tall as the head. All of the aliens seemed to be only about five feet tall, shorter than Villas-Boas. He made a point of telling researchers that he was sure that he could have beaten any of them in a fair fight, but that five of them were too many for him.

Three of the aliens moved Villas-Boas to another small square room. They entered through a swinging door that fit so snugly into the wall that he could not see where it had been. Two other aliens, carrying a large vessel with rubber hoses, approached. The hose was fastened to his chin, he felt a scratching, and saw the clear, glass vessel fill with his blood. The procedure was repeated. When the hoses were removed, Villas-Boas felt a burning and itching on his chin. When the creatures finished, they gathered their equipment and they all left.

Villas-Boas inspected the room for a few minutes, seeing only a large couch in the middle of it. Because he was feeling tired, he went over to sit down and then noticed a strange smell in the air. From the walls, about head high, he noticed a gray smoke pouring into the room. Its thick, oily smell made him sick. For minutes he fought the feeling, but it continued and he finally vomited.

Feeling better, Villas-Boas sat back on the couch, waiting. After thirty minutes, maybe longer, there was a noise at the door. He turned in time to see a naked woman entering. She came in slowly, watching Villas-Boas. She stepped unhurriedly to him and embraced him.

She was short, under five feet tall. She had light-colored hair, almost white, as if it had been bleached heavily. She had blue eyes that were slanted, giving her an Arabian look. Her face was wide with high cheekbones, but her chin was very pointed, giving her whole face an angular look. She was slim, with high, very pointed breasts. Her stomach was flat and her thighs were large. Her hands looked normal and were small.

When the door closed again, the woman began to caress him, showing him exactly what she wanted. Given the circumstances, Villas-Boas was surprised that he could respond, but he felt desire for her growing. She kept rubbing him, leading him on and in moments they were on the couch, Villas-Boas forgetting everything except her. Almost before he realized what was happening, they were joined and according to him, she responded as any woman would.

They stayed on the couch, petting, and in minutes both were ready again. Villas-Boas tried to kiss her, but she refused, preferring to nibble his chin. When they finished a second time, she began to avoid him. As she stood up, the door opened and one of the alien men stepped in, calling to the woman. Before she left, she smiled at Villas-Boas, pointed to her stomach and then to the sky. It was then that he realized that she had flaming red pubic hair.

One of the men came back and handed Villas-Boas his clothes. While dressing, he noticed that his lighter was gone. He thought that it might have been lost during his escape attempt.

The alien directed him out of the small room and into another where the crew members were sitting and talking, or, rather, growling, among themselves. He was left out of the discussion, the aliens ignoring him, so he tried to fix the details in his mind. On a table near the aliens was a square box with a glass lid and a clocklike face. There were markings corresponding to three, six, and nine, and four marks at twelve. As he looked at it, the idea that he should take it, as proof of his adventure, gripped him. He edged his way closer and when none of the aliens were looking at it, Villas-Boas grabbed it. Before he could even take a closer look at it, one of the creatures jumped toward him and pushed him away.

At last another of the aliens motioned for him to follow. None of the others even looked up as they walked to the entrance and the door. It was again open, with the ladder extending to the ground, but they didn't go down it. Instead, they stepped onto a platform that went around the ship. Slowly they walked along it as the alien pointed out various features. Because he didn't speak, Villas-Boas didn't know the purpose of any of the things he was shown. There were machines with purplish lights. He glanced at the cupola that emitted a greenish light and that was making a sound like a vacuum cleaner as it slowly spun.

When the tour was over, he was taken to the door. The alien pointed to the ladder and motioned Villas-Boas down it. At the bottom, he stopped and looked back, but the alien hadn't moved. Instead, he pointed to himself, then to the ground, and finally toward the sky. He signaled Villas-Boas to step back as he disappeared into the UFO.

The ladder telescoped into itself as the door began to vanish. When it was closed, there was no seam or crack visible. The lights began to brighten as those on the cupola began to spin faster and faster until the ship lifted quietly into the sky.

It stopped to hover about a hundred feet above the ground. The buzzing from it increased as it spun faster, until it was revolving at blurring speed. The colors flashed through the spectrum before settling on a bright, blinding red. As it changed color, it changed direction, causing a loud roar. It then shot to the south, disappearing in seconds.

Villas-Boas returned to his tractor and noticed it was nearly 5:30 A.M. He had been on the UFO for over four hours. He tried to start the engine, but it still wouldn't work. He climbed down to look at the engine and discovered that the battery cables had been disconnected. When he hooked them up, the tractor started easily.

He was sure that the cables hadn't come loose by themselves and, in fact, claimed that he checked them before he left the house. He said that he believed the aliens had done it so that he couldn't escape from them if he had been able to break their hold on him.

Villas-Boas didn't tell anyone, except his mother, about the sighting until February 1958. Then, after reading several UFO stories in a Brazilian magazine, he contacted Jaoa Martins, who, with the help of APRO's Dr. Olavo Fontes, interviewed him. Both were impressed with Villas-Boas's sincerity. Martins told him that he didn't think the story would be published because it was so strange. Villas-Boas seemed disappointed so they suggested that he contact a newspaper. He declined.

The whole thing leaves us with one big question. Did Villas-Boas spend four hours on a spaceship crewed by creatures from another planet? His story suggests that he did. He wasn't sophisticated enough to invent a story that avoids the pitfalls of a hoax. He didn't have the education or knowledge to know how to fool the investigators. Based on what he told them, and the way he told them, we almost have to conclude that it is the truth. But with a case like this, more evidence is needed. Something more needs to be added, and until that happens we are left with more questions than answers.

November 1957: Levelland, Texas

Late in 1957 the UFO picture changed dramatically and radically. Witnesses not only saw strange lights and weird machines, but also watched UFOs land—causing car engines to fail, radios to fade, and even power losses in some cities. Now, instead of reporting a point of light that could have been anything, the witnesses could report a solid object with observed side effects. It moved the UFO from the realm of the imagined to the realm of the measured.

The many sightings of November 1957, were foreshadowed by a mysterious object seen in Indiana. On October 15, 1957, Robert Moudy was in his fields near Foster, Indiana, when he saw a large, flat oval shoot overhead. As the screaming ball passed, Moudy claimed the engine of his combine died. When the UFO disappeared, the engine sputtered back to life. Like most of the sightings, the Air Force ignored the case, even though it was widely reported.

The following day, October 16, the first of many sightings was made at Holloman Air Force Base near White Sands, New Mexico. Ella Louise Fortune was traveling near Holloman when she saw a large, white, cigar-shaped object. Like dozens of others, she took a picture, but unlike others, she used color film. Later analysis showed it was a lenticular cloud.

On November 2, Russia announced that they had launched another Sputnik. In Levelland, Texas, the news was overpowered by reports of a large red UFO. Pedro Saucido was the first to see it. He was driving toward Levelland when the glowing UFO swept across the highway in front of his truck. As it landed, the lights of the truck went out and the engine died. Saucido dived out the door and rolled out of the way. His passenger, Joe Salaz, sat terror-stricken, his eyes glued to the UFO. The blue-green glow faded into a red so bright that Salaz could no longer look directly at it. During the three minutes the UFO sat on the highway, both men thought they heard noises coming from inside it. Suddenly, the torpedo-shaped object, still glowing red, shot silently into the night sky.

Saucido was afraid to continue toward Levelland because he thought that he might run into the object again. Instead, he drove to another West Texas town and called the police in Levelland. A deputy sheriff listened to the report but laughed it off as another flying saucer story. The obvious distress of Saucido was overlooked.

About an hour later, Jim Wheeler saw a red glowing UFO sitting on the road. As he drove closer, his car engine died and the lights went out. The egg-shaped object then blasted off swiftly and silently. Wheeler's car started again and he, too, called the Levelland police.

Police had just finished talking to Wheeler when José Alverez called to report that he had seen an egg-shaped object that killed his car engine. A few minutes later, Frank Williams walked into the office and reported the red UFO.

The sheriff's office had now received several calls about the giant red egg. All had reported that a red UFO, almost two hundred feet long, had killed their car engines. The deputies were discussing the possibility that someone was playing an elaborate joke. But shortly after midnight they decided that it was no joke. As the discussion progressed, they received still another call. James Long said that he was driving on a country road northwest of Levelland when he came upon a landed, bright red UFO. His truck engine died and the lights went out. He got out and started toward the UFO, but it took off before he got more than a few feet from his truck. After the UFO was gone, the truck started easily.

Levelland's sheriff, Weir Clem, did not like the idea of chasing lights in the sky, and like his deputies, he had ignored the first reports. Thunderstorms had been causing problems, but it was no longer raining in town. All the phone calls and separate witnesses were making the Levelland sightings very hard for authorities to ignore. Any multiple witness case with the same object reported independently is impressive.

About 12:30, Ronald Martin, a college student, was nearing Levelland. He glanced at the dashboard ampmeter, saw it jump to discharge, then back, as the engine died and the lights went out. He got out of the car to look under the hood but found nothing wrong. As he turned, he saw the red UFO on the road. Unsure of what to do, he got into the car and tried to start the engine. After a few minutes, the UFO rose silently out of sight and when it was gone, the car started.

Finally, just after midnight and Ronald Martin's call, Clem decided to investigate. He left the office with Deputy Patrick McCullogh and about 1:30 they saw the glowing UFO in the distance. About the same time, two highway patrol officers and Constable Lloyd Bollen saw the UFO. In all, five police officers reported the object but none were very close to it.

At Project Bluebook in Dayton, Ohio, the teletype started shortly after the sheriff saw the lights. He called Reese Air Force Base in nearby Lubbock, Texas, and they relayed the sightings to Bluebook. A copy of the weather report was included. Officers sitting in warm, dry offices at ATIC found their answers almost immediately. Thunderstorms were reported in the area so all the witnesses must have seen ball lightning. They had been excited at the time of the sightings and because it was wet, they probably killed the engines themselves. Not long after they had received the initial sighting reports, the Air Force had the answers. Now all they had to do was investigate the case and prove they were right.

There was a complication. About two hours after the rash of Levelland sightings, two men on patrol at White Sands reported that they saw a bright egg-shaped object. It fell for a distance, the light went out, and they lost sight of it. Just before it hit the ground, or landed, the light came back on. Of course, they reported what they had seen, but no one seemed to care or believe them.

At least there were no believers until 8:00 P.M. the following night. Then, a second patrol reported the same thing. The second patrol had no way of knowing about the first report. No stalled engines or dimming lights were reported in New Mexico.

The White Sands sightings, following so closely behind the Levelland reports, were dangerous to Air Force explanations. The men on patrol at White Sands were supposed to be reliable and their sightings could prove troublesome. The Air Force wasted no time. The patrols were made of young and impressionable men. Because they had been talking of UFOs, said the Air Force reports, it was decided that the alleged sightings had been suggested by the discussions. The sightings were a direct result of the rash of reports from Levelland.

On November 4, 1957, James Stokes was driving toward El Paso when near Orogrande, New Mexico, the engine of his car began to sputter and the radio faded out. As the engine quit, Stokes guided his car to the side of the road. Ahead, he could see a group of people talking and pointing to the sky. Looking up, he saw a large, oval-shaped object shooting toward the road. It buzzed the highway, turned to the northwest, and then reversed for another pass at the cars before disappearing.

As the object passed over the cars, Stokes could feel its heat. He saw no portholes and thought that it was three thousand feet above the ground. The speed was estimated at 760 miles an hour. Hours after he saw the UFO, Stokes noticed an itching on his face, hands, and wrists. The areas that had been exposed to the UFO reddened as if they had been sunburned.

One of the men in the group had a camera and took several pictures of the UFO. Later investigations by the Air Force failed to find either the pictures or any of the other witnesses. Considering the Air Force's handling of the wave, that is not too surprising.

On November 5, Stokes made an official report to the Air Force about the sighting. Newsmen from all over the country were calling and trying to interview him. He was called from his post at Holloman Air Force Base to talk with the curious. Stokes was obviously agitated by the ordeal of both seeing the UFO and the interview that followed.

The same day, a Washington news release explained the Levelland sightings as exaggerations or misinterpretations of natural phenomena. At Holloman, however, the Air Force spokesman said that Stokes was an employee of the Air Force Missile Development Center, had been in the Navy for twenty-four years, and was believed to be a very competent observer. In other words, the Air Force was accepting the story as Stokes reported it.

While Stokes, the people at Levelland, the patrols at White Sands, and the Air Force were fighting it out, R.O. Schmidt walked into the Kearney, Nebraska, police station. He claimed that while he was inspecting grain he found what he, at first, thought was a wrecked balloon. When he was thirty feet away, he was stopped by a beam of light that paralyzed him.

Two men from the UFO—Schmidt now knew it wasn't a balloon—searched him for weapons and then invited him on board. Inside, he saw two women and three men working on instrumentation and was told that the people meant him no harm. They couldn't tell him where they were from but did say that they might announce their presence in the near future. When Schmidt left, there was a flash of light and the UFO was gone.

Police did search the area but could not find imprints. They found a greenish, oillike substance that they took to the Kearney College for analysis.

Schmidt's story was the beginning of a rash of occupant reports. Although none of the witnesses could have known of Schmidt's story because it wasn't carried in the morning papers, several of them were remarkably similar. Schmidt saw his UFO in the early evening, and early the next morning, on November 6, Everett Clark saw a landed UFO. In a field near his home in Dante, Tennessee, were four men and women. Clark talked to them briefly before they got back into the UFO. It shot quietly into the sky.

Neighbors and friends described Clark as intelligent and honest. They didn't think he made up the story. In the field, they found that the grass had been depressed as if something very heavy had rested there. Weeks later, he said that he had never heard of Schmidt and his claim.

About an hour after Clark saw the landed UFO, several cars were stalled by another UFO near Santa Monica, California. Richard Kehoe was driving to work when the engine of his car died. Kehoe noticed that there were two other cars stalled, and when he got out, he could see a brightly lighted object on the beach.

Kehoe and the men from the other cars, Ronald Burke and Joe Thomas, were talking when two humanoids got out of the egg-shaped UFO and walked toward them. The creatures were yellowish-green in color and they tried to talk to the terrified men for several minutes, but no one could understand them. Finally, the creatures left, the UFO took off, and all three men drove off.

One of the men called the police, but no one seemed interested in another UFO report. The sun wasn't even up yet and already it had been the busiest day of the flap. Air Force files would show that nearly a hundred people reported UFOs on the sixth of November.

When Clark first saw the UFO occupants, they had been trying to grab a dog, apparently to take onto the UFO. John Trasco of Everittstown, New Jersey, claimed that he saw a brilliant egg-shaped object hovering over his barn. Underneath, he saw a small, putty-colored humanoid trying to grab his dog. Trasco yelled at the creature, but it said that it only wanted the dog. Trasco told it to get the hell out and leave his dog alone. The creature dropped the animal and ran for the UFO. It took off in a vertical direction.

Edwin Leadford, also on November 6, claimed that he took a picture of a cigar-shaped craft over Anaheim, California. Official Air Force records show that Leadford was involved with a series of complaints that ranged from malicious mischief to missing car keys. They wrote the sighting off as a hoax because of the police reports and because Leadford was "pleased and excited about the publicity given him."

Further investigation by civilian researchers showed that Leadford was not the trickster but the victim. He had called the police on six separate occasions to report others had been damaging the gas station where he worked or had stolen his car keys. It gives a different impression of Leadford when seen that way. He was not the troublemaker.

Air Force records show that Leadford said he had advanced the film so that there was no chance for a double exposure. An unidentified Air Force investigator circled that statement in the report and wrote above it, "Strange that he mentioned double exposure." It implies that Leadford had made a double exposure to fake the picture. However, if Leadford had, in fact, advanced the film to prevent a double exposure, there is no reason to believe that he wouldn't tell investigators about it. The Air Force was trying everything to discredit the witnesses of UFOs. This is quite obvious from the investigations and reports dealing with the Leadford picture.

Later in the evening, four campers at Lake Baskatong, near Ottawa, Canada, saw a bright sphere hovering over a hill. The light was so bright that it lit the clouds above it. Their shortwave radio failed shortly after the object appeared and would work only on one frequency, giving off a strange, Morse-like code. When the UFO disappeared fifteen minutes later, the radio began to work.

And finally, on the same day, Rene Gilham saw a UFO hovering over his farm. After it disappeared, he began to itch and his skin began to redden. Before the rash disappeared, Gilham had to be hospitalized for eleven days.

In Washington, on November 6, came the official release that there had been over 5,700 sightings, and of those, none had been confirmed. There was no physical evidence or footprints or anything that showed any so-called flying saucers existed. Then from Dayton's Wright Field came the statement that no physical evidence had ever been found and that although 3 percent of the sightings were unidentified, they would have been solved if complete reports had been submitted. What they didn't mention was that nearly 30 percent of their files were stamped "insufficient data," which meant that no investigation of the case had taken place. That raises the number of cases with no explanation to 33 percent, or about 1,885.

The seventh of November brought no relief. Sightings continued with many containing occupant reports. Melvin Stevens was driving near Meridian, Mississippi, when he saw an object on the highway. As he approached, three men, about four and a half feet tall, got out of it and came toward him. Stevens said that they wanted to talk, but he couldn't understand what they were saying. After what seemed an eternity, they gave up, climbed back into the UFO, and took off. Several minutes later, a very scared Stevens arrived in Memphis and made his report. He looked like he had just seen a ghost.

On November 10, a Madison, Ohio, woman said that she had been gardening when she saw a very bright triangle-shaped object over her house. For thirty minutes she watched it but finally had to look away because it hurt her eyes. A few days later a rash developed over her body. Her doctor said that the rash might have been a result of what she had seen. She became ill in less than a week, the third American to report an injury or burn while watching a UFO.

On November 14, a hovering UFO flashed brightly and the power in Tamaroa, Illinois, failed. Power was out for about ten minutes in a four-mile area. It was just one of several such outages that were attributed to UFOs.

Then, on November 15, the Air Force again announced that the whole series of sightings was due to misinterpretation of natural phenomena. Included in this package of explanations was the Stokes sighting. But on November 20, they changed their minds and their statements about Stokes. They believed his story to be a hoax, suggested by "the natural phenomena at Levelland." They had tried to find the other witnesses but had failed to find either the witnesses or the pictures. APRO did find one other witness. A man had gone to the hospital to have his burns looked at but balked at the idea of reporting to the Air Force. His hesitation was justified.

About the same time, R.O. Schmidt was being examined by psychiatrists who found him unstable and very ill. He was committed to a mental institution. After he was released, he made many more UFO "contacts" and joined the lecture circuit.

After November 20, the number of sightings began to drop off. Apparently, no one wanted to be connected with a hoax or accused of being unable to identify natural phenomena, or even worse, to be committed. That was one of the reasons that the man burned with Stokes kept quiet. He didn't want to be called incompetent. During the period of November 2 to November 15, there were hundreds of sightings, not only in New Mexico or Texas, but also all over the world. Some of the sightings seemed to confirm what Stokes had reported.

On November 7, Mr. and Mrs. Linsey Trent were driving near Orogrande, New Mexico, when they noticed the speedometer jump from sixty to 110 and back. Then, to the south they saw a bright, metallic oval flying high. The object had well-defined edges and was in sight for several seconds. When it disappeared, the speedometer began working perfectly. The location and the description seemed to confirm the Stokes sighting.

When the Air Force changed their conclusions of the Stokes sighting, they said that Stokes admitted to having radio problems in the area before the UFO sighting. The other reports—the man who was burned and the couple who saw the UFO—volunteered the information in such a way as to suggest that they did indeed see something. All said that they were afraid of Air Force ridicule and that was why they didn't officially report the sightings.

After November 20, the Air Force tended to ignore the growing number of sightings. Part of the reason could be that the treatment of Stokes and Schmidt reduced the number of sightings being reported to the Air Force. If they are not reported in official channels, the Air Force believed, they must have never taken place. At any rate, sightings continued, but the press, public, and Air Force stopped reporting them.

In the years following the November 1957, sightings, dozens of explanations have been offered. Some said that the launch of the Russian Sputnik was the cause of all the spacecraft reports. They say that there were no sightings before that and the fact that it was a spacecraft put the idea into the heads of the people. Their claim is that all UFO waves can be reduced to one cause, one major sighting, and then dozens of others that follow the leader.

The easiest way to shoot down the theory is by pointing out that the wave of 1957 sightings really began in Asia in August, started building through October, and peaked about November 6–7. After that, there were still dozens of sightings, but where the Air Force received over a thousand reports in 1957, they only received six hundred in 1958. Even though the Russians launched their Sputnik on November 2, not all the people at Levelland had heard about it. Those sightings seem to have happened at the time the news was being released so it cannot be claimed as the cause of the sightings.

If anything could be the cause of the UFO wave of 1957, it would seem that it would be the *Fortune* picture taken on October 16. Although it was taken in the middle of the wave, and if anything suggests space travel, it is the picture of an extraterrestrial spaceship. But the picture hardly caused a ripple. By November 2, most had forgotten about it.

Others say that the wave caused by the Russian satellite instigated the sightings because nothing was heard about UFOs after November 20, but there were hundreds of sightings. It was in December 1957 that the first of the pictures of the Trinidad Island UFO were taken. The wave did not just dry up suddenly; the numbers slowly dropped off.

As an interesting sidelight, there were the waves of 1964, 1966–67, and 1973. The UFOs didn't disappear because the Air Force said they don't exist, but were/are still being reported. The end of a wave doesn't mean the end of UFO sightings.

April 24, 1964: Socorro, New Mexico

Before the mid-1960s, there was little written about physical evidence from UFOs. Part of the reason was that the Air Force, with its restrictive categories, placed everyone who had seen a landed UFO in the crackpot file, because they would not believe that an extraterrestrial spacecraft would land on earth. Project Bluebook officers were willing to waste tax money chasing high-flying discs but refused to even look at early cases that involved landings. For this reason, many of the early physical evidence cases were rejected before there were any investigations of them and the evidence was lost before it was recovered.

This changed in 1964 with the Socorro, New Mexico, landing. It could be that too much of the case made the papers before the Air Force had a chance to ridicule it or it could be that a police officer made the report, but regardless, the evidence was still visible days and even months later. Whatever the reason, the Air Force didn't ridicule the case, Hynek didn't call it swamp gas, and the police officer wasn't laughed at. After the Socorro case, other physical evidence reports and landing cases began to receive serious treatment by the Air Force.

The details of the Socorro case are important because it is a landmark. It is the first case where the Air Force admitted they had no answer for the physical evidence found. It was the first time that a large part of the public didn't scorn a case involving a landing, and it was the first time that the Air Force at least listened to a description of the creatures that rode inside. Since 1964, the details and facts of the report have been argued by the believers, the Air Force, and the debunkers. The only success they have had in ridiculing the report is by overlooking the facts or distorting them. The Air Force has left it as "unidentified."

It was early in the evening, about 6 P.M., when Socorro police officer Lonnie Zamora took off after a speeder. Near the outskirts of town, Zamora heard a loud roar, saw a flash of light, and thought that a dynamite shed had blown up. He altered his course and drove toward the shed.

Zamora was driving near a gully and over four hundred yards away, at the bottom of the gully, he could see a bright, white object. At first, he thought that it was an overturned car and near it he could see two "people." Zamora stopped the patrol car and got out. He couldn't see the figures in the gully well but thought that they were smaller than normal adults. They were wearing some type of "white clothes," but he couldn't see any other details. Zamora realized that the object was not an overturned car, and as he started forward, the humanoids apparently saw him. Everyone turned to run, the aliens scrambled back into the UFO, and Zamora bumped into the patrol car. The UFO rose, spitting a blue flame.

Seconds after the UFO disappeared, Zamora called Sergeant Chavez, a state police officer. Chavez didn't see the UFO or the occupants, but he did see the markings where the UFO stood. One bush was still smoking, several clumps of grass were burned, and there were four holes pressed into the ground. Both he and Zamora examined the evidence.

During the next few days, several investigators from various Air Force bases arrived. They examined the landing site, took Zamora's statements, checked his background, searched for other witnesses, and photographed everything in sight. Dr. J. Allen Hynek was brought in and he eventually spent days trying to find a hole in the case. Like the Air Force officers, he failed.

Finally, with nowhere else to go, the Air Force wrote its official conclusions. They said that the sighting could not be identified. This was a real break with their tradition of writing off every report of occupants as a psychological problem. Usually, they had ignored all sightings involving occupants and had always worked hard to destroy any reports of physical evidence. Apparently, this case grew too big too fast and they left it alone. They didn't think that the Socorro report would ruin their stand and felt that any controversy caused by an attempt to discredit it would be damaging to their other investigations. Maybe they counted on the short attention span of the public and hoped that the story would die quickly.

A few months after the sighting, Hynek went back to Socorro, New Mexico, to see if there were any significant changes in the story or the people. He visited with Zamora, Chavez, and the editor of the local newspaper. Hynek's final report said, "The more articulate Sergeant (sic) Chavez still firmly believes in Zamora's story . . . although I made a distinct attempt to find a chink in Zamora's armor, I simply couldn't find anyone, with the possible exception of a Mr. Philips, who has a house fairly near the site of the original sighting, who did anything but completely uphold Zamora's character."

Hynek's full report continues for eight pages but does not once suggest how the sighting could have been faked or why it would have been. He mentioned that Mr. Philips lived close to the landing site but did not hear anything strange, even with the windows and french doors open. Hynek is not concerned with this seeming discrepancy because "the wind was blowing down the gully" and the Philips house is in the opposite direction. "This, of course, can make a tremendous difference in the ability to hear. Further, there are trucks passing along the highway quite close to Mr. Philips's house and he undoubtedly is used to hearing backfires and truck roars of one sort or another." That last bit of information is very important in the light of some debunkers' claims that the case is a hoax because Philips didn't hear anything.

The final conclusion by Hynek was that he could not identify what had landed in Socorro. He didn't like Philips's claim of a hoax because "there are just too many bits of evidence that militate against this hypothesis." Until a better idea is presented, Hynek was satisfied to make his conclusion as unidentified.

The debunkers, never satisfied with a good case, worked to stir up a storm of controversy. One man, using a scaled map of the landing site, stuck four knitting needles into a scouring pad. He showed that the needles were at four different angles and claimed that this proved the case either a hoax or, at least, a plasma discharge, but certainly not a spaceship. If it had been a real spacecraft, he believed, then the needles would have had a regular pattern. The random pattern suggested that someone had dug the holes and claimed he saw a UFO, or that he had seen a plasma cloud create the marks with electrical discharges.

He overlooked one important fact. The terrain of the gully is rough. If a craft had been landing there, the legs of it may have compensated for the terrain. If he had used a model of the gully, rather than a map, he may have found a regular pattern. The legs were equidistant apart, but they were not rigid and compensated for the rise of the terrain to keep the craft level.

Because he quoted heavily from the official Air Force file on the case, I will do the same. It is his belief that the random pattern had never been satisfactorily explained and was purposely overlooked by UFO "buffs." However, Hynek's report from the Air Force files seems to cover the point. "We can recall that although the figure was drawn poorly, when it was redrawn according to dimensions given, it was found that the diagonals of the quadrilateral intersect at right angles. Mr. Powers pointed out that one of the burned marks was directly at this mean center."

That point, in Hynek's report, was overlooked by the debunker. He is as guilty of leaving out parts of the information as those who supported the spacecraft idea. That one paragraph does more damage to his argument than any other part of the file.

The debunker has also shown how the facts about a UFO case can be distorted. He quoted from Frank Edwards, using all the mistakes about the landing against Edwards. The APRO *Bulletin* covered that in April 1968. Editor Coral Lorenzen says that Edwards made thirteen errors in recounting the Socorro case, "the most glaring of which was his insinuation that Zamora had approached to within a hundred feet of the 'little men.' "

It wasn't that Edwards tried to deceive the public or wrote only to sell his books but that he wrote from memory. Most of the time he didn't go back to check his facts so that, in some cases, they "became better." He should have checked them, but he didn't. His accounts of sightings are still good, with only minor details being incorrect, and, because Edwards wrote that way, it shouldn't be used as evidence against all UFO researchers and writers.

A year after the Socorro sighting, a newspaper man from El Paso, Texas, interviewed several of the town's officials, including the mayor. In an article for an El Paso newspaper, he explains how there are plans to use the sighting as a tourist attraction. The road to the site has been improved, signs were going to be erected, and publicity was going to be staged. They were big plans but, for some reason, they were never carried out.

The mere mention of money in connection with a UFO sighting has always been enough to prove that the sighting was a hoax. Dozens of sighting accounts end with the simple statement that so and so did not receive any money and was not interested in gaining fame, as if this somehow proved the authenticity of the case. If they became too excited with the attention paid to them, it proved, at least to some researchers, that the case was a hoax. I have never figured out the connection between being excited by your name in the papers and the credibility of your statements. However, to become too excited about the publicity ruins the sighting.

Along with the possibility of making money, the debunker said that the mayor of Socorro owned the land where the UFO touched down. I'm not sure why this is important, but I think it has to do with the theory that someone was trying to invent a tourist attraction. An easy response is that someone had to own the land. Had it been a government reservation, would that mean the government had "faked" the landing? Of course it wouldn't and it certainly wouldn't prove that the craft was some type of government test vehicle. The debunker, however, tried to use the ownership of the land to discredit the sighting.

During the next several years, I'm sure that this sighting will be told and retold. Facts will become lost or added and this version will be disputed. In this account, I have tried to present both sides, have used the official files, and tried not to embellish the account. Zamora did see something in the gully and it is the interpretation that is in dispute. I believe that it was some kind of extraterrestrial spacecraft.

September 4, 1964: Glassboro, New Jersey

The Air Force has been accused by many of bungling its UFO investigations by wrapping them in a cloak of unnecessary secrecy. It has been suggested that the Air Force UFO project was a poorly run investigation, hampered by "official" requests for solutions and a hierarchy that wanted all reports identified. The question about their investigations becomes, "Did they hide facts and purposely try to cover their investigations or were they just guilty of being a bunch of incompetent investigators, trying their best with their scanty funds and limited knowledge?" The best way to discover

exactly what happened is to e⸺
investigations, as it appears in the⸺
then draw on a few outside facts.

Early in the evening, on September 4, 19⸺
a red glowing object hovering over the woods ne⸺
New Jersey. They watched as the UFO descended,⸺
and finally landed. When it was gone, several minutes ⸺
they searched the woods and found a burned crater in a clear-
ing. The next day, the two men went back to the woods and
reexamined the burned area. As they were leaving, they told
two boys who were fishing about the burn and they told their
father who was the local NICAP (National Investigations
Committee on Aerial Phenomena) representative.

Residents of the area said that they, too, had seen strange,
flashing red lights in the sky for several nights before the
landing. Mrs. Freda Dufala saw a spherical, red glowing
object hovering close to where the crater was found on September 4. Three nights later, on September 7, Carol Smith
saw an orange-yellow object near the woods. From under it
came a bright red glow. Smith told police that she watched
it land, take off with a thundering roar, and then saw it land
again.

Word of the September 4 sightings and landings spread
through the eastern United States and accounts of the sightings
were reported in the Sunday, September 6, editions of many
eastern newspapers. The next day, several papers carried
follow-up stories about the landing. Local police were "mystified" by the crater and "took samples to forward to the Air
Force."

Air Force accounts of the sighting begin with reference to
the newspaper articles and "numerous" phone calls to
McGuire Air Force Base. On September 10, 1964, the official
Air Force investigation was conducted. They failed to find
anything strange when they examined the crater, used their
Geiger counters, and took several pictures. In the crater,
however, they found a firecracker, which an Air Force colonel
seemed to think was very significant. There are several mentions of the firecracker in the Bluebook report. By September
14, 1964, the Air Force had completed its investigation. The
final report was in and they thought nothing more of the

1964, Glassboro, New Jersey

examine one of their Project Bluebook files and

1964 two men saw
over Glassboro,
later,

119

...ed. The Air Force ...s a hoax and in the ...of potassium nitrate

...Air Force officers. The ...se and that gave them a ...archers were restricted by ...by not being able to overlook ...tors had done. They began a ...d many holes in the Air Force story.

NICAP ... the first to publicly dispute the Air Force stand ... ing. They had made measurements of the crater and the ... od indentations. They took samples the day after the crater was found, photographed it before the curious arrived, and interviewed the witnesses within hours. The Air Force failed to even find the witnesses, but that didn't worry them because they knew it was a hoax before they got there.

One of the witnesses, identified as Mr. Frank Sergi, said that the Air Force arrived after thousands, maybe as many as four thousand curious people had trampled through the woods. A professor was with the men from McGuire and he returned several times. When Sergi asked what had caused the strange marks, the professor replied, "Nothing, nothing."

On September 12, 1964, a group of students from a high school science club went to Glassboro to conduct their own investigation. They were disappointed and wished that they hadn't decided to wait until the twelfth. By then, the area had been picked over by the police, the Air Force, and the curious. The most valuable evidence had been taken, lost, or trampled.

Their measurements, as well as those by the Air Force and NICAP, disagreed with the newspaper accounts. They didn't find a perfect triangle but rather that the measurements differed slightly. Instead of being twenty-seven feet on a side, the distances between the indentations were twenty-six feet by twenty-three feet by twenty-three feet. The holes were slightly inclined from the vertical, in toward the center. The smaller holes were squared, about nine inches across and nearly eighteen inches deep. The roots in the smaller holes were crushed, as if they had been pressed into the ground. This refinement indicated that the holes had not been dug but that something had been evenly and forcibly pushed into the ground. If the holes had been dug, the roots would have been cut, not crushed.

Geiger readings were taken in case there was radiation in the soil or the surrounding area but nothing above the normal background radiation was found. NICAP and the Air Force investigations confirmed this. In fact, an Air Force consultant in Earth Science at Southern Connecticut State College said that no indication of radioactivity was found. "For this reason [lack of radioactivity] there was a delay in receiving the final analysis," he wrote in his report to Project Bluebook.

One other piece of evidence was very important. Over the crater, several tree branches were broken by the UFO. Apparently they were splintered as the UFO descended. All the investigators examined the broken limbs and Sergi said that the professor climbed the trees several times to make measurements. All the investigators, those from NICAP and the high school science club, those from the Amalgamated Flying Saucer Clubs of America and from many police departments, found this evidence significant and did not support the contention that it was a hoax.

In January 1965, newspapers printed the final story about the New Jersey "hoax." A young man had come forward and admitted that he had rigged the Glassboro landing for the publicity he would receive and the money that he would earn. The newspaper explains how the boy with the aid of two friends "punched some holes in the ground, broke some tree limbs, and spread some chemicals around, to get the rumor started." During a camping trip, the boys dug the crater, set fire to the center of it, and then spread some sulfa potassium and radium dioxide about the area to make it radioactive.

Police uncovered the "hoax" after the boy tried to sell the story to a local newspaper. In the trial that followed, the boy told the judge that he needed money to continue his college career and thought that he could make some money from the UFO story. He told the judge how he had faked the sighting, impressing him, the police, and the Air Force with his ingenuity but was fined fifty dollars anyway. The sentence was suspended and he paid the ten dollars in court costs. With that, an official record that the sighting had been faked, the Air Force closed the case.

Others wondered about the trial, the "confession," and the hoax. Where had the boy obtained the radium dioxide? It is obtainable only in small amounts and is extremely dangerous as well as expensive. A person would hardly have access to it if he was "broke" and trying to "earn money for college." The amount of return on the investment would make it a very poor risk. Someone would have to pay a lot of money for the UFO story and no one pays that much.

None of the reports, from the Air Force, local police, or the high school science club mentions radioactivity. All checked for it but none found it. What was the point of the boy going to all the trouble of spreading the radium dioxide since the quantity was so insufficient? It didn't add any credibility to the case because no one found it.

Several tree experts were consulted to determine how the branches had been broken and the weight needed to break them. They later said, in a signed report, "It would have required heavy machinery or the combined weight of ten men to break the limbs. The root system was sprung downward. There was a scar of recent origin at the base of the trunk that would have required a powerful piece of equipment and a smooth metal cylinder." They didn't know how it could be done and not leave some identifiable traces. There should have been tracks for the machines or cable burns on the tree but none were found.

Leaves from the top of a forty-foot oak tree were examined by experts. The leaves were singed to the last degree of being destroyed. There was no evidence of disease, insect, fungus, or any other known condition to cause the leaf damage. NICAP's investigator said, "If it is a hoax, it would require some type of flame-thrower, in very skillful hands to singe but not burn the leaves."

The physical evidence investigated and examined by the tree experts left them with only one conclusion: "It is patently impossible to artificially produce the damage that we investigated." These results, along with all the other reports, appear in the Air Force file on the sighting. The crater was the next item on the list. As outlined earlier, it was surrounded by three smaller holes about nine inches in diameter. There was no evidence that any of the holes were dug but that they were pressed into the ground and that the crater was blasted into it.

The outside of the crater was singed, as if by a very intense heat. The sand had fused, forming glasslike particles. The heating of the crater had been relatively uniform because the depth of the burning was uniform. It had been extremely hot but present for only seconds because the ground was not burned very deeply.

There are several ways that this burning could have been done, but all of them leave residue. No nitrates, the residue of gunpowder, were found by anyone except the Air Force. No chemicals from a flame-thrower or blowtorch were found and no trace of machinery that could produce the burning was found. Of course, none of this concerned the Air Force. They had found the remains of a "blackcat" firecracker and that proved the sighting to be a hoax.

All of this would indicate that three teenage boys rigged the UFO landing. They spread an expensive chemical, radium dioxide, around the site to make it radioactive, but no one found it. They used heavy equipment to break tree limbs but left no traces. They dug uniform holes to resemble the marks left by landing gear but were sophisticated enough not to break the roots. They crushed them to give the impression that something heavy had been forced into the ground. And, they burned the inside of the crater with something hot enough to fuse the surface sand quickly but not burn the subsoil. They did all this expertly, quickly, and quietly. Then, they left the secluded area for others to find and suspect a UFO landing.

The biggest problem with all this is that the boys could not have gotten the equipment, the chemicals, or the expertise. They could not have gotten so many other Glassboro residents to come forward with UFO sightings to support their hoax and there is no reason to believe that anyone would find the crater unless directed to do it. The only hoax involved with this case seems to be the Air Force conclusion. The hoax is the story about the boys faking the sightings and the Air Force acceptance of their story.

As a matter of fact, a few days after the landing, another UFO was reported in the area. The Air Force and Navy responded with several airplanes, six helicopters, and three police cars. The new sighting added weight to the UFO landing reports, but the Air Force continued to scream "hoax."

This brings several questions to mind. Did the Air Force somehow provide the perpetrator of the hoax? Did they induce someone to come forward claiming it was his work so that the evidence and sighting could be written off? And, if they did it once, did they do it again?

In the Glassboro landing, we can only speculate about the Air Force role in perpetrating the "hoax of admission." No one has said that the Air Force asked them to claim that they faked the sighting. That the Air Force did it is only a guess, but it is a guess based on the facts, the admissions of former Air Force personnel, and deductions made about it from other sightings.

Air Force directives and orders issued during the years that Project Bluebook was in operation were often intended to hide the facts. Someone very high in the Air Force wanted all UFO sightings identified and then written off. This can be seen by the number of sightings with explanations that are obvious covers such as Venus being seen in the middle of the day and outshining the sun. Or balloons and swamp gas that fly into the wind and can outrun jet interceptors. Just explain the sighting and don't worry if the explanation is weak as long as it can be said that the case has been solved. Then, stick to that explanation even if it doesn't fit the facts. Tell a lie often enough and eventually someone, somewhere, is going to believe it.

But again, this is not conclusive evidence of a cover-up. It is highly suggestive, but it doesn't mean that the Air Force was faking its sighting solutions. It supports the theory but doesn't prove it.

Several years ago, a former Air Force sergeant had talked to researchers for the UFO Archives about UFO sighting solutions that he faked while in the Air Force. He said that, under orders, he faked solutions to "keep the local civilians calm and to keep the sightings from reaching the wire services, the press, or network news broadcasts.'' It worked quite well because many of the sightings are buried so deep that they will never be found.

The sergeant worked for a secret project that involved the use of giant balloons like those the Navy called Skyhooks. They were hard to launch because they required ideal weather, but once airborne they would travel great distances. ''When there was a UFO sighting in an area, members of our unit would go to the local authorities with one of the balloons and claim that it was the UFO. Most of the time, the people listened.'' he told researchers.

There were several questions, however, that I, as an investigator, wanted to be quite clear about. This was a new twist to an old problem and I didn't want to be responsible for starting any rumors. Again and again, I asked the same questions. I was trying to make sure that I had all the facts and had them right.

So I said, again, trying to keep things accurate, ''Let me get this straight. You would go into a city, say El Paso, after there was a UFO sighting and show your balloon. Then, you would tell the police or anyone who would listen, that it was your balloon they saw. You did this, even if there was no balloon in the area?''

The sergeant looked at me. ''I never went to El Paso to do it, I went into Roswell, New Mexico, but that is essentially correct.''

At the time the sergeant made the statement to me, I didn't realize the significance of it. It was important to know that someone at the Pentagon was initiating activity to cover up good sightings, but whether the sergeant had gone into Roswell or El Paso made no real difference. Then. Now . . . !

''And your orders came from the Pentagon?'' I wanted to be quite sure about that point.

''Well, of course, mine came from our CO, but his came from the Pentagon. The orders for all these units were from the Pentagon.''

''They ordered you to go out and fake UFO sightings?''

''They weren't really orders and some of us believed that we were telling the truth. If you tell someone a lie and they repeat it then they are not lying. They are passing false information, but they believe it too. We were told that these people were sighting our balloons and believed them to be the UFOs. We were to spread the word to the people.''

The main problem was trying to pin down exactly what happened. It wasn't an attempt to be vague but more of a failure to communicate exactly what had taken place. ''You knew what you were doing? You didn't really have a balloon in the area, but since the people wouldn't know that you told them that their UFO was your balloon?''

''You got it. These things needed perfect weather to be launched. In one case, we hadn't launched a balloon in five days, but we took one into town on a truck. We said that it was the UFO.'' He stopped for a moment.

I scribbled a few notes. ''There was no way that it could have been the balloon?''

''None whatsoever. We tracked these things until they came down. We knew where they all were and when they were there. The UFOs were not our balloons.'' He was quite sure.

''And your orders came from the Pentagon? They ordered you to go out to fake the UFO sightings?''

''Well, as I said, they weren't really orders, but they were about the same thing. Well, yes, they were orders. We knew that someone at a higher headquarters knew what the UFOs were and they were trying to hide the answers. After all, it is all one Air Force.'' That seemed to be it, the Air Force trying to use the balloons to cover the real problem.

''Was this a common practice?''

''I only did it once, but it did become common. In the meantime, this all (UFOs) became balloons which was ridiculous. And we were sworn to secrecy and all scared stiff.''

''Okay. What you are saying is that you told people that their UFO sightings were your balloons and you did this on orders that came from the Pentagon?'' I asked to make sure that we weren't assuming something.

''Yes.''

''And you don't want to qualify that in any way?''

''No.''

''You knew that you were faking these solutions?''

The sergeant drained his coffee before answering. He was still worried about repercussions from the Air Force. "We weren't told to go out and start hoaxes. Just show the balloon and say that it was the UFO. But it was the same thing. It all comes down to the fact that we were using the balloons to explain sightings that couldn't have been the balloons. None of them were up or in the right area. We all knew that, but some of us thought that there was a good reason for it."

The questioning and resultant discussions continued for almost an hour. The main point was that the sergeant said that he had, in fact, faked UFO sighting solutions for the Air Force. It proves that the Air Force wanted answers to sightings and that they didn't care how they got them, even if they had to manufacture them. What would be the point of doing this if it wasn't to cover up the facts? The Air Force, not Project Bluebook, not the interceptor pilots or the official spokesman, but only a few, select, high-ranking officers knew and know what the UFOs are. These would be the men of the MJ-12, who had their answer on July 7, 1947, when they received the material from Roswell. From that point, they were controlling everything and it was they who decided that it is best if the general public is kept in the dark.

In 1969, the Air Force, with the help of the infamous Condon Committee, "proved" that UFOs don't exist. No one believed that report and apparently even the Air Force is unhappy with it. It has been claimed that since then the Air Force still investigates UFO sightings. If asked, Air Force officials claim that they are no longer interested in UFOs. Like the former cover-up and the manufacture of answers, the new theory, at first, was just speculation. And, like the cover-up, there is now proof that it is happening.

In March 1973, the crew of a DC-8 cargo plane, while on a night flight, saw a large, disc-shaped object. Both the pilot and the copilot saw the UFO, and in separate interrogation sessions gave the same story. They were at 21,000 feet when the copilot saw the lights of what he thought was another plane. He pointed it all out to the pilot and they watched it turn toward them, catch them, and then begin to pace them.

In the bright moonlight, they could see a domed disc with two vertical fins in the back. Through the clear dome they could see figures moving. The copilot reached down and turned on the weather radar. The disc showed on the scope. For nearly eighteen minutes they watched the UFO both visually and on the radar. Finally, the UFO shot out in front of them, doubled back at incredible speed, and disappeared.

Everything seemed to confirm the sighting. Both men saw the same thing; they saw it on radar and they had no reason to lie. On the ground, they made an "official" report. The Air Force officers interviewed both pilots at length and when they left, the Air Force officers suggested that the pilots keep the story quiet by not discussing it with anyone but "authorized persons." The pilots could not talk for fear of losing their jobs, but for a promise from NICAP that they would remain anonymous, they agreed to tell the story.

The important thing is the fact that Air Force officers investigated the case. They then requested silence from the pilots and they did this four years after the end of the official Air Force project. At no time did any of the Air Force officers tell the pilots that they were no longer interested in UFOs. They took the story and then told the pilots to keep quiet. This proves that there still is an official investigation and that there still is a cover-up. The Air Force did not want the story circulated and they felt safe because they could silence the witnesses by threatening to have them fired. The threats worked for over a year.

But what does all this mean? The Glassboro landing showed how the Air Force ran their investigations. It proved that they were interested only in writing off the cases. They would grasp at straws, or in this case, a firecracker, to explain the report. If enough controversy could be artificially injected into a case, then its effectiveness could be destroyed. That was what they attempted to do in Glassboro.

The Air Force sergeant showed how the Air Force would make up solutions if they could find none. In an organization that was interested in giving an outward appearance of calm control, it is necessary for them to be able to answer all questions about UFOs. To do it, they had to be able to explain sightings and many times they had to manufacture the explanations. Everyone outside the elite Air Force group be-

lieved an effective investigation was being conducted. The
sergeant showed how effective it was.

The DC-8 crew showed that the Air Force is still doing it.
Air Force investigators, probably from a new Air Force project, rumored to be named either Project Aquarius or Bluepaper, interviewed and then silenced the pilots. It's much
easier for Air Force spokesmen to say that they are no longer
interested in UFOs instead of having them claim some out-
landish explanation. As it stands now, the lack of interest is
much more effective and doesn't strain the credibility the way
the balloons and Venus did.

Combined, all the information, all the regulations dealing
with the release of UFO information, and the results of investigations mean that the Air Force is hiding something.
Maybe they think that they are protecting us or protecting
some important classified data, but we're learning so much,
even though we've had to move slowly, that it's time to let
us in on the secret, if there still are any secrets.

March 2, 1965: Brooksville, Florida

Some cases are important because of the evidence that
comes out of them. Roswell would be the first and foremost
example of that sort of case. Others are important for what
they tell us of the quality of research by both private researchers and Air Force investigators. Brooksville, Florida is
a good example of that.

On March 2, John Reeves, a retired longshoreman who
lived on the outskirts of Brooksville, had trouble sleeping
and decided to take a walk. In the woods behind his house
he came upon a landed object. From the left came a "robotlike" creature that was walking toward the craft. It
stopped, turned, and raised something to its face, almost like

a tourist raising a camera. There was a flash, like a flashbulb going off, and Reeves was convinced that he had been photographed.

The robot returned to the ship; the landing gear, a four-legged affair, retracted, and the UFO took off with a roar and a whistling sound. Reeves, somehow having lost his glasses in the excitement, couldn't see all that well. His description of the craft and the creature were vague. The object was twenty to thirty feet in diameter and eight to ten feet thick. The creature wore a stiff, silvery suit and had an inverted glass bowl on its head.

But the Reeves case isn't important for the description of the object or the creature. After the UFO was gone, Reeves searched the ground near where the creature had first appeared and found two sheets of paper covered with strange writing, almost like hieroglyphics. Reeves described it as a combination of Oriental pictographs and shorthand symbols.

Shortly after the sighting, Air Force investigators arrived, interviewed Reeves, took the papers, and left. A few weeks later the Air Force returned the papers and claimed that they had decoded the message. It was from "Planet Mars" and was a request for a traveler to return home.

If it was a hoax, it certainly wasn't a very clever one. But then one of the deputies who had talked to Reeves in the beginning told me that the papers returned by the Air Force were not the ones they had taken away. According to the man, the documents brought back by the Air Force didn't match the writing on the photocopies made before the arrival of the Air Force.

And, when the papers were first shown to them, one of the deputies cut a corner from the paper, touching a match to it. It burned like flash paper—a quick, bright flame with almost no smoke and very little residue. The papers brought back by the Air Force didn't react that way. The Air Force investigators claimed that the papers they returned were the same ones they had been given. The sheriff's deputies claim they aren't.

Several months later, a second landing took place in the same area as the first. This time footprints were found and photographed. Also found were some small metallic objects and a short piece of wire. The metal turned out to be titanium, rare in a pure state because of its high melting point. The chemist who later analyzed the metal said that he believed the story because of the samples.

There was some unfortunate controversy about the case. Early on, some of the sensation-seeking press, most notably the tabloids, tried to change the case from an encounter into another abduction in the vein of Antonio Villas-Boas (*see October 1957: Antonio Villas-Boas*). To keep the thrill seekers out of the area, investigators for APRO said the case was a hoax. It kept the thrill seekers away and let the serious researchers investigate. As it turned out, according to a deputy, ''On Friday and Saturday night it's impossible to get close to where the saucer landed. There are people out there from all over, just waiting for the thing to land again. Some of them camp out all night.''

The controversy still surrounds the case, but that is no longer important. What's important is the deputy sheriff's claim that the Air Force took the physical evidence and then brought back something different. There is no reason for the deputy to lie about that. And there is no reason for the Air Force to do that unless they were trying to hide something, and given what's been going on for the last forty years, that isn't hard to believe.

June 24, 1967: Austin, Texas

One of the strangest of the Project Bluebook unidentifieds is also one of the last. Ray Rosi had been driving near the north side of the Mansfield Dam, in the area of Austin, and had stopped to let his dog out. It was about 3:12 A.M. when his attention was drawn to a bright, elongated, solid-looking blue object just above the horizon. A minute before the UFO appeared, two men in a small red sports car had driven by, slowing down near Rosi, but then speeding on their way. He thought nothing of that until he saw the UFO.

The car pulled to the side of the road only 250 feet from him. "I wondered why they would be at such a place that time of night. They parked with lights tilted up the hill and flashed their beams several times. It was a short time later when the strange object appeared on the northwest horizon. Occupants of the red auto pulled over to the other side of the hill, and stopped the car again—out of my sight."

After seeing the apparent signal, Rosi took out his big spotlight and started flashing the "only code that I could think of that anyone might understand (mathematical: 3.14, pi)." He flashed it a few times, and the object "stopped dead still." The illumination faded for a second or two, and then brightened again, but the UFO continued to hover. Finally it started again, following the same path.

As the UFO continued, Rosi got out a pair of binoculars. Through them, he could see a blue cigar-shaped UFO. When he flashed the light code again, the UFO slowed, the brightness faded, then brightened, and then the UFO resumed its original speed. At 3:22 A.M., the UFO disappeared into a low cloud cover moving in from the south.

After the UFO disappeared and Rosi had collected his dog, he drove to the nearest phone to call the Air Force. They responded with the standard form and one officer, Lieutenant Robert Foreman. As he was completing the form and discussing the case with Foreman, Rosi mentioned that he had the feeling that he was being watched. He compared it to "a youngster doing something wrong in the backyard of a home who all of a sudden felt that he was being watched." He said that it was a feeling of communication "somewhat like mental telepathy, yet not strong enough because I have never experienced or received any message by brain wave."

Foreman completed his investigations, took the completed Air Force form with its quagmire of questions and drawings, and left. He submitted them to the project headquarters. Rosi, of course, had an interest in the case and later asked what was being done. Finally, he received word of the decision on his sighting. It was stamped INSUFFICIENT DATA FOR SCIENTIFIC ANALYSIS.

Rosi was furious. He filled out another form to forward to the Air Force but added a lengthy comment to question thirty-five, which asks for "information which you feel pertinent, and which is not adequately covered in the specific points of the questionnaire or a narrative explanation of your sighting." Rosi wrote: "It is a real mystery to me why you state in your August 21 missive, 'The information which we received is not sufficient for a scientific evaluation,' in consideration of the fact that the very thorough report which Lieutenant Foreman took and supposedly submitted to you contained far more definitive information . . . than could be elicited via your questionnaire."

Rosi continued, adding that more information was available through Foreman's report than in the form that was being sent, but that their handling of the case "leads me to believe . . . that the accusations of negligence heaped upon you . . . by some independent investigations in recent years may NOT be entirely unfounded."

Rosi, like others, was caught wondering what was missing from his reports and those of Lieutenant Foreman. What data was needed so that a "scientific analysis" could be made, and why wasn't that point covered in the forms? It seemed that a great deal of time and effort was being expended to gather data that was later found to be lacking some important factor.

After reviewing Rosi's new forms, reevaluating the Foreman report, and doing more research into Rosi's background, the Air Force changed the status of the report. No longer was it "insufficient" but "unidentified." Considering Rosi's rather technical background, his education and obvious sincerity, the Air Force had found itself in another of its famous holes.

Rosi's experiences, both with the UFO and with the Air Force, were interesting. His report was one of the best found in the files. And, it had received no public dissemination. No one outside the Air Force knew about it, and, if the Air Force had its way, no one ever would.

July 10, 1967: Meridian, Mississippi

One of the very last cases reported to Bluebook that was labeled as unidentified occurred in Meridian, Mississippi. Philip Lanning was driving south of town, on the evening of July 10, 1967, when his car coasted to a stop and the radio faded. Lanning got out and started to look under the hood when an object of "excessive size passed forward of my position and perhaps two to three hundred feet over my head." The object was moving silently except for the "rushing of an extreme wind." It was heading to the east and Lanning thought that it was about to crash-land in a clump of trees.

"Just before reaching the trees, it tilted upward, appeared to be moving to the immediate right, and then accelerated rapidly at an angle almost straight up and disappeared into low-flying clouds." Lanning thought the object was in sight for three to five seconds and one Air Force officer thought that was important. In his opinion, no one could have observed all that Lanning claimed he had seen in only five seconds. The officer overlooked the fact that most people are notoriously poor at estimating time, especially when excited.

The object itself was "like a cymbal on a drum set and was a dirty metallic gray in color on the underside. When it tilted upward, Lanning was able to see the top, which he said was colored "like the bluing of a good weapon." He saw no portholes or hatches, and could hear no sound. He was not sure how big it was but felt that "it could be compared with the length of a house."

Lanning wasn't sure who would be interested in the report, but he felt that it should be sent to "someone in the U.S. Government," so he forwarded it to a friend in Naval Intelligence. The Air Force received it and began an investigation.

Once again, they were impressed with the background of the witness. Lanning, as a former military officer, had received a great deal of training and was, therefore, considered reliable.

Nearly a year later, a further outline of the sighting was made. One man noticed that some of the statements made by Lanning were "characteristic of this type of sighting." The object tilted upward and accelerated, disappearing into the clouds in a matter of seconds.

Maybe it was Lanning's background, or maybe it was the detail of the sighting that caused the Air Force to label it as unidentified. Whatever the cause, they were breaking with tradition. This is one of the very last cases in the files to receive the unidentified tag.

January 17, 1969: Crittenden, Virginia

On January 17, 1969, the last report to be classified as "unidentified" was made to Project Bluebook. There would be other reports, including several photographs, but the January report from Crittenden, Virginia, would be the last real UFO.

The witness, an employee of NASA, did not want his name connected with a UFO sighting, and, although I am not required to do so, I will respect his wishes by using the name John Kincaid. Kincaid claimed that he had been asleep since 10:30 P.M. that night, but that he had been awakened at 3:24 A.M., by an extremely loud hum. The sound fluctuated from very loud to a low buzzing, then back to loud. Kincaid got up and walked to the window, staring out toward the sound, but saw nothing. After a few seconds, a lighted object appeared in the southeast.

As Kincaid watched the UFO come slowly toward him, he saw that the bottom seemed to be elliptically shaped with blunt ends. The UFO was about a hundred feet above the ground, about thirty feet wide, and over a hundred feet long. It moved slowly and came within a hundred feet of Kincaid so he was able to get a very good look at it. He called to his wife, but she didn't hear him, apparently because the noise from the UFO smothered his words.

Around the bottom of the UFO, Kincaid could see a series of windows that were all brightly lit except for one at the rear that blinked. It may have been blinking in time to the changes in the pitch, but Kincaid couldn't be sure. The windows were rectangular and appeared translucent. They would allow the light out, but Kincaid couldn't see in and each seemed to be surrounded by a glow or haze, further restricting his vision. Kincaid could see the center of the craft in that light and said that it was solid, apparently metallic, and reflected some of the light.

The UFO continued to drift across Kincaid's field of vision. It rocked gently as it moved, making it appear to move up and down slightly, but it never gained or lost much altitude. Finally, Kincaid said that it made a very gentle turn, tilting slightly and moving to the west. A few seconds later, the craft faded from sight.

Kincaid also reported that he felt a "tingling of his nerves" as the UFO flew by. He complained that he had unusual mental impressions and felt a hypnotic relaxation pass over him that calmed his fear. He was at a loss to explain any of the feelings.

When the UFO disappeared, Kincaid's wife asked what he had seen. The hum was still audible when Kincaid picked up the phone to call the operator. He asked the operator if she could hear it over the line, and she replied that she could. Kincaid, surprised, asked, "Are you sure?"

"Yes, I can hear it."

When the noise finally faded, he decided that he should report the sighting to the authorities and asked the operator to connect him with nearby Langley Field. He was routed to the local "Project Bluebook" officer who took the report and then told him how to file an "official" report. The officer didn't stay on the phone too long and was obviously unimpressed with the fact that the UFO had just been sighted. By

3:35, Kincaid was back in bed, the whole episode having lasted less than fifteen minutes.

The next morning, on the way to work, Kincaid told the others in his car pool about the UFO. They listened politely but didn't seem to care about a UFO report. At work, he told some of his friends and they seemed more interested. One of them called the local paper and Kincaid was interviewed by a reporter.

Later that day, Kincaid tried to find the operator that he had talked to during the night. He failed at first but kept trying. On January 22, he was connected with the supervisor and was told that the operator could not have heard anything other than a plane. Kincaid persisted, claiming that the operator had heard the strange hum and not the engines of a plane. The supervisor was equally insistent and refused to give Kincaid the operator's name or let him talk to her.

On the afternoon of January 17, Kincaid tried to find others who may have seen the craft because he wanted some confirmation of the sighting. He located one woman who thought that her mother, Susan Johnson, may have heard the UFO. Mrs. Johnson and a three-year-old granddaughter had heard the sound and had both awakened, frightened. Mrs. Johnson didn't get up to look but said that the sound was so close that she thought something was "coming through the roof."

Kincaid continued the search for other witnesses. In nearby Eclipse, Virginia, he found another woman who had heard the UFO. It had awakened her four-year-old daughter and had badly frightened her, to the extent that she didn't look out the window. She said that it sounded as if "it was going to land on top of us."

A few days later, he found a couple who had heard the strange, electrical hum. Kincaid interviewed them, and all decided that they had heard the same thing. Still later, he found yet another witness in a nearby town. Kincaid then filed a report with a private UFO research group before trying to forget about the incident.

One point should be made about this sighting. Several debunkers have said that the witnesses' activities after a sighting are very important. Anyone seeing what he or she thought to be an extraterrestrial spacecraft would be very excited about it. By finding out how the witnesses reacted hours after the sighting, we can gain a clue to the accuracy of the case. Kincaid was very excited. He had lain awake the rest of the night. He told his friends immediately, and he had tried to find others who had had a similar experience. His reactions were not those of a person playing a hoax.

The Air Force reactions, however, were not impressive. Two months after Kincaid filed his report, the Air Force finally began its investigations. After such a long time lapse, the trail was cold. First, the investigators tried to find out if there had been any helicopters in the immediate area, but Langley Field showed no traffic of any kind. Next, they tried the civilian airport, but were told that such records are kept only for fifteen days and that they were forty-five days too late. None of this bothered the Air Force men, who tried to convince Kincaid that he had seen a helicopter. The official Air Force record shows that Kincaid "was unreceptive to this line of reasoning." When that failed, they tried to convince him that he had seen the Goodyear blimp or an aircraft taking night photographs of the area. However, all attempts to prove to Kincaid that he had not seen a UFO having failed, they finally concluded that the case was "unidentified."

1969: The Condon Committee

Throughout the late 1950s and the 1960s, the Air Force and the government tried to think of ways to get the Air Force off the spot it thought it was on (*see January 1976: The Search of the Bluebook Files*). Various officials, both civilian and military, supplied ideas, but the one that came to the forefront was to find a civilian committee that would study the UFO phenomenon, say a few positive things about the Air Force investigation, and then conclude the study the way the Air Force wanted it concluded.

The outgrowth of all this was the study done at the University of Colorado headed by Dr. Edward U. Condon. UFO researchers hailed it as a breakthrough. Finally the public would have a chance to see what lay hidden in the Bluebook Files. And finally, there would be an unbiased investigation of the phenomenon.

But the eighteen-month study was riddled with controversy. Staff members quit, claiming that a serious investigation wasn't being made. Even before the final report was written, researchers were saying that it was a whitewash. The study was nothing but a public relations gimmick designed to fool the public.

Within hours of the report being finished, the UFO researchers knew they had been had. It rehashed old conclusions, reinforced ridiculous labels such as the Tremonton movie showing birds (*see July 2, 1952: The Tremonton, Utah Movie*), and suggested that the Air Force close Project Bluebook because nothing concrete had been found. On December 17, 1969, the Air Force, following that advice, announced that Bluebook was being shut down. In all its years of investigation, it had never found conclusive proof that UFOs were real or that they posed a threat to national security.

The question about the University of Colorado study becomes, Did the Condon Committee succeed in its mission? And that leads to the second question: What exactly was its mission?

Early in the study, a memo written by Dr. Richard Low to Condon suggested that there was no scientific impartiality. Key members of the research team set out to systematically debunk the subject, as had been the policy of the government since early 1953 (*see January 1953: The Robertson Panel*).

Couple all that, the Low memo, the Robertson Panel recommendations, and the various letters and documents concerned first with debunking and demystifying UFOs and then with getting the UFO investigation out of the public eye, and the answer becomes, "Yes, they accomplished their mission."

Unfortunately the mission wasn't to investigate UFOs but to end the Air Force's public investigation of them. With the Condon Report in hand, the Air Force could close Bluebook.

It died with a whimper as people, worried about the Vietnam War, inflation, and President Nixon, moved on to other things.

October 1973: The UFO Occupants

October of 1973 was a time of unusual UFO activity. It was a time when many people were reporting UFOs, but more important, they were reporting the objects on the ground and the creatures from inside the craft gathering samples of the plants, animals, and minerals. Had we been alert, instead of arguing about the reality of the situation, we might have been able to initiate communication with the occupants of the objects. Instead, we argued about the sanity of the witnesses because the October 1973 wave brought a number of new, frightening aspects to the UFO field.

The first indications that October 1973 was going to be different came a few weeks earlier. In the middle of September, a family from Sydney, North Carolina, reported a creature with red glowing eyes, long hair, pointed ears, and a hook nose on a gray face. The limping creature was missing a hand but could leap fifty or sixty feet at a time. They found no physical evidence, but they weren't alone in the sighting. A radio disc jockey and a group of boys saw the same creature and fired six pistol shots at it.

October started with a bang. On the first, three men reported they saw a huge creature that walked mechanically. In the distance they saw an egg-shaped object and an examination of the field where it had landed revealed imprints from it.

Three days later, Cary Chopic, a Simi Valley, California, man saw a triangular-shaped object hovering in a cloud of dust. In a clear bubble on top of the UFO, Chopic reported seeing a humanoid creature in a silvery wet suit. When the creature saw Chopic, it leapt out of sight. The bubble began to rotate faster, seemed to disappear into the craft as it emitted a whirring sound as a fog began to envelope the object. Seconds later the UFO vanished. It didn't seem to move; it just vanished.

The next evening a retired schoolteacher and her daughter were on the highway near El Centro, California, when they noticed a Greyhound Bus and several cars pulled to the side of the road. Standing near all the vehicles was a group of people watching a large, disc-shaped object surrounded by a glistening vapor. The object rose vertically to twelve hundred feet, turned, and vanished, leaving a vapor trail that drifted toward the ground. After a minute or two, the trail evaporated without reaching the ground.

On October 6, a man and his wife saw a bright spotlight bouncing over a field close to their house. They assumed that it was the police chasing cattle rustlers. Minutes after they first saw the light, it winked out and they thought nothing more of it.

The next day, however, the man was working behind the house when his wife came out to tell him that she could see dense black smoke coming from the field where the light had been. While watching the smoke, a dome-shaped tent of orange-yellow appeared. Both witnesses said they didn't think the smoke had anything to do with the UFO.

A few minutes later, a "bulldozer" about a quarter of the size of the UFO came into view. As it moved away from the witnesses, five "scouts," humanoids in yellow-colored clothes, appeared, running between the two objects. The woman thought the creatures wore helmets, but she couldn't be sure.

Both witnesses returned to their chores. When they looked back, the object and the scouts were gone. They didn't bother to search for evidence in the fields but did wonder how the men and equipment could get into the field without passing the house.

About noon their daughter returned. When she heard the story, she rushed out to the area where the objects had been seen. She found flattened grass and a few broken bushes. Several days later more flattened grass was found, leading to speculation that the creatures and their equipment had returned more than once.

On October 11, in Tanner Williams, Alabama, a three-year-old boy told his mother that he had been playing with a nice monster that had gray wrinkled skin and pointed ears. Had it not been for confirmation of that description a few days later, no one would have thought much about the boy's strange playmate.

Also on October 11, in Connersville, Indiana, and just after 4:30, Terry Eversole and his sister reported a disc-shaped object with a segmented compartment on the bottom. They said the object was silver with a dome on top and three green doors on the bottom. After several seconds it shot off toward the horizon and vanished.

Three hours later, Bill Tremper and fifty other people in Connersville watched an oval-shaped object with a pale yellow light on top. They reported a segmented compartment on the bottom. The UFO crossed the sky until it was over a restricted area where it hovered briefly and then settled to the ground. After thirty minutes, the object rose, hovered, and disappeared.

About the same time, Randi Stevens, Joel Burns, and three others saw a UFO hovering near Laurel, Indiana. They claimed the object looked like two saucers put together but more important, they reported that the bottom was segmented. The object hovered until a truck driver who had been watching got into the cab and blew the horn.

It was on that same day that two men walked into the Pascagoula, Mississippi, sheriff's office and reported they had seen a strange object land while they were fishing. Several robotlike creatures, described as wrinkled, gray, and with pointed ears, came out of the UFO, swooped toward them, grabbed them, and took them into the craft. For twenty-five or thirty minutes, the men were subjected to a physical examination on the craft. Within hours of making that report, Charles Hickson and Calvin Parker would be known across the country and all national reporting of UFOs would be centered in Pascagoula.

In Boulder, Colorado, Allen Robbins and his wife reported a strange object there. Robbins's wife saw the UFO first, a mass of lights approaching from high overhead, and called his attention to it. The slowly rotating craft maintained a steady speed as it silently flew. Interestingly, they saw a string of lights on the bottom that divided it into thirds.

In Berea, Tennessee, James Cline was awakened by barking dogs. A farm family reported a UFO with blinking lights in the woods and Cline saw a creature with a glowing white head across the road. Tracks from both the creature and the UFO were found the next day.

On October 15, a cab driver claimed that his cab was stalled by a blue UFO that landed in front of him. He then heard a tapping on his windshield and saw what looked like a ''crab-like'' claw. There was speculation that this was the second of the October abductions.

Howard Moneypenny, a weather service specialist, saw a bright light glowing in the distance on October 16. He pointed the UFO out to others and a private pilot volunteered to give chase to the object. He had to give up after several minutes when he realized that he wasn't getting any closer. On his way back to the airport, the object seemed to be chasing him. The UFO finally disappeared in the distance.

Also on October 16, William and Donna Hatchett were traveling on an Oklahoma county road when they saw a bright light in the south. At first they believed it to be a farm security light on a pole, but it seemed to be pacing the truck and getting closer. As the UFO turned toward the truck and began descending, Donna begged her husband to stop for a moment.

When Hatchett stopped the truck, the object stopped too, hovering near the front of the pickup. Both Hatchett and his wife could hear or feel a penetrating, low-pitched hum. There was a blinding white light from the object that Hatchett thought to be about the size of a Boeing 707 jet.

While Hatchett sat there staring at the UFO, his wife got out and moved to the rear of the pickup. Hatchett, now frightened, ordered his wife to return. She did as told but got out twice more.

Finally, with his wife back in the truck, Hatchett drove away. As he did, the UFO moved off in the opposite direction, gaining altitude as it did.

Later, both Hatchett and his wife reported they felt the

creatures in the UFO knew everything they were thinking (*See June 24, 1967: Austin, Texas*). Donna Hatchett claimed that the flashing lights she saw as the object pulled away reminded her of the lights on a computer.

The last October 16 sighting was reported by two children who saw a craft with a pointed dome that made a buzzing sound. The older boy claimed strange creatures offered him a chance to look inside, but he was too frightened to accept. The boys' father reported the family dog was frightened when he went into the backyard after the sighting.

The seventeenth brought no relief. In Watauga, Tennessee, a copper-colored UFO hovered just above the ground while a tall creature reached out, apparently to grab two children. The creature had clawlike hands and wide, blinking eyes.

In Falkville, Alabama, Police Chief Jeff Greenhaw photographed a tall creature in a silvery suit after he was called into the area to check on a UFO report. Greenhaw stopped his car when he saw the creature as it moved slowly toward him. After a few moments, it turned and began running. Greenhaw pursued it until his car spun off the road. Various investigators and UFO organizations have labeled the case a hoax after NASA produced pictures of their metallic firefighting suit that bore a resemblance to the creature in the Greenhaw photos. If it was a hoax, it was not one perpetrated by Greenhaw. He certainly gained nothing from it if he did.

On the same day, small creatures in a cone-shaped object landed in front of a car driven by Paul Brown, forcing him to stop. As he got out, two creatures in silver suits and white gloves confronted him. Seeing Brown, they returned to their craft, which took off immediately. Brown fired several shots from his revolver at it.

In Mississippi another UFO landed on a highway, blocking traffic. As one car approached, its lights went out and the engine died. Occupants of the car saw a humanoid with a wide mouth, flipper feet, and webbing between the legs.

Another abduction was reported near Loxley, Georgia. Clarence Patterson claimed that his pickup truck was sucked into a huge, cigar-shaped craft. He was jerked out of the cab by several robotlike creatures who seemed to read his mind.

He blacked out after that and the next thing he knew he was on the highway driving at ninety miles an hour.

The most important case of the seventeenth came from Utah. A woman there, Pat Roach (called Pat Price in a few reports), claimed that she, along with a few of her children, were taken from their house by several tiny creatures just before midnight. The beings, from a UFO that landed in a secluded field near her home, also took some neighbors. Only Roach's youngest daughter remembered anything of the incident. The woman, however, believing that a prowler had been in her house, called the police. It would be two years before the details of the sighting would be learned. It was a landmark case because it was the first time that anyone had reported the aliens coming into a private house to get them. Now that seems to be the standard.

The next day there were more UFO sightings. Near Chatham, Virginia, two boys reported they were chased by a white thing about three or four feet tall. It had a large head, no eyes, and ran sideways.

Near Savannah, Georgia, a small silver creature was seen standing by a highway. Dozens of cars zipped by it, but none of them stopped. No craft was seen.

Herchel Fueston, a patrolman for the Noblesville, Indiana, police reported a cigar-shaped object just before midnight. When he turned his spotlight on it, it began moving to the southwest as its lights brightened. It flew over the Morse Reservoir and hovered briefly. Fueston reported a row of portholes but could see nothing behind them. Finally the object descended to treetop level and disappeared.

On the nineteeth, a woman near Ashburn, Georgia, reported her car engine died and she lost the power steering and the brakes. As she coasted to a stop at the side of the road, a small man in metallic clothes appeared. The woman reported that the creature had a bubble head and rectangular eyes. It walked around the car and then vanished, much to the woman's relief.

Later that same day, a farm couple in Copeland, North Carolina, discovered an oval UFO hovering near their home. There was a small humanoid in a gold metallic jumpsuit moving near it. They observed no other detail, being afraid of both the craft and the creature.

The last reported sighting on the eighteenth involved a landed disc. Susan Ramstead said that her car engine stalled when she approached a domed disc sitting in a cornfield. Minutes later the craft shot skyward and vanished. Four years later, it was discovered that Ramstead was taken on board for a physical examination. It wasn't until a time discrepancy was noted that the details of the whole sighting were learned. Ten years after the sighting, even more astonishing things were discovered (*see July 1983: Ramstead Revisited*).

The next day, October 20, a college student vanished on her way home for a few days. When she finally reappeared, she claimed to have been taken on board an alien craft and subjected to a series of long and painful stress tests. Investigations of the sighting progressed slowly because of the agitated nature of the young woman. Like the Roach case and the Ramstead case, the significance of the sighting wouldn't be realized until years later.

On the twenty-first, a mother and her son in Ohio sighted a gray humanoid near a landed UFO. A search of the fields produced ground traces.

On the twenty-second, a series of sightings began in Hartford City, Indiana. Debbie Carney spotted two creatures wearing silver suits on the road in front of her car. She drove past them quickly and didn't see any kind of craft.

But fifteen minutes later, De Wayne Donathan and his wife were returning home when they saw a flash of light in the road in front of them. Thinking they were about to hit a farm tractor and had only seen the reflector on the back of it, Donathan slammed on the brakes. In the field near them, they saw two creatures jumping around. Donathan described their movements as dancing.

Two hours after that, Gary Flatter drove through the same area looking for the creatures. He noticed a high-frequency whine and saw a line of small animals running across the road. An instant later he saw the creatures standing in a plowed field. Flatter turned his truck's spotlight on them and was nearly blinded by the reflection from their suits. Flatter described the creatures as four feet tall, with egg-shaped heads and gas masks with tubes running to their chests. Shortly after he turned the light on them, they leapt away. The next day footprints were found in the field.

After the Harford City sightings, the wave declined rapidly. There were one or two occupant sightings on the twenty-third in Kentucky. A lone woman saw two small creatures and the object from which they came. A day later a North Carolina man's car engine was stalled by a low-flying oval UFO. He is reported to have seen a creature with blazing red eyes.

On October 28, the last of the October abductions took place. Dionisio Llanca was taken to a hospital near his home in Bahia Blanca, Argentina, where he complained of amnesia and loss of appetite. Doctors, using hypnotic regression, learned that he had been picked up by two men and a woman from a UFO. On board the craft he was subjected to a physical examination during which blood samples were taken. After nearly three quarters of an hour, he was returned to his truck and left alone. There is still controversy about this case, with some researchers claiming it was a hoax.

Llanca's was the last occupant sighting of October 1973, but not the last of the year. On November 1, a series of sightings began in New Hampshire when Florence Dow heard a thump on her front porch. She turned to see a motionless creature wearing a black coat and a wide-brim hat pulled down over a face that looked as if it had been covered with masking tape.

The next night, Lyndia Morel saw a strange yellow light in the distance as she drove to work. As she watched it, it appeared to come closer until she could tell that it was spherical and covered with a honeycomb. There was a single, oval window and behind it was a creature with gray wrinkled skin and large slanted eyes.

As she drove along, she felt drawn to the UFO and kept looking at it. She finally became frightened and pulled into a farm driveway. Leaping from the car, she ran to the backdoor, which was shielded from the craft. After several minutes of hammering on the door, the farmer opened it and she convinced him that she wasn't crazy. While she was in the house, the UFO vanished.

Two days later, Rex Snow and his wife were awakened

just after midnight. Outside, Snow saw two small creatures wearing silver suits gathering samples. Snow ordered his German shepard to attack, but it stopped far short of them. It ran back to the house, obviously afraid.

After the New Hampshire series, there weren't many more sightings. The wave had crested and dropped off. It would be several years before the significance of the wave would be understood. The number of occupant reports, with the creatures gathering samples, suggested one thing and the abduction cases reinforced it. October of 1973 seemed to be the time that the aliens were attempting to learn all they could about us and the Earth. When they finished with it, they headed off to study the data they had gotten—but not before they had given us another good look at them and their motives.

February 1975: The Minnesota Mutilations

Late in November 1974, rumors began to connect the sightings of UFOs with the mutilated cows that were being found in large numbers in various Minnesota counties. Several individuals and a couple of institutions were linking the two, claiming that the UFOs were responsible for the mutilations. There was a lot of circumstantial evidence involved and before the entire episode was over, two people would appear on a network talk show explaining two opposing points of view, there would be hundreds of newspaper and magazine articles, and the evening network news would be reporting the deaths of cattle as if they had been important statesmen or major Hollywood stars.

Although there had been stories of mutilations in South Dakota in the fall of 1974, there had been no reason to associate the deaths with UFOs. Then, on November 29, 1974, the Meeker County, Minnesota, sheriff, Mike Rogers, received a call from a local farmer reporting that one of his pigs had been killed sometime during the night. This was apparently the first such death in Minnesota and both the sheriff's deputy, who responded, and the farmer, who had found the pig, were baffled. They could not explain how the pig had been killed.

There was one other point that several self-styled UFO investigators who entered the case later harped on as being important. At 11:30 P.M., the farm's security light had gone out. The farmer, at first, thought that it had just burned out, but it came back on about fifteen minutes later. Electrical interference is a well-known side effect of UFOs, they claimed (*See November* 1957: Levelland, Texas), and this was just one more indication that UFOs were deeply involved.

In the next few weeks, dozens of UFOs were reported in Minnesota and dozens of cattle were found dead and mutilated. Although the sightings and mutilations never correlated, many felt that the number of sightings was added proof that the UFOs were somehow involved. It appeared, from the number of reports in Minnesota, that there was a minor flap in progress.

The evidence for the UFO involvement seemed to grow. On one farm, a mutilated cow had been found "inside a circle of melted snow with a perfect diameter." Several other burned areas were found near the cow and on a small lake there were indentations in the ice. Some investigators claimed that UFO landing gear had caused the holes.

The Meeker County sheriff continued to investigate. Frank Schiefelbein had called him to look at the body of a dead black angus cow. Rogers found that the lips of the animal had been cut off, the tongue was cut out, and the jugular vein was sliced. There was almost no blood on the ground, although the left ear was missing and the reproductive organs had been removed. The injuries should have caused massive bleeding.

The sheriff also noticed that there were no footprints in the area, other than his own and Schiefelbein's. The snow around the dead cow had melted in a circular pattern. This seemed to be more evidence that UFOs had somehow been involved in the death of the animal.

In December 1974 and January 1975, the mutilations began

to receive national attention. Newspapers, magazines, and even network TV shows were carrying the story of UFOs and the mutilations. So far, there had been no concrete evidence that UFOs had killed the cattle, but some investigators were willing to make the "logical" step. All the evidence pointed to that conclusion, even if "all the evidence" was circumstantial at best. Someone finally remembered "Snippy" the Colorado horse, supposedly killed by death-ray-toting aliens in the 1960s, and that seemed to settle the matter. Aliens were flying through the night skies killing and mutilating animals for no apparent reason.

During the next weeks, reports of mutilations began to come from Texas, California, and Oklahoma, and the reports matched those in Minnesota in every aspect except one. There were no indications that UFOs were involved. In fact, the possibility was not suggested except for one man in Oklahoma who had a reputation for chasing the sensational and never worried about the facts. He had found that they sometimes got in the way.

By March, the story had been widely circulated and many of the major UFO organizations were involved. APRO asked several of its field investigators, including me, to look into the mess. They wanted an answer quickly.

One of the first people I contacted was Michael J. Douglas, the news director for WYOO radio in Eagan, Minnesota. Douglas had been investigating the rumors from the very beginning, knew the principals, had personally inspected several of the mutilation sites, talked to the veterinarians, and had received dozens of phone calls about UFOs. He became so involved that he was spending ten to fifteen hours each day running down the leads. He had, in fact, investigated the original mutilation and had talked to the man who claimed a UFO had done it.

At first, Douglas had gone along with the theory that UFOs were responsible. He believed that UFOs were something real and they could have caused the deaths. It was one of his contacts who told him that he had proof that UFOs had done it, so in the beginning, Douglas accepted that answer.

However, his investigations soon led him elsewhere. He spent several days in Meeker County and found the real facts.

It seemed that someone, or a group of someones, were trying to lay the blame for the mutilations at the portholes of the UFOs. Douglas began to suspect that humans and not aliens were the culprits.

He spent some time with Schiefelbein and learned the truth behind all the evidence. The burned circles on the hillside, one of the big reasons some believed UFOs were responsible, were actually silage piles. Heat from the decaying vegetable matter had created the circles and not UFO heat-producing engines as claimed.

The indentations in the lake ice had an equally mundane explanation. Schiefelbein had been chopping holes in the ice to get water for the cattle. He had made the "markings" and if anyone had bothered to ask him earlier, he would have told them that. The original "UFO investigators" hadn't bothered but assumed UFO landing gear.

A veterinarian was called to perform the autopsy on the dead angus. He sent sections of the liver, kidney, portions of the skin, and some blood to the University of Minnesota for analysis. Nothing extraterrestrial was found and the vet didn't believe a UFO had killed the cow. The facts pointed to the Earth and to humans.

That left the lack of footprints and blood as the biggest problems. The autopsy had revealed chemicals that would cause the animal's heart to pump at an accelerated rate. It was the opinion of the doctor that the chemical had been injected to cause the heart to race, pumping all the blood from the body. The slit in the jugular vein suggested that someone had collected the blood before leaving the site.

Only the footprints, or rather the lack of them, was left to explain. Evidence, some of it uncovered by Douglas, suggested that the killers had used sheets of cardboard to distribute their weight and mask their footprints.

By the middle of March 1975, Douglas knew that UFOs had nothing to do with the mutilations. He told serious UFO researchers that it was his belief that humans were responsible and would then go to great lengths to explain his reasons. When asked about "all the evidence" he would tell of his investigations, and then leave the final conclusion to the individual.

It was about this time that APRO asked its investigators what they had found. I had made a trip to Eagan to talk with Douglas, while others had followed leads in New York, Arkansas, and Texas. In Minnesota, I learned that Douglas had the right answers to the questions, but I wanted to talk with the man who had the proof that UFOs were responsible. Douglas arranged the interview and for nearly an hour I talked with him. The evidence he had had nothing to do with his belief that UFOs had killed the cattle. It was his own invention of a flying disc that convinced him.

The man, who claimed that he was a lecturer with the University of Minnesota, was spreading the story that the cattle had been "shot" with a weapon that "collapsed their blood structure," and this was why no blood was found in the bodies. The man had only recently invented the weapon and wasn't sure what the wound would look like until he saw one of the mutilated cows. Then he knew. The cow had been shot with a weapon similar to his.

Of course, this wasn't his only proof. He had also invented a disc, and the weapon was part of the armament. After all, the craft had to be defended. And, because he had included a weapon system, it stood to reason that the aliens would do the same thing. A friend of his reinforced this insanity by saying the Apollo spacecraft were armed. He had no proof of that, other than heresay, but he was convinced it was true. Using all this information, the lecturer formulated his theory that the cattle had been shot by aliens.

During the hour I talked to him, he mentioned several strange cases of the past. He asked me if I knew that the Navy had teleported a ship during World War II (*see April 1956: The Allende Letters*). All the discussion about the Navy teleportation convinced me that the man didn't have all the facts, or that he didn't want to hear them.

The final blow to his credibility came from the APRO *Bulletin*, which says, "An interview [conducted separately from my research] with this man disclosed a complete preoccupation with achieving notoriety. His attempts at technical discussion were pitifully naive. Couple this with the fact that recently in Bellingham, Washington, he claimed to be a Sasquatch or Bigfoot contactee [he visited their homes] and that his touted evidence connecting UFOs with dead cattle disappeared in the light of objective investigation to complete the picture.''

The other APRO field investigators sent their reports to headquarters. Although they had not discussed the case among themselves, they all came to the same basic conclusions. UFOs were not involved with the mutilations. Their reports were also published in the APRO *Bulletin*. ''Most of the cattle deaths,'' wrote the editorial staff, ''resulted from the usual causes; disease and malnutrition. The missing parts were those usually attacked first by small scavenging animals simply because they are easiest to sink small teeth into; i.e., lips, tongues, ears, udders, etc.''

Douglas had been aware of this answer for some time. He made it clear that he no longer believed that UFOs were connected with the deaths. In late February, he found a possible source of some of the other mutilations. A few weeks later he knew that worshipers of Satan, and not aliens from space, had killed some of the cattle. They needed the animals to make sacrifices for Satan and it was the practice of certain rituals that demanded the mutilation.

A great deal of evidence now pointed to this idea. The APRO *Bulletin* even reported the ''modus operandi'' of the Satanists. ''The group would approach its intended victim at night, walking on large sheets of pasteboard. The victim was shot with a tranquilizer dart, immobilizing it [traces of nicotine sulfate were found in the livers of some of the animals]. Then a heart stimulate was injected, an artery in the throat was punctured and the blood was caught in a plastic bag . . . Organs to be used in the Satanic rites were then surgically removed with a minimum of bleeding.''

Further proof of this was given by Douglas. After he had broadcast that Satanists were responsible, he was threatened by them. They didn't want any publicity—yet. For weeks after the broadcasts, Douglas had to be careful about who he talked to because he didn't want any personal information about him to reach the members of the cult.

Another investigator working for the Center for UFO Studies had a brief run-in with the Satanists. He, too, had discovered that UFOs were not the force behind the mutilations and had told others about the cult. Like Douglas, he was threatened. It was more proof that the cattle had died at human hands.

The publicity and news reports made it increasingly hard for the Satanists to operate in Minnesota and they moved south. As the mutilations ended in Minnesota, they began in Texas. "In the weeks that followed," according to the APRO *Bulletin*, "the members ran afoul of the law and were apprehended." That certainly seemed to end part of the problem.

But the UFOs kept flying, the cattle kept dying, and the researchers kept trying to link the two. In the summer of 1975 several hundred head of cattle, and dozens of other animals including sheep, buffalo, horses, dogs, and cats were found dead and mutilated. No one seemed to have an answer that covered all the mutilations and investigators were continuing to try to find a clue about the mess.

As the mutilations spread, some UFO researchers began to spread rumors. One man, after trying to investigate a UFO sighting, found that a cattle mutilation had occurred only a few hours before the UFO shot through the area. On a regional TV news broadcast, the man said, without justification, "It seems that every time we get a UFO sighting we get a cattle mutilation." That evening, in an area covering some of the most populated cities in the country, millions heard that claim. A few weeks later, after the sightings had been investigated fully and the mutilations explained, the news media had little to do with the researcher who uncovered the truth.

In Texas, another group trying to gain some national attention was making wild claims about UFO landing sites and cattle mutilations. It was their belief that a close proximity, either in time or space, proved the extraterrestrials were responsible for the deaths.

In fact, throughout 1975, dozens of rumors about the mutilations were being circulated and none seemed to cover all the events. The only place where everyone was in agreement was in Minnesota. Even the most radical of the UFO investigators agreed that UFOs were not involved there.

In May and June 1975, cattle began to die in Colorado. The police, sheriffs, and newspapers were, at first, caught off guard and completely mystified by the deaths. They had no idea where to start their investigations when on May 29, 1975, Daryl Evans reported the death of one of his cows during a snowstorm. The animal was mutilated with a "surgical skill" that included the removal of several organs. The rancher reported he had seen a helicopter on the night of the incident.

In June, daily stories of the mutilations began to appear in the papers. As that happened, all the theories to cover the mutilations began to make the rounds. Some said it was the Satanists again, others claimed UFOs were at the bottom of it, one man said that it wasn't Satanists but it was human, and a lone man claimed that the government had found some mysterious disease in the animals and had to kill them to keep the information from the public. But still the animals died and no real clues were found.

On June 28, 1975, stories appeared telling of still another mutilation. A purebred Hereford bull calf was found dead and that brought the number to twenty-two killed in eastern Colorado since the beginning of April. Sheriff George A. Yarnell said that the only way that this mutilation broke the pattern was that coyotes had attacked the carcass. There were jagged tooth marks in the animal's hide as well as the clean "knife cuts" that had been reported in other areas.

Sheriff Yarnell said that he had found no bullet holes or any other wounds in any of the animals so he had no clue as to how they had been killed. By the end of June 1975, sixteen animals had been killed and mutilated in his Colorado county alone.

On July 10, 1975, the first of the horse mutilations was reported. Once again Sheriff Yarnell was called to investigate. He reported the horse had been alive about 9:30 P.M. on a Sunday night and was found dead on Monday. There were no signs of a struggle and no physical evidence at the site. The animal was found lying in deep grass.

Following closely, another dead cow was found the same week near Canon City, Colorado. The cow's tongue, sex organs, and eyes were gone and there was no sign of blood where the cuts had been made. Once again, the authorities were puzzled by the mutilations.

By July 10, the number of mutilations had jumped to over forty. Animals were being killed at an alarming rate and no one seemed to know who or what was doing it. Several Colorado organizations tried to stop the flood by offering rewards for information leading to the arrest and conviction of mutilators, but that did no good. When armed patrols were fielded, the mutilations happened in another country or state. Nothing seemed to work.

In August, newspapers tried to solve the mutilations. However, over a period of weeks, they carried stories outlining all the answers that had been offered. The APRO *Bulletin* was again quoted in one article explaining how cultists had killed the cattle.

Following the article about why UFOs were not involved, there was another explaining why some researchers thought that UFOs were involved. A Colorado group claimed that a study of the magnetic lines of force around the Earth gave clues to the identity of the mutilators. Because one site in Colorado was near an area of magnetic disturbance, UFOs became a logical suspect. "UFOs," according to a group spokesman, "which use magnetism as a form of power, would naturally be interested in any aberration in the magnetic lines around the Earth. The correlation is hard to ignore." He didn't explain what the correlation was.

The group took pains to explain why helicopters and crazy cultists could not be responsible. They claimed that there was no way that the equipment necessary to drain the blood from an eight-hundred-pound steer could be carried on a small helicopter. The fact that scavengers didn't touch the dead animals was another reason that UFOs and not cult-carrying helicopters were suspected by the UFO group.

Following closely to that report, a Wyoming newspaper carried stories about strange lights in the night skies and the bodies of mutilated animals found nearby. Although no one had seen UFOs near the mutilation sites, no one saw UFOs mutilate the animals and there were no sightings at the time the mutilations occurred, a few made the connection anyway and believed the two events were related.

Throughout August and September, the mutilations in Colorado continued. The number grew to over two hundred and the rewards grew to thirteen thousand dollars. Law enforcement agencies, including the Colorado Bureau of Investigation (CBI), joined the search for the killers. Little physical evidence was being found at the sites and the lack of it helped those claiming UFOs to make their point.

There were exceptions to that. Footprints were found at a few of the sites, tire marks from a four-wheel drive vehicle were found with footprints leading to a fence but disappearing on the other side of the fence, and in one case, a small blue bag containing a scalpel and a cow's ear were found at a mutilation site. But these were the only clues.

In October 1975, the mutilations returned to the Midwest. Nowomen in and around Prairie du Chien, Wisconsin, reported that several cattle had been killed and mutilated, but this case had a twist. Some believed that a gas grenade had been used to tranquilize the cattle and all the bodies were found in the same field. For days afterward, the people were burning up the lines to local talk shows trying to put the blame on someone.

Iowa was struck in late October and early November. Mutilations were reported in several southeastern counties, most of them centering around Monroe, Iowa. The sheriff and local veterinarians had no explanations for the deaths. That didn't stop others from speculating. Solutions ran from the Satanic cult to predators to a Bigfoot-like creature hunting for food. The Iowa secretary of agriculture, Robert Lounsberry, thought that many of the cases could be solved if the insurance records were searched.

A few weeks after that, the UFOs made their first appearance in connection with the midwestern mutilations. Sightings were reported by the dozens in a small area in Wisconsin, but there was only one mutilation. Some were saying the UFOs had somehow been responsible for the death of the cow.

During this time in Colorado, there were only a few mutilations. The wave that had peaked in the summer seemed to be dying. The CBI had been working on the case for several weeks and was claiming that very few of the mutilations were done by humans. In November, they were leaving the impression that only 30 percent of the deaths could be attributed to causes other than natural. They were saying that only sixty cows had been mutilated instead of the staggering two hundred.

In December, in Iowa, six cows were found mutilated on one farm. The owner, Don Stickle, wasn't sure when they had been killed, but the evidence indicated the first had died about six weeks before the bodies were found. The last had apparently died only hours before the bodies were discovered. Iowa law enforcement agencies moved in and the Iowa State University School of Veterinary Medicine received samples from the dead animals for analysis.

Not long after the animals were found, the farmer saw a UFO in the eastern sky. It hovered there for hours, shooting rays of light toward the ground. It was only a point of light and disappeared as the sun came up. Later that day, a woman in Sioux City reported that she, too, had seen the strange light in the sky.

Finally, in January 1976, the Colorado Bureau of Investigation released their final conclusions on the mutilations in their state. In all the two hundred cases that had been reported, the CBI could find only one mutilation that had been done by humans. They were saying, in essence, that all the reported cases were the result of hysteria and media invention. There were no mutilations and therefore, no problem.

Sheriffs, ranchers, and cattlemen associations were not listening to that kind of nonsense. They responded, calling the CBI report a fairy tale and pointed out that the CBI had made no on-site investigations but relied on samples sent to their labs. The ranchers conceded that part of the problem may have been hysteria and that not all the mutilations were caused by cultist killers, but they believed that the CBI had dodged the majority of the problem. Someone was killing the cattle.

They had believed for a long time that they were chasing a group of humans, humans who were very good at what they did, but humans nonetheless. Very few people in Colorado thought that UFOs were killing and mutilating the cattle.

In September 1975, the helicopter supposedly used by the cultists was photographed. The Teller County, Colorado, sheriff's office released pictures of a blue Hughes 500 helicopter near trees and what appeared to be a man standing or hanging in the door.

After the picture was released, another helicopter pilot told reporters that he had chased a Hughes 500 helicopter one night. He had been flying late and was directed by radar to the location of an unidentified craft. It took five passes for him to spot the other helicopter because it was flying without lights. He was able to identify it as a Hughes 500. The pilot said, "Up until that time, I hadn't believed the stories of helicopters, but now they make sense. There are places out there [near Rush, Colorado] that you could hide a freight train."

The real question is whether or not UFOs are in any way responsible for the mutilations. Most of the leadership of the UFO organizations have said no. Jim Lorenzen, the international director of APRO, has said, time and again, "There has not been one case linking UFOs to cattle mutilations."

NICAP's Jack Acuff has been quiet about it, but the UFO *Investigator*, published by NICAP, has carried articles and letters about the mutilations. For the most part, they tend to agree with APRO by saying they don't believe UFOs are involved.

An APRO field investigator who supplied some of the information used here also ruled out UFOs. His investigations in Wisconsin were able to dispel many of the rumors from that area. For example, he learned that the cattle killed near Prairie du Chien had not been gassed but had died of blackleg, a spore-borne disease. Predators, according to the vets there, were responsible for the mutilations. The Grant County, Wisconsin, sheriff, Percy Stitch, knew about the alleged mutilations and answers to the questions.

The November 1975 sightings of UFOs and mutilations in Grant County, Wisconsin, were investigated in depth by me. I found that most of the sightings were of Jupiter and the mutilation involved only one cow with an ear hacked off. The cow died of natural causes and there was nothing to indicate that the mutilators that might have been operating in other areas were responsible.

A Bloomington, Wisconsin, vet, Dr. Jeff Davis, confirmed that analysis of the case. He said that the cow had been sickly from birth and had died of respiratory failure. He wasn't surprised that it had died.

The December Iowa UFO sightings and mutilations fell into the same category. The UFO was identified as one of the bright stars visible at that time of the year. It hovered over the area for four hours and was reported as far west as Nebraska, indicating it was very bright and very high. Linn Country, Iowa, deputy sheriffs called to the scene easily identified it.

Once again, the mutilations didn't fit the pattern that has developed. The wounds were not like those made in Colorado; the sex organs, tongues, and eyes were all intact. Autopsies of the animals indicated that blackleg might have been responsible for the deaths. The farmer, unhappy with the Iowa State University analysis, had some of his own conducted. His tests showed that there was no blackleg.

A NICAP regional investigator pointed out that the "surgical skill" supposedly displayed by the mutilators was not that impressive. He talked to butchers who have admitted to "mutilating some already dead cows as a joke. They got a big bang out of the vet's reports saying that the surgical skills would be hard to duplicate."

As 1976 rolled into 1977, the whole picture began to change. After the CBI analysis, the numbers of mutilation reports began to drop off. The UFO groups were quiet and it seemed that the thing was going to be allowed to die a natural death. The evidence still didn't show anything extraordinary.

Some UFO groups claimed they were continuing their research. A St. Louis committee that was formed at the height of the phenomenon still sent letters to researchers, but they seemed to be doing little else. A group in Washington wanted to prove UFO involvement, but they had no success.

Nothing new was being added. It seemed that every case that was objectively researched ended in the same manner. UFOs were not the cause. They could be ruled out because no one had yet to see a UFO mutilate a cow and the circumstantial evidence suggesting it just did not stand up.

That still left the question unanswered. If it wasn't UFOs,

then who was doing it? The cultists, who had taken a large part of the burden in the beginning, were starting to look like less likely mutilators. There was no doubt that some of the mutilations had been committed by humans; the little blue bag showed that. But was it the large, organized effort that some had reported?

Reports began to leak that two prisoners had been interviewed by Federal Agents. They claimed they were members of a cult, hooked on drugs, and led by a weirdo in Texas who practiced sacrificial rites for Satan. They claimed that they used the cardboard, drained the blood, and drank it. They cut up the cattle as one more step toward the ultimate —a human sacrifice.

Several newsmen obtained copies of the report, giving the whole story. When that happened, more investigation began. Later it was said that the prisoners had made up the stories so that they could get some time outside the prison, giving their stories to authorities. They told a good story, but according to Federal Agents, it was a hoax.

But it was obvious from some of the reports that a human agency, meaning a person or group of persons, was mutilating some of the cattle. One of the motives was insurance. In the case from Wisconsin, the farmer had hacked off the ear so that he could recover his money. If the cow died of natural causes, which it had, he received no money. If crazy cultists carved it up, then he was reimbursed.

But was that an answer in the rest of the cases? Reports claimed that as many as a thousand animals have been mutilated in the western part of the country. It was just too many to believe in cultists. There couldn't be that many crazies running around.

A complete and simple answer wasn't possible. It seemed that three things were operating, but none of them in UFOs. First, there were the cultists. The ear in the blue bag, and an ear sent in a shoebox to a California newsman showed that. Second, there were imitators and jokers. The butchers proved that. It also proved that humans were responsible for some of the mutilations, if not the deaths of the animals.

Finally, there was an answer so obvious that no one wanted

to believe it. They would prefer to think that the U.S. Government was killing the cattle to hide some new and rare disease, or aliens from space were swooping in to destroy the animals. It was an answer suggested by the CBI and a few other levelheaded individuals. The cattle weren't being killed and mutilated. They were dying and being attacked by scavengers.

The CBI, in their report, said they thought only 30 percent of the cases were real mutilations and they may have been generous with that. It also meant that something no one noticed before was something that they were now looking for. Ten years ago, when a cow died, no one paid any attention to the condition of the body. Suddenly, the condition of the body was of importance if some of the organs were missing. And, those that were taken were always the ones that it was easiest for the scavengers to eat.

The support of that conclusion can be seen everywhere. There never was any evidence suggesting UFOs. The lack of blood has been explained by the vets. Blood oxidizes after death so the inexperienced, looking for it, might be unable to recognize it. The unidentified vet making pronouncements about a case should be disregarded. If his identity is unknown, there is no way to verify him, his credentials, or if he said anything about the situation.

Until someone offers something more than a dead cow, we have no place to go with the cattle mutilation story. The things that happened today are the same ones that happened last year. And when one gets reported, it is followed by a dozen others. No one worried about their dead cows until it became possible that they had been mutilated. The farmers began seeing predator damage and reporting it as mutilations.

Now, ten years later, there are no reports of mutilations; No stories of UFOs killing cattle or cultist crazies running around the country in four-wheel drive vehicles and helicopters. This has gone the way of so many other "great" mysteries. It was something created by the media, exploited by a few who wanted to get their names in print, and was something that had very little basis in fact. Now, finally, it has been laid to rest.

January 1976: The Project Bluebook Files

During my years of UFO research, I had heard stories of a UFO cover-up by the officers of Project Bluebook. I had heard that there were things hidden in the files that would answer all the questions that private researchers had. I had heard that there was information buried there that would astound. In 1976, before the files were released to the general public in the National Archives, I had a chance to find out how much of it was true. Although the overall search was disappointing, there were things there that hinted at the answers we all wanted.

Air Force records of the UFO phenomenon began in 1947. Before Project Sign, the Air Force's first UFO study, there was an unnamed study conducted by the CIA. Their conclusions, although absent from the Bluebook files, are quite obvious. If they didn't believe there was anything to the UFO problem, they would not have recommended a continued study and "Sign" would never have been born.

After several months, on September 23, 1947, Lieutenant General Nathan F. Twining forwarded a report about the "flying discs" through channels to the chief of staff. In the report he concluded that UFOs were real, that they were metallic, high-performance, disc-shaped objects that outclassed anything the Air Force had at the time. He recommended that a classified study be made of the objects. This was the beginning of Project Sign.

General Twining's letter and the resulting communications were stamped "secret." Air Force Major General L.C. Cragie set up the investigative project and gave it the security classification "restricted." This original report remained secret until 1961.

UFO sightings continued throughout 1947 and into 1948. Some were quite spectacular, but no single sighting aroused much public interest. By late summer 1948, dozens of puzzling reports were coming into the Air Technical Intelligence Center (ATIC), but it wasn't until a DC-3 was buzzed near Montgomery, Alabama, that ATIC decided it was time to make an "estimate of the situation" (see August 1948: The Estimate of the Situation). They "estimated" that UFOs were real and interplanetary! The report was stamped "top secret" and forwarded to General Hoyt Vandenburg. Vandenburg didn't believe it and returned the report to ATIC. But this was the first top-secret Air Force study of UFOs that reached the conclusion that they were real craft.

By the end of 1948 the UFO threat was diminishing. "Sign" claimed to have investigated 122 sightings and identified all but seven. Someone at ATIC apparently believed that the UFOs would go away so the final report recommended that the project be continued, but at a very low priority level. It also thanked various agencies, including the FBI, for their help with "background investigations as well as for other investigative assistance."

In 1949, Project Sign was downgraded and its name was changed to Grudge. The change was necessary, the Air Force claimed, because the old name had been compromised. With the new name came a new Air Force attitude concerning UFOs. All the reports were now evaluated on the premise that they were misidentifications that had to be explained. If the report claimed that the object behaved as if it might be a natural phenomenon, it became that phenomenon. Many reports were not evaluated because they could be explained without any investigation.

This attitude can be readily seen in the "Montana Movie" case (see August 1951: The Great Falls Movie). Air Force analysis of the films didn't take very long. It was reported that two jet fighters might have been in the area at the time of the sighting. Air Force officers picked this up in the initial report, circled it, and wrote next to the remark, "This is probably it." They simply did not care that witnesses said they saw the jets just after the objects disappeared and that they viewed the UFOs at relatively close range. A later Air

Force study revealed that for the objects to be mistaken for jets, they would have to be over twelve miles away. But the jet theory remained the official Air Force explanation.

Two years later, in 1952, the Air Force again asked for the Montana film so they could run more tests. Mariana originally accused them of taking the first thirty frames that clearly showed the objects to be discs and never returning them. After several months, Mariana wrote an angry letter to the officers at Bluebook demanding his film back. They complied, but no one can be sure whether the Air Force took the thirty frames or not. Bluebook files deny it, but Mariana had friends who claim to have seen the unaltered film. No one, not the Air Force, its corps of debunkers, or any of the private UFO groups have ever found a good explanation for the Montana movie. All of this didn't affect the Air Force because they had already written off the case.

This lack of concern on the part of the Air Force investigators continued through 1950 and into 1951. Not many UFOs were being reported and those that were had been largely ignored by the public and press. The only exception was a series of articles written by Major Donald Keyhoe, which stirred considerable interest, but no one pressured the Air Force for answers.

In late 1951, another Air Force reorganization took place, and Project Grudge was changed to Project Bluebook. Captain Edward Ruppelt, the officer in charge, and his staff again attempted a serious study. But in 1950 and 1951, only 379 UFOs were reported and the Air Force claimed they identified all but forty-nine.

Everything fell apart in 1952 as far as the Air Force was concerned. By the end of the year, there were over 1,500 new UFO reports in Air Force files and 303 of them would remain unidentified. That might not have been too bad, especially if the public didn't know about it, but at the end of July 1952 (*see July 1952: The Washington Nationals*), fleets of UFOs were seen over Washington, D.C., and the Air Force was powerless against them.

At 11:40 P.M. on July 19, 1952, eight UFOs appeared on the radar of the CAA's Air Route Control Center at Washington's National Airport. The objects weren't airplanes because they were charted, at first, flying at a hundred miles per hour and then accelerating to unbelievable speeds. During the night, several airline flight crews reported seeing strange lights on their approach to the airport.

As more unknown blips appeared on the radar scopes, the men in the center called for help. At first the supervisor thought that there was a malfunction in the radar equipment, but a technician could find nothing wrong. As they watched, the UFOs moved at 130 miles per hour, then one of them broke formation, accelerated to seven thousand miles per hour, and disappeared. Before the night was over, operators at Andrews Air Force Base, Bowling Air Force Base, and several nearby airports had sighted objects on radar and visually.

A week later the UFOs were back. It was almost at the same hour as the previous sightings and the same radar crews again reported them. The supervisor contacted key personnel including military officers, as he was under order to do so. Newsmen were invited into the control room to watch the intercept but were quickly asked to leave on orders from the Pentagon. "They'll be using classified orders," said a spokesman. "Newsmen will have to be barred."

As is standard operating procedure, the military was put on alert status. Three officers rushed to the control tower at National Airport and watched as interceptor jets vainly tried to catch the objects. At times the fighter pilots saw the lights, and their radar sets locked on target while at other times nothing was seen. Throughout the night, sightings were made and intercepts attempted. As the sun came up, the UFOs disappeared and the fighters returned to base—but the mystery remained.

The news media pressured the Air Force for an answer. Finally, a press conference was called and a partial answer was given. The Air Force felt that some of the targets were the result of temperature inversions! However, all the radar operators and interceptor pilots were familiar with inversions and they didn't believe that they could have spent the night chasing something they knew was a natural phenomenon. Several weather experts said that an inversion was over Washington at the time, but it was much too weak to have caused radar returns. The Air Force received a lot of bad publicity as a result of the inversion explanation, but they never really said that was the answer, only that it might have been. These sightings are listed in the Bluebook files as "unidentified."

The sightings continued into August. All over the country people reported UFOs and many of them were listed as "unidentified." In July, fifty-three sightings were left unidentified and in August, twenty-two were unexplained. The press and the public were now intrigued and the Air Force was being hounded for answers. Again in September, another twenty-two reported UFOs could not be identified. By October the flap was waning and in December there were only three UFOs that Air Force officers couldn't explain. But there were 303 unexplained UFOs for the year, an all-time high.

The Air Force knew they had to do something to explain the UFOs and the old answers would no longer carry any weight. In January 1953, the Air Force, probably at the insistence of the Central Intelligence Agency, created the Robertson Panel (*see January 1953: The Robertson Panel*). No one hid the fact that most of the scientists were very skeptical about UFOs and that CIA agents would be leading the discussions.

ATIC officers were also present with what they thought were the best UFO cases. These included the Mantell incident of January 1948, the 1950 Montana movie, the Tremonton, Utah, movies taken in 1952, and several multiple-witness, radar-confirmed sightings. All were eventually explained away by the panel.

Because the CIA had "salted" the panel with scientists who would see things their way, it was fairly easy to lead the direction of the discussions. They were able to ridicule the cases, show how they might be explained, and eventually push for the conclusions they wanted. In just three days the Robertson Panel did what the Air Force had been unable to do in the past five years—they explained the whole UFO phenomenon.

The panel made three recommendations, including, "that the national security agencies take immediate steps to strip the Unidentified Flying Objects of the special status they have been given and the aura of mystery they have unfortunately acquired.'' They didn't believe UFOs were real and they wanted the Air Force to debunk them. It marked a definite shift in emphasis that can be seen in the Bluebook files. The panel's recommendations were followed by AFR (Air Force Regulation) 200-2 and JANAP 146 that made it a crime for military personnel to release information about unidentified flying objects.

The attitude before the Robertson Panel had been to take the matter and try to evaluate the problem. Edward Ruppelt tried to make the project a solid study. During the first five years (or until the end of 1952), there were 394 unidentified sightings in the files. In the remaining fifteen years of the project, only 308 were added to the unexplained list.

From the 1952 high in prestige and manpower, Bluebook was dropped as a special project with a drastic cut in personnel made in 1953. After the Robertson Panel conclusions, Bluebook simply became a debunking agency without any power. Sightings were to be identified—no matter how. The list of early sightings explained after the panel met is extraordinary: Kenneth Arnold saw a mirage; Thomas Mantell chased a balloon; and the Montana movies definitely showed jet fighters. All these cases were explained by the "improved methods of scientific research." What it really meant was that all sightings were to be explained regardless of the facts.

This policy continued until Project Bluebook was ended. In 1957, the famous Levelland, Texas, (*see November 1957: Levelland, Texas*), sightings were called misidentified natural phenomena. This incredible wave began in the early evening when Pedro Saucido and a passenger in his truck saw a bright red object. It touched the ground briefly, causing Saucido's truck engine to die and the lights to go out. Seconds later, the huge, cigar-shaped craft shot up into the sky. During the next five hours, several people, including five police officers, would see the UFO and have their car engines stalled. (It is interesting to note that the Air Force found only three witnesses who claimed to have seen the UFO on the ground, although at least five had called the sheriff.) It made no difference to the Air Force that the witnesses saw the object close to the ground and gave detailed descriptions. Because it sounded like ball lightning it was ball lightning.

The Levelland sightings marked the beginning of a new round of press coverage. Like the UFO waves of the past, the press had ignored the subject until there was one exceptional case and then they jumped right in. The fact is, however, Levelland didn't begin the flap; it only marked the peak. But the sightings convinced many military men that UFOs had to be taken out of the public realm. Like the 1952 wave, the Air Force was getting too much bad press about their investigations and solutions. Several ranking officials again began looking for a way to end these problems and keep the public satisfied.

In December 1958, there was additional proof that the Air Force wanted every sighting explained. An officer assigned to the UFO project claimed that he found "certain deficiencies" that he felt "must be corrected." Specifically he referred to AFR 200-2, "dated 5 February 1958 (revised on that date), which essentially stipulates the following . . . to explain or identify ALL UFO sightings." This requirement, set down in two separate regulations, JANAP 146 and AFR 200-2, made the investigations difficult to conduct, but the conclusions were very easy to find. The sighting was of a common object. But if there was nothing sensational or extraordinary to hide, what was the purpose of those regulations?

Interest in UFOs again tapered off in the late 1950s. After the December 1958 study, there was an attempt to transfer Project Bluebook to some other Air Force agency, specifically to the secretary of the Air Force, Office of Information (SAFOI). This would have been the final blow to the prestige of the project, but no one wanted the burden of Bluebook and all transfer attempts failed.

On April 1, 1960, in a letter to Major General Dougher at the Pentagon, A. Francis Archer, a scientific adviser to Bluebook, commented on a memo written by Colonel Evans, a ranking officer at ATIC, about Bluebook. He said, ". . . [I] have tried to get Bluebook out of ATIC for ten years . . . and do not agree that the loss of prestige to the UFO project is a disadvantage." This is one of the first written indications of Bluebook's diminished status. It also shows that for over ten years the project had been fighting for its life.

In 1962, Lieutenant Colonel Robert Friend, who at one time headed Bluebook, wrote to his headquarters that the project should be handed over to a civilian agency that would word its report in such a way as to allow the Air Force to drop the study. At the same time, Edward Trapnell, an assistant to the secretary of the Air Force, when talking to Dr. Robert Calkins of the Brookings Institute, said pretty much the same thing. Find a civilian committee to study the problem, then have them conclude it the way the Air Force wanted it. One of the stipulations, of course, was that this organization say some positive things about the Air Force's handling of the UFO project.

Others suggested closing Project Bluebook but realized that the public would have to be "educated to accept the closing." They wanted Bluebook changed to a public relations outfit to convince everyone that UFOs were mirages and then fold up the whole operation.

By 1966, the Air Force managed to get Bluebook's press releases to come through SAFOI. Letters to the public no longer carried the prestigious ATIC letterhead but only the information office stamp. The Air Force was making its attempt to eliminate the UFO headache once and for all.

The major stumbling block was a new wave of sightings. Police Officer Lonnie Zamora and his New Mexican "egg" started it all over again in 1964 (*see April 24, 1964: Socorro, New Mexico*). Throughout 1965 and into 1966 the wave continued, with UFOs gaining ground with nonbelievers. Television networks and several prestigious magazines began to treat the subject a little more evenhandedly. Air Force explanations were being held up to ridicule and more witnesses were coming forward to tell their stories. Congressmen and senators were clamoring for an investigation and an end to the censorship. The outgrowth of all this was the Condon Committee.

In October 1966, negotiations were finished and the University of Colorado agreed to investigate UFOs for eighteen months (*see 1969: The Condon Committee*). In the summer of 1968, their investigations ended and the task of writing the report began. The committee claimed that they studied the best sightings, but a close reading of the final report showed that many outstanding sightings were ignored. They also claimed that, just as Colonel Friend and Edward Trapnell suggested in 1962, the Air Force had done a good job of investigating and that the project should be closed. In December 1969, after twenty-two years, Project Bluebook was declared "officially closed."

All of this can be seen two ways, depending on how you interpret it. One might say that the Air Force didn't try to cover up UFO evidence and the project was riddled with bunglers and a lack of coordination. However, other information, some of it obviously missing from the files, proves that Project Bluebook was a well-coordinated, well-planned cover-up. Much of the evidence involves only a passing reference to certain cases, though other information points to blatant attempts to lead the search in the wrong direction.

During the first few months that Bluebook was functioning there was a series of progress reports. Bluebook Reports 1 through 13 were apparently all regular reports, including administrative details and a briefing on the sightings during the period. Reports 1 through 12 were in the Bluebook files, as was Special Report 14. All were originally stamped either "secret" or "restricted." Bluebook Report 13 was missing. Many researchers have copies of Reports 1 through 12 and 14, but only one or two have seen Report 13. If everything is open and aboveboard, why is that report missing?

Many of the most spectacular cases that have been reported over the years are also missing from the Bluebook files. For example, in the Bluebook reports there is a mention of interceptor gun camera films (*See 1955: The Gun Camera Films*). Page two of one of the project reports says, ". . . and a section of gun camera spectrographic film furnished by the Air Force for analysis was examined by experts on spectroscopy." Gun camera films would be almost conclusive evidence that UFOs are real. The reference to spectroscopic films also indicates that special filters were put on the cameras to get the pictures. It implies that the planes were equipped to intercept UFOs. But none of this appears in the Bluebook files. The master index contains no reference to gun camera movies and no one seems to know where these films might be. The reference in the report says they do exist and the index says they don't.

Another prime example of the whitewash that must have taken place before the information was released to the Condon Committee is the Kinross file. In November 1953, an F-89 jet interceptor, flown by Lieutenant Felix Moncla, disappeared while chasing a UFO over Lake Michigan (*see November 23, 1953: The Kinross Disappearance*).

One of the first cases that I asked to see while studying the Bluebook files in Alabama was the Kinross incident. The file consisted of a cardboard folder with two sheets of paper pasted inside and the heading that this was an aircraft accident and not a UFO case. One page said that because of all the publicity and queries about the accident, the file had been opened but that there was no UFO involved. The other page was a galley proof from a book by Donald H. Menzel claiming that Kinross never encountered any UFOs and that the plane had accidentally crashed. He did say that many authors of "UFO lore" have latched on to the case to build their extraterrestrial theories. But the entire incident, according to the Air Force and Menzel, was an aircraft accident.

One other fact stands out in the Kinross incident. A Michigan newspaper carried the story of the missing F-89 in an afternoon edition. After that there were no references to it and none of the major Iowa, Michigan, Wisconsin, or Illinois papers carried the story. The Air Force moved quickly to kill the story, something they don't normally do in an aircraft accident. What made this case so special? Why didn't they want the story printed? And, why are there no references to any Kinross (Truax Air Force Base) sightings in the Bluebook files?

Still another example of the whitewashing is the case involving the Florida scoutmaster who claimed to have been burned by a UFO. Again, the case is missing from the master index, but reference was made to it in the Bluebook reports. On page three it says, "Regarding the 'Florida' samples . . . the lower leaves, those nearest the ground . . . slightly deteriorated, apparently by heat. No logical explanation is possible . . .'' Where is that case file now? Who removed it and why?

Did the Air Force really cover up their UFO investigations? Is this the answer that the information, the various regulations, and letters point to? Although the Air Force may not have set the policy, there was a cover-up. All the information, taken separately, isn't enough to prove it, but when added together it becomes quite obvious.

If there was no cover-up, then why were secret reports hidden in files for twenty years and why are so many of them missing today? Even the master index has cases listed as missing. If there was no cover-up, why did press releases say one thing, namely that there was no secrecy, when there are at least two reports classified secret that claim UFOs are real. And more important, if there is no cover-up, why is there no mention of the Roswell incident in the files? Perhaps the most damaging evidence comes from one page of the Bluebook index. It has six entries that have been removed or altered.

This becomes even more interesting when it is remembered that the CIA and FBI were involved from the beginning. In the early 1950s, when Bluebook was issuing periodic statements, the CIA was at the top of the distribution list. It was evident they were very interested in UFOs. It was possibly the CIA that started the policy of secrecy and they kept it going with the Robertson Panel.

The original project carried a restricted classification and that was never removed. All UFO projects carried this classification and that would mean that all files were to be "safeguarded." AFR 200-2 required that all "unidentifieds" be classified immediately and releasing any such information carried a ten-year prison sentence and a ten-thousand-dollar fine. What this means is that somewhere along the line, someone lost several dozen classified reports about UFOs. This is something that would not be taken lightly by the military.

It might be claimed that the reports were missing after the project has been declassified, but that is not true. The master index was made before the project lost its classification and the reports are carried as missing there. It means that they were removed under someone's direction so that they would not be included in the files.

One other fact suggesting a cover-up becomes obvious when looking at the Bluebook files—almost no reports came from any of the other services. Hundreds of members of the Air Force reported sightings to Bluebook, but the other services—the Army, Navy, and Marine Corps—are represented by only one or two listings. Does this mean that only Air Force personnel see objects they can't identify, or did the reports from the other services go elsewhere?

Evidence in the Bluebook files suggests that other services had their own secret projects. After the movies were taken at Tremonton, Utah (see July 2, 1952: The Tremonton Movie), and were examined by Air Force analysts, the Navy requested the films. They spent over a thousand man-hours making a frame-by-frame analysis. Their conclusions were that the movies showed spherical, internally lighted objects.

The distribution lists on the Bluebook reports also carry a reference to the Navy. Both the Office of Naval Research and the Office of Naval Intelligence received copies of the reports. Interest in the Tremonton UFO ranged over a wide cross section of government.

There is no mention of Army Intelligence on the distribution lists, but other facts may cover that. UFO investigators uncovered one instance that showed there was a cover-up that might have included Bluebook (see September 24, 1947: The Majestic Twelve). An Army Intelligence Officer, after investigating a UFO report on an Army post, sent his findings to a post office box in Arlington, Virginia. Although JANAP 146 and AFR 200-2 spell out the responsibility for UFO sightings, it seems evident that there was a second, more highly classified project. The really explosive, relatively unpublicized, and easily silenced reports were sent elsewhere. BLUEBOOK WAS ACTUALLY A COVER FOR THE REAL INVESTIGATION!

Since 1947, the government, through the Air Force, has claimed that there is no evidence of UFOs. They have said that there are no secret government reports and no cover-up. This is not true. The first secret study saying that UFOs are real was made in 1947 and there have been many others. Every statement that has been made by spokesmen about censorship is false. There *were* secret studies, there *were* classified reports, and *there is a secret project today*.

The final and most damaging evidence of a cover-up comes from the Air Force, as well as all other government agencies that claim that they are no longer interested in UFOs. There is a new, more secret project under a new code name, possibly Project Aquarius or Project Bluepaper, according to several researchers. Headquarters for it may be Alamogordo, New Mexico, and evidence indicates an important branch of it is based in Montana. The UFO project is not dead; it has only moved more deeply underground.

The Bluebook files have been edited, names have been changed, locations have been deleted, and cases have been removed entirely. If there is no cover-up, then why all the changes? Why all the missing cases and why all the lies about UFOs?

February 1977: Pineville, Missouri

The first call came into the Kansas City headquarters of the North American UFO Organization in mid-March 1977. Monty Skelton, president of North American, took the call and reacted immediately. Within a week, Skelton, along with other staff members, went to McDonald County, Missouri, to begin fieldwork on one of the most puzzling strings of UFO sightings since the Exeter, New Hampshire, case in 1965.

Pineville is a small town in southern Missouri less than twenty-five miles north of the Arkansas border. The sheriff's office is located near the town square and next to the newspaper office. Skelton and I arrived just before noon on a cool, cloudy day. The sheriff and his deputies didn't know much about the UFO sighting but said that the town marshal, Carl Armstrong, had been involved with some of it.

Armstrong arrived and said that he hadn't seen anything except for a couple of lights in the distance. He had, however, talked to many of the people who had seen the lights and he agreed to take us to Huckleberry Ridge where most of the action had taken place.

Although Armstrong didn't say much, both Skelton and I were stunned by his comment about the sightings. We hadn't known that there had been more than one. We had heard that one man claimed that his car engine had been stalled and we wanted to talk to him, but Armstrong said that several people had their engines stalled and that dozens had seen the lights.

We followed Armstrong out of town. He wanted us to meet Lawrence McCool, but he wasn't home. We managed to locate him at a nearby country store. McCool was at first reluctant to talk to us, but slowly his story emerged.

About the middle of February—we were later to establish the date as February 14—McCool was driving along Highway 90 and was near the intersection of 90 and Route K. He had been trying to find the strange orange light that others had reported during the last few nights.

The weather was terrible. The wind whipped through the trees, blowing the sleet diagonally across the road. Later that night, a tornado hit Joplin, Missouri, causing some damage. McCool was heading toward his house after checking out reports of the light near the highest point in the country. He reached the crest of the hill and there it was. The light was hovering over the trees, not more than seventy-five feet above the ground. In the midst of the bright orange glow, McCool could see a domed disc.

As he sighted the object, McCool tried to call others, including Armstrong, on the CB radio. His truck crept forward and, as he approached the object, his truck's lights went out and the engine died. McCool tried to maintain radio contact with the others, but the CB wasn't working. The bright orange of the disc penetrated the sleet and lighted the trees a few feet under it. For minutes, the UFO hung there while McCool stared, the windshield of the truck accumulating sleet.

This was something more than the light seen by others. McCool could see a definite disc shape and a slight dome on top. He thought that the outer edge and the center were brighter than the rest. From its position over the highway, he estimated that the UFO was eighteen feet in diameter and between four and six feet thick.

The UFO hovered for several minutes and then faded from sight. After it was gone, the truck engine started and the lights came on. McCool called the others, indicating that the CB was working properly now that the UFO was gone.

McCool said that, after that experience, he was no longer skeptical. He had seen the object at close range and he knew that it wasn't a natural phenomenon. He started looking into all the stories reported in the area, trying to solve them. By the time we arrived in March, McCool and several others had already done the preliminary investigatory work.

McCool went on to say that the last sighting he knew of had been only a few days before we arrived. Although the object wasn't making the close approaches that it had in the beginning, people were still seeing it. McCool mentioned the names of other witnesses but thought that most of them were at work. If we could wait until later, he would try to line up several interviews.

At 7:00 P.M., we arrived at McCool's house. He had talked to some of the others and, although they were worried about talking to strangers, most had agreed to at least meet us. First on the list was Ivan Kanable.

Like McCool, Kanable had come into the case near the beginning. He had spent long hours driving the backcountry roads, trying to find an explanation for the lights, and although he had discovered every artificial source of light, he had been able to solve very few of the UFO reports.

One of the first sightings in which Kanable was involved happened on February 26, 1977. Kanable, along with cousins Evelyn and Virgil Hottinger, and at least four carloads of people, went to the county high point. As they drove up, they spotted a bright red glow coming from the woods several hundred feet away. They all thought that it was some kind of fire and Evelyn was worried because her husband "has respiratory problems. I thought the smoke would be bad for him."

They soon realized that the glow wasn't a fire but something else. Kanable had spent so much time on that section of the road that he knew every source of light around it. He knew that the light they saw wasn't a farm light, he knew there wasn't a road in the area, and he no longer believed that it was a fire. With binoculars, he could see the glow better.

The Hottingers, Kanable, and all the others saw two rectangular, metallic objects near the bottom of the hollow. Virgil Hottinger later described them as "bridge markers, complete with the stripes on them."

After he said something about the bridge markers, Kanable pointed out that there was no bridge down there and there were no markers. The next day, Kanable and the Hottingers returned so that they could examine the area. The road that Hottinger thought led to the bridge turned long before it got to the place where the markers had been seen. There was nothing there that even remotely resembled bridge markers.

Kanable said that others had seen the light recently and, if we wanted, he would show us the best location to watch for it. Before we went out, we interviewed one more witness. He had seen the lights on several occasions and described them as looking like the shuttle that NASA was building.

According to him, he could see the lights nearly every night from one of the windows of his house. Many had seen them from there also and, although one woman tried to photograph the lights with a polaroid camera, she didn't get anything unusual.

The man's story and drawings were interesting because they didn't fit into the normal type of UFO craft. Instead of being disc-shaped, the man claimed that they looked more like rounded airplanes. His drawings resembled a craft that had been reported in Minnesota in 1975. However, none of the others were reporting anything quite like it, so it seemed to be in a class by itself.

After interviewing the man, Kanable and McCool took Skelton and me to the high point. We stopped the car and they pointed out the lights around us. There weren't many lights because the area is thinly populated. About midnight, we saw a strange light bobbing through the trees near the horizon, but McCool said that there was a road in the area and we were probably seeing a car.

Time was beginning to press us and we had to leave. We

had only talked to about a dozen people about a couple of sightings, so we knew that we would have to come back for a longer period. Less than a month later, Shelton and I returned. The first thing we did was to call McCool and he again helped set up interviews for us.

On the second trip to Pineville, one of the first people we interviewed was Ron Cargile. Like most of the others, he had heard about the sightings on the CB radio, but he didn't really believe the stories that were circulating. After a number of calls were made on the CB, Cargile decided that he would go out to look, but he didn't expect to see anything. He drove out of his driveway, turned east on Route K, crossed E, and finally stopped on the high point. The view in all directions was virtually free of obstruction. Directly in front of Cargile there was a large tree and about fifty feet behind that was another. Slightly lower and off to both sides were woods. About a mile in front of him was a metal building with a bright security light, and in the far distance were several lights from several farms, but all were miles away.

Just after 10:00 P.M., Cargile noticed that the CB was buzzing with static. The signals from the other CBs were fading and the static was growing. Suddenly, off to the left he saw an orange glow rise from the woods and begin drifting toward the large tree in front of him. The object was very bright. Cargile thought that it was small, no more than five or ten feet in diameter. He could see that it was disc-shaped, domed, and that a band of colored metal ran around the center of it.

The object seemed to be coming toward him and he tried to call the others, but the radio wouldn't work. The UFO suddenly veered away from him and passed behind the closest tree. For a minute and a half, Cargile watched the UFO, the glow from it illuminating the ground.

The radio interference continued for another few seconds and then it, too, faded. Cargile started the engine of his truck and turned homeward. He had seen the object and now knew that the others were telling the truth. He had no reason to stay.

During the course of the investigation, we realized that we hadn't talked to the people who had the first sightings. Everyone that we had seen said that they had heard about the orange light on the CB and then had gone out to look. Evelyn Hottinger monitors the local React (a CB emergency group) and had heard the stories the first night. She had kept records of the calls and that allowed us to date some of the sightings.

Using that as a guide and the statements of McCool, we found that Carl "Snuffy" Smith was the first eyewitness and we went to talk to him. Although we didn't have any luck tracking him down, we did run into Edward Fletcher. According to the stories we had heard, Fletcher was one of the first witnesses. Smith had spotted the light and called Fletcher.

Smith had first seen the light in January of 1977. He had watched it bob above the trees. He said that it was bright orange, about the size of a bright star, but the color was different and it was much brighter. He saw it several times, but he didn't mention it to anyone until February.

Smith called Fletcher and, although his house was about a quarter of a mile away, Fletcher could see the light. Fletcher couldn't tell how far away it was, but he did say that he thought it was spherical. The bright orange color impressed him because he had never seen anything like it. Smith and Fletcher, separated by half a mile but talking on the CBs, continued to watch the light. It hovered over and darted about the tops of the trees. Fletcher said that it finally angled toward the ground and he lost sight of it because of the trees.

Later that evening, Hottinger received a call on the CB emergency channel saying that someone had seen some lights near the ground and had thought that it was helicopters rustling cattle. Minutes later there was another call, but this time there was no question about it. The man wasn't seeing helicopters but strange orange lights. Hottinger noted in her log, "They aren't helicopters. They're UFOs!"

By the end of the evening, Hottinger had stopped noting the calls. She had received over fifty of them. The word was out.

Using her log, we were able to put dates on many of the sightings. Many of the witnesses couldn't remember the exact dates, saying that it was near the first of February, or near the end, or in the middle. The log gave us the exact dates.

We continued to interview the witnesses. Late one afternoon, McCool took us to a small house near the outskirts of Pineville. We weren't too concerned about the sighting because it sounded like it was going to be just another in the long series we had already put together. June Hilton was outside her home, waiting for us. She told us that she had seen the lights on three different nights, but she didn't think that they were the same ones that everyone else was seeing.

On one of the nights, all she had seen was an orange light in the distance. It had been so far away that she hadn't seen anything but the color and the motion. On another night, however, she had seen one fairly close. She was returning late from a chore and saw the bright light in the valley between two hills. The light was white and at first she thought that it was the light from a farmhouse. Later, she realized that it wasn't.

As she approached the light, it began to take on a shape. She studied it carefully, so that she could be sure that it wasn't just something natural. The white light's shape changed slowly, dissolving into a craft that looked something like an airplane. It had a long fuselage.

Her description wasn't too clear and we asked her to sketch it for us. When she handed it back, we were shocked. She had drawn the same thing that the man we had seen during our first trip had sketched. McCool assured us that Hilton hadn't talked to him and he hadn't talked to her.

It was amazing that her description of the object was similar to the man's. He had described a white light instead of an orange one. He had talked of it hovering near the ground. Its characteristics differed from those of the orange light. We were given the impression that two separate craft were buzzing around.

On the final day, as we were returning to Joplin before heading for home, we discussed the case at length. I pointed out that it was the first time that we had ever gone into an investigation like that and not been able to find one solution. Skelton thought that it was because McCool, Kanable, and the others had already weeded out those cases that were obvious natural phenomena.

We had taken some of it a few steps further than McCool

and Kanable. We stopped by the local power company to see if they had recorded any drains of the electrical power. Several residents had mentioned that their lights had dimmed once or twice. We were told that the power company would have no way of telling, unless someone complained. Skelton and I had hoped that there would be something in the power company records so that we could confirm at least that one aspect of the case, but there wasn't anything.

We also stopped by the local airport in Neosho in the hope that some radar confirmation could be found. We were told that all radar traffic was handled either through Kansas City or Tulsa, so there was no way the people there could help. We thought that Joplin might have something, but they didn't.

According to the people at the FAA control center in Kansas City, radar coverage in that area is spotty at best. The mountains and terrain are such that accurate coverage has yet to be extended to all of the area. Radar coverage begins at eight thousand feet and, because no one was looking for anything strange on the scopes, nothing was seen. The number of VFR (visual flight rules) aircraft who don't file flight plans makes it impossible for the radar operators to spot anything that doesn't belong, unless it does something out of the ordinary. Because most of the sightings were made below eight thousand feet, there was no reason to expect anything on the scopes.

There was only one other thing to check that we could think of. Because we were convinced that everyone was telling the truth, and because we hadn't been able to find an answer to any of the sightings, we felt that we should get as many of the main witnesses as possible to take lie detector tests.

It was my opinion, however, that such a move was an exercise in futility. If the tests showed that the people were telling the truth, we had proved nothing. The lie detector would tell us only that the people honestly believed that they had seen the strange orange light. It certainly wouldn't identify the light. If, for example, McCool sincerely believed that the object he saw was a spaceship from another planet, the test could confirm that he believed it. That didn't mean that it was a spaceship, only that McCool believed it to be one.

As we wound up the investigations, we asked some of the people if they would take the lie detector tests. McCool gave us a flat "no." He said, "If they don't want to believe me, I don't care. I have always been considered honest." He viewed the question as an insult. We tried to convince him that it would make the people who didn't know him believe him, but he wasn't interested. As long as his neighbors knew that he wasn't crazy, that was all he wanted. Some of the others, however, agreed. They said they didn't mind and, in fact, wanted to take the tests.

There are a few conclusions that can be drawn about the case. There are some sightings that have to be investigated and there are the polygraph exams, but neither of these matters is vital to the case. While in the area, Skelton and I talked to at least seventy-five people, and possibly as many as a hundred, and we didn't scratch the surface. McCool estimated that five hundred people had seen the lights.

The question is not *if* they saw something, but *what* they saw. It obviously wasn't Venus because the lights were seen in all parts of the sky at all times of the night. Venus, even at maximum elongation, will set within three hours of the sun. It wasn't some kind of artificial light because McCool and Kanable checked every such source. McCool said, "One night we walked a mile of fence until we found the light. It was one of those small boxes that attached to fences to electrify them. Another time, we saw a dull red glow. It took an hour to pinpoint the source, but we found it. Someone had left the heat lamps on in their greenhouse."

While we were there, we saw several meteors, and McCool knew what they were. He pointed out constellations and even some of the brighter stars. "I've become quite familiar with the sky since all this started," he told us.

There was nothing that we knew of that could account for everything that had been seen. Naturally, none of the cases *proved* conclusively that the Pineville UFOs were extraterrestrial spaceships. UFOs might, indeed, be some kind of atmospheric phenomena that we don't understand, or they might be some kind of psychic phenomena, or they might be spacecraft. The point is, we don't really know yet. By continuing the Pineville investigations, maybe we will be able to answer some of the questions.

April 1981: Van Allen on the Tunguska Explosion

Dr. James A. Van Allen, former head of the Department of Physics and Astronomy at the University of Iowa, is one of this country's most eminent scientists. He is best known for his discovery of the belts of geomagnetically trapped radiation that encircle the earth. In this exclusive interview, Dr. Van Allen discusses the popular theory that the 1908 Siberian explosion may have been the result of an alien spaceship crash, and advances some of his ideas on interstellar flight and scientific method.

(Q) Dr. Van Allen, there has been a great deal of speculation in the popular press recently that the famed Siberian explosion of 1908 was, in fact, the result of the crash of an interstellar spacecraft. What do you know about the incident, and what is your best estimation of the cause?

(A) The famous Russian meteor expert, E.L. Krinov, has compiled a massive amount of scientific evidence, including dozens of eyewitness reports, microbarograph records, and seismograph records from various stations around the world, on the 1908 Siberian "explosion."

Now, the evidence is that there was an extremely great acoustical blast in the atmosphere. There was a series of loud explosions heard from ten to thirty kilometers away by individual observers. Not a single one, but a sequence, which was described as being similar to artillery fire. There was a large flame that shot up from the spot of impact, and a very large cloud of dust that lingered in the atmosphere for many days, spreading around the world. Of course, there were also the seismic records from scientific observatories in many other countries and the microbarograph stations that recorded the air wave, or what the pressure of the atmosphere was. So you can see that Krinov has assembled an immense amount of objective data.

Now, Krinov's conclusion is one that I accept, and that I think is generally respected and accepted, at the present time, by scientific workers, and that is that this was very likely a cometary impact. No large pieces of physical matter have been recovered that are extraterrestrial in origin, but there has been a substantial amount of small magnitities and silicate globules found in the soil in the center part of the impact. These were carefully scraped out and have been analyzed in the laboratory. So it appears that there is good evidence for the belief that in this object there were bodies of material of the same type that are characteristic of well-known and well-recorded meteorite falls. But all of it broke into fragments a millimeter in diameter or less, and no really large chunk of material has been found.

Now all this evidence corresponds to what we know about the composition of comets, which consist of a relatively small nucleus, possibly ten or twenty kilometers in diameter, surrounded by volatile material, gas, and fine dust. The spectra of comet tails is well known and consists of CO^2 and water, and similar lightweight materials. The general picture of the development of the comet tail as it approaches the sun is that these volatile materials are heated and evaporate, and in so doing create the fragile structure of the comet which may be a kind of loose structure of ice crystals. Still, in the spectra of comets, the heavier elements of the cometary head such as iron, nickel, manganese, silicon, and in some cases, sodium and other metallic elements, are positively identified. So all of the findings in the Tunguska meteor fall seem to me to be compatible with the hypothesis that a comet struck the earth.

(Q) So, a comet would account for the shock wave, the flash of fire, and the other observed phenomena?

(A) Oh yes. All these phenomena are quite reasonably accounted for by a cometary fall. Of course, the basic thing about a comet is that it has a very high speed in relation to the earth. So a typical comet velocity is twenty kilometers per second up to fifty or sixty kilometers per second, relative to the earth. At this speed the kinetic energy of a comet is a good deal greater than its total energy at vaporization. That is, if it is brought to rest, it has enough kinetic energy so that it can completely evaporate its own substance, and that includes iron. At least, the energetic capability is there so that with the impact with the ground, it's altogether reasonable to believe that it will vaporize in a great blast of hot gas.

(Q) Would such a blast be, in any way, similar to an atomic explosion?

(A) Atomic explosions release a certain amount of hot gas, so I would say that there would be a certain gross resemblance. What I'm not clear about is if any of these investigations included a search for any radioactive residue. It's not mentioned in Krinov's account. I don't know whether it's been investigated and been found to have negative results, or whether it's never been investigated. It's a very basic point.

(Q) In their book, *The Fire Came By*, John Baxter and Thomas Atkins claim that traces of cesium 137 were found in the area. What does this do for your cometary theory?

(A) What's their authority for that?

(Q) They cite a 1959 investigation of the area led by Plekhanov.

(A) That's a very important finding if it is true. It is also very important to know the distribution of the material and also whether this was above normal levels, and if they took into account that the Soviets may have done atomic bomb tests in the area. (Author's note: Soviet nuclear tests have been conducted in the Tunguska area.) It's very important to make such investigations, but as I said, Krinov does not mention any, and he does discuss at some length the findings of the 1959 investigative party.

(Q) So the mere finding of some type of radiation isn't that impressive?

(A) They have to check the whole run of all the fission types of isotopes that result from a bomb explosion. The finding of one is significant, but I think that it has to be a much more searching investigation if you want to decide a major question like this.

(Q) Since we're not really concerned with an atomic bomb, but with a nuclear-powered spacecraft whose reactor supposedly went critical and exploded, what are the possibilities of such an event actually occurring, and, say, leaving behind some sort of residue?

(A) Well, an atomic engine is already critical when it's working normally, but not at an explosive level. It's under control. Otherwise, if it's not critical, you're not getting any energy out of it. It has to be critical, but in a question of loss of control—"Could it explode?"—I think that atomic engines have been worked on extensively in the United States and although I think it's possible for them to explode, it's what you'd call a low order of explosion. Getting an all-out explosion is a very technically difficult thing. In fact, it's not even easy to make an atomic bomb explode high order as it's called, like bombs are designed to do. In the case of a nuclear engine for a spaceship, it would be, at the most, a kind of fizzle, a low-order disintegration and not a high-order explosion.

(Q) Baxter and Atkins claim the explosion was on the order of thirty megatons. Is that possible?

(A) I think that thirty megatons is about the biggest bomb anyone admittedly made, and such weapons are extremely skillfully designed and undergo a lot of testing to make sure that they are capable of a high-order explosion. But a nuclear rocket doesn't have that kind of engineering at all. It's designed to basically run critical and to produce hot gas that goes out the exhaust of the rocket, but I would think that at the most you would get a very low order of explosion. Thirty megatons is somewhat larger than the biggest bomb ever burst. The biggest was something like a ten-megaton blast.

(Q) So you are convinced then, that the Tunguska explosion was the result of a cometary impact, and not a thermonuclear explosion?

(A) That's correct. I don't know of anything that I've seen or read on the subject that is inconsistent with a comet.

(Q) Could a comet carry out a maneuver, seem to change course, as it is claimed some witnesses described?

(A) Not very much. No. The only thing that it could really do in the way of changing course would be when it plunged down into the atmosphere and its course would be slowed down somewhat, but it would still be more or less a straight line through the atmosphere. So it could not change course. Nor is it feasible for any spacecraft to change course, spacecraft moving at velocities required for this line of thought. To change course very dramatically would require a huge amount of thrust.

(Q) What effect would the atmosphere have on a body passing through it?

(A) The main thing about the atmosphere is that it is a resisting medium and therefore, any object flying through it at high speeds gets quite hot due to air resistance. There is a mechanical tendency for the disintegration of a fragile body. There's also the so-called ablation process, which means the melting and blowing off of the outer skin of the body. This ablation process and the red-hot appearance of the reentering spacecraft is pretty well known in the manned spacecraft program. You get a great tail of ionized gas behind the object and a radio blackout with this ablation process, which melts and blows away the outside of the heat shield. If the heat shield isn't thick enough, the whole spacecraft will disintegrate. So you have a combination of thermal and mechanical forces acting to break up the incoming body.

(Q) So any body entering the atmosphere at high speed would look pretty much like a meteor?

(A) Yes. Pretty much indistinguishable as it passes through the atmosphere.

(Q) And a roar from it wouldn't be completely out of the ordinary?

(A) No. I think that would be what you would expect.

(Q) In the wake of all the claims about the Tunguska fall, it has also been claimed that the Winslow, Arizona, crater is the result of an alien spaceship crash, and that such a cause accounts for the alleged square shape of the crater. What do you know about this?

(A) I've flown over that myself and it certainly didn't look square to me. Nor has any picture I've seen of it. They all look more or less like a bowl shape, an irregular bowl shape. I suppose that there is something of a square shape in a very general sense. It isn't very pronounced. It must be a feature of the surrounding terrain, the rock formations, and how resistant the surface material is. I think that it is a very great stretch of the imagination to say that it is square. Actually, there have been a very large number of atomic bomb bursts produced in the surface of the earth and they turn out to look exactly like a spherical or bowl shape, no square tendency. I don't have any reason to think that an atomic burst would make a square crater. Everything I know tends to the contrary. The bomb craters tend to be circular.

The Barringer Crater at Winslow is very similar to craters on the moon, craters on Mars, craters on Mercury. That doesn't prove anything one way or the other, but it is an interesting comment on the whole question.

But I would like to come back to the radioactive question. The most crucial, most objective evidence that I can think of to put to the problem is the presence of radioactivity and whether or not the full spectrum of radioactive products is or is not present in the samples. With cesium you already begin to perk up your ears, but all of these fission products result from every atomic explosion that has been done by the Soviets and ourselves. Now, there is a certain amount of cesium even in snowfalls. In Iowa City, about twenty-five years ago we could scoop up snow and find cesium. This is as late as 1961. It was fairly common. The mere presence of cesium at the site, unless you know the absolute activity, and know that it isn't present in the surrounding area or is a common feature at that level, is indecisive.

(Q) Are there any naturally occurring atomic blasts?

(A) No. Not within human knowledge. There are many nuclear processes that occur naturally on the sun. The sun is, so to speak, a fusion reactor. There is no combination of circumstances on the earth which could make a natural atomic blast.

(Q) It's been reported that a glasslike substance was found, both at Tunguska and at Winslow, which is similar to samples of fused earth found at desert test sites after our atomic bomb tests. How can you account for these particles of glass?

(A) Glass beads and little iron nodules are a common feature in meteorite falls. They are frequently recovered from the surrounding spray of material in cases where the meteor has been seen to fall. One of the major aspects of meteoric study is concerned with the collecting and analyzing of these nodules and beads, which are characteristic of the natural meteoric dust. So atomic bombs are by no means unique in producing molten material. All you have to do is melt the material by atmospheric heating, and the kinetic energy of a meteorite is adequate by a factor of ten or so, more than adequate, to vaporize it completely. So in an actual impact you get a mixture of vaporization and melting and production of hot gas.

(Q) So a meteor or comet fall can account for the glass globules then?

(A) Oh, absolutely.

(Q) Would an average comet be of sufficient size to cause damage of the magnitude observed at Tunguska?

(A) Sort of a typical comet, if there is such a thing, would be about fifty kilometers in diameter. I can't tell you offhand what that weighs, but an object that size has enough kinetic energy due to its motion relative to the earth, to do all of this damage and a good deal more.

(Q) The comet could burn the area and bend the trees, snap them off?

(A) Heavens, yes. It has . . . I could figure it for you . . . probably a one-ton comet moving at fifty kilometers per second is equivalent, energetically, to a rather large atomic bomb. The same would be true of a fairly large meteor.

(Q) All the evidence suggests to you, then, that the 1908 explosion and fire in Tunguska, Siberia, was a cometary impact?

(A) I think that there is nothing that I've heard about the evidence which excluded a comet as the most reasonable possibility. Now I don't mean that you should have a closed mind about it, but once again I would like to return to the radioactive evidence, which is, in my opinion, what the decision would hinge upon, if it is properly investigated.

(Q) Would you like to see a good investigation of the composition and levels of the radioactivity in the area?

(A) Right.

(Q) And an investigation of the distribution of the radiation?

(A) That's correct. Now people might claim that it's been eroded away and covered up by vegetation and this kind of thing, after all, this was eighty years ago, but there are a large number of smaller fragments that have been recovered and the radioactivity of these fragments is of a very high interest. I'm really astonished that this hasn't been investigated. I think that's the most crucial physical evidence, and to my knowledge, it has not been brought forward.

(Q) Is there any evidence that there has ever been another comet fall on earth?

(A) This is unique to my knowledge.

(Q) So one might reasonably expect a certain degree of uniqueness in the physical evidence recovered from Tunguska in the event of either a comet fall or a spaceship crash?

(A) I agree with that. I think that's true.

(Q) What would it take to convince you that the Tunguska incident was indeed a spaceship crash?

(A) I don't want to be tiresome about the radioactive thing, but that would be one source of important evidence. If you take just a conventional spaceship, without appealing to any type of atomic propulsive power, it would have to have been of an enormous mass to have produced this widespread effect. I mentioned that you would have to have a comet maybe fifty kilometers in diameter, maybe as small as ten kilometers would be adequate. That's a massive object. You would have to have a truly enormous spaceship to have the kinetic energy capability to produce such widespread destruction. As you probably know, our spaceships, satellites, fall back into the atmosphere every day all around the earth and most people don't even notice them. During July and August of 1976, about two hundred objects, artificial satellite objects, entered the earth's atmosphere. Of course most of them were fairly small pieces like clamp rings or various items of that sort. During those two months, I venture to think that ten or twenty rather large Soviet spacecraft reentered the atmosphere. Most of them aren't even seen. They never get to the ground in any way that ever makes a substantial impact.

Now, of course, if you want to be hypothetical about this you could say that the Tunguska impact was due to a spacecraft weighing many hundreds of tons. You can't do this, make this widespread destruction, without many thousands, tens of thousands, of tons of material.

(Q) If it had been a spaceship, would you expect to find some kind of metallic material suggesting a spaceship, at the site?

(A) I would think that it would be extremely unlikely to find iron magnetite globules, silicate globules, such as have been found, if it were a spaceship crash. I guess you could say, "How do we know?" If you want to be altogether open-minded about this, you could say that we wouldn't know. It just seems rather unlikely. It's very difficult to exclude, if you want to just let your mind roam to any number of hundreds of thousands of tons you would need to do the job, produce the destruction. I suppose you could make it out of aluminum or something else that is easily vaporizable. I don't think that I could positively exclude that. It's just that it seems rather unlikely, don't you think?

(Q) In your opinion, then, none of the physical evidence, air shocks, seismic records, rule out a comet?

(A) I think that all of these things are very naturally interpretable as resulting from a cometary impact.

(Q) And there have been no other cometary impacts, which, in itself, makes this impact a unique case?

(A) Yes, to the best of my knowledge, this is a unique case.

(Q) It would seem we're very lucky it didn't hit Chicago or New York or Iowa City.

(A) Yes. It could any time. We never know. It's very unlikely, that's all. Comets appear in an unpredictable manner. Some comets are so-called periodic comets, meaning that they travel around and around the solar system like Halley's Comet, which comes back every seventy-six years.

(Q) Why wasn't the Tunguska comet seen before it hit the earth?

(A) Good question. It is possible that it was of such a size that it couldn't be seen while it was in interplanetary space, but still big enough that it could produce the effects. I don't think there has ever been a meteorite that was detected before it hit the atmosphere. They're below the limits of detectability when they're free-flying in space.

(Q) Let's move for a minute to the larger question of interstellar travel. Is it feasible that somebody could build a starship?

(A) Well, the most important fact to consider is that any other star is an extremely long way away from the earth, any star other than the sun. The nearest is the Alpha Centauri system and it's about 400,000 astronomical units from the sun. At the present time, at the highest spacecraft velocities that we can get, it would take us about a hundred thousand years to get there. And that's being fairly generous in the expectations of what we can do in the way of propulsion. That's with the present type of propulsive capability. There's no reason to think that it can't be done. Using present types of propulsion it would take about a hundred thousand years.

Now if you want to think about the more advanced types of propulsive systems, in principle, you can get there a lot quicker using atomic propulsion. But even then I don't think that you can cut it down by an awful lot with anything practically visualizable at the present time. Perhaps you could conceivably get it down to ten thousand years. That's the basic thing. Otherwise there is no reason why you can't do it. It just takes a rather long time. The hundred thousand-year estimate is more like the proper realistic number to think about at the present time. Even then I'm being pretty generous.

(Q) What is the ultimate limiting factor in interstellar travel?

(A) There is an enormous amount of experimental evidence that within the bounds of present knowledge, the speed of light is the ultimate velocity for any physical object.

(Q) Is this because of Einstein's theories?

(A) That's not so much to do with Einstein as it's an experimental fact, at the present time. I'm thinking here of speeding up atomic particles. No one has ever succeeded in demonstrating any velocity greater than the velocity of light.

(Q) There is, then, no way of short-circuiting the distances between stars, say by some method like *Star Trek*'s warp drive?

(A) There is no known evidence for doing that, so if you want to base any suggestions on existing knowledge, you'd have to say that light's the ultimate velocity. Let me say that it's only about four light years to Alpha Centauri, so if you could travel at the speed of light it would only take you four years to get there. Then, of course, you'd have to slow down when you get there.

I might mention another fact that I've never seen mentioned in discussions of interstellar flight in anything resembling the velocity of light. At the velocity you have to travel through the interstellar gas, which is, so to speak, standing still and you're running through it. Now that amounts to the fact that the interstellar gas, being mostly hydrogen, would constitute an enormous radiation hazard to the spacecraft because, if the spacecraft is traveling at the velocity of light through the gas that is standing still, it is the same as bombarding the spacecraft with that same gas moving at the velocity of light. Now, I calculated that at one time and concluded that this consideration, and never to my knowledge has it been mentioned, would absolutely devastate any type of human life in any spacecraft that we could imagine. So even apart from the propulsive difficulties of getting up to the speed of light, you'd be absolutely fried by radiation. The proton beam bombardment of the spacecraft would be devastating to any living organisms or electronic equipment.

(Q) Would the spacecraft tend to carry this radioactivity with it?

(A) Indeed! It would become radioactive like a target in a cyclotron.

(Q) Would we expect a radioactive residue from it?

(A) It would be the metal parts and things like that that would become radioactive so it wouldn't necessarily leave a residue. However, if it came in and disintegrated, then it would. Then the material that was radioactive would be disintegrated by the impact and spread all over the impact site. But I was referring more to the radiation exposure to which any occupants would be subjected.

(Q) So the limiting factors then are the speed of light and the amount of hydrogen gas in interstellar space?

(A) The most basic limitation is the propulsive capability. Sending an unmanned spacecraft is one thing, a manned craft quite another. Of course *Pioneer* 10 (Author's note: *Pioneer*

10 is an unmanned deep space probe designed to explore the outer planets before leaving the solar system) is escaping in the general direction of Aldebaran in the constellation of Taurus at the present time. Aldebaran is the brightest star in Taurus and it's about ten times as far away as it is to Alpha Centauri. Eventually it's going to get there, if you wait long enough. The time required is, I think, on the order of a million years. Sometime in the next million years, if there are intelligent creatures on Aldebaran, they'll have a real UFO.

(Q) Speaking of *Pioneer*, if, in a million years from now there are any Aldebaranians, what are the chances of them being able to figure out where it came from, based on the plaque *Pioneer* carries?

(A) It depends on how bright they are. Frankly, I had trouble understanding it myself even when I had the explanation right there next to it. I had to refer back and forth. It would be a terribly good piece of detective work if they did.

(Q) Is interstellar flight really only a mere whimsical notion?

(A) I don't really want to say that interstellar flight isn't possible. I consider that it is possible, but there are these enormous flight times that must be dealt with, and the fact that one had to develop a regenerative, closed ecological system that allows you to grow food. You would have to do it without the benefit of sunlight. Basically, you would have to do it, presumably, with some type of atomic power plant. You have to have self-contained quantities of water and organic materials. Succeeding generations would have to live and die totally within the confines of the ship. You have to be very careful about what you throw away; even bodies would have to be saved for their organic content. It's all a pretty grandiose plan.

(Q) One final question, Dr. Van Allen, pertaining to the Tunguska incident. There are bound to be those who prefer the explanation of a crashed spaceship to the explanation of a cometary impact, and who will point to the 1803 decision of the French Academy of Science that concluded that meteors could not fall from the sky, and say, "Organized science won't listen because it's too locked into its own way of thinking." How do you respond to their charge?

(A) I realize that I'm subject to that charge, that I might be said to have a vested interest in that type of explanation, that is, a scientific explanation. I realize that I may be accused of being generally of such a rigid mental framework that I'm unwilling to consider any other aspects. But I would like to say this. One of my favorite sayings is one my daughter uses, and that is if you're in the middle of a ranch in Wyoming, and you hear the thundering of hoofbeats, you don't expect a herd of zebras. It doesn't mean that they couldn't be there, but one should at least exhaust known natural phenomena and possibilities before grasping at exotic possibilities.

June 1983: Susan Ramstead Revisited

I first met Susan Ramstead in 1977 after I had spoken to a local service organization about my investigations of UFOs. At the time she was a young businesswoman who worked for one of the major corporations and had no interest in flying saucers. In October 1973 (*see October 1973: The UFO Occupants*), she saw a landed craft in a cornfield as she headed to a business conference. Later, under questioning, we learned that there was more to the sighting than just the landing.

At the lecture Ramstead told me of the disc-shaped craft with the slight dome on top. It gave off a blue glow that seemed to be reflected by the ground around it. As she approached it, the car engine stalled and the lights went out. A few minutes later, it took off, disappearing in the distance.

It was an interesting story, especially since she had been close to the UFO. She had been in contact with her husband on the CB radio describing the sighting to him, but when the car stalled, the radio faded.

During our discussion of the sighting, we realized that Ramstead thought she had been out of touch for five minutes, but her husband said it was closer to twenty, maybe thirty. A time discrepancy is one of the flags of an abduction case (*see June 12, 1988: Don Schmidt*), and we made arrangements to explore that aspect of the sighting.

A few days later, under hypnosis, Susan Ramstead described the aliens coming to her car, actually standing around it: short beings with no real facial features. She tried to raise her husband on the radio, but it wasn't working.

The next thing she remembered was that she was in the ship, being examined. Like other abductees, she described the interior as cold and bright, almost antiseptic. There were machines and computerlike screens. She was strapped to a table and examined, just as others have claimed to have been.

Ramstead described the aliens as cold and unfeeling. As with the others, the impression she was left with was that they wanted their information and didn't care about the traumatic side effects to the victim. After they had gathered their information, she was left to herself to get dressed. Although escorted from the ship, there was nothing in the demeanor of the aliens to suggest they were sorry for what they felt they had to do.

When Ramstead woke up, she was sitting in the front seat and the ship was in the sky. It vanished rapidly and Ramstead continued her journey, arriving late. She didn't tell anyone there she had seen a flying saucer. Her business friends would have laughed.

At the time, I thought her story fairly typical of the abduction reports: a lone victim on a deserted stretch of highway, taken on board the craft, examined, and then returned to the car. Some type of memory block had been used, but it was of such a flimsy nature that we easily broke through it. That was just another indication that the aliens didn't really care what we knew and what we learned.

That, briefly, was the Susan Ramstead story. I thought nothing more of it, and went on to other things, other investigations. Then, in June 1983, Susan Ramstead called again. She wanted to know if the aliens ever returned.

I told her that it was common for the creatures to suggest they would be back, but I didn't think it happened. It was more like the threat that robbers used when telling the victims not to move for five or ten minutes. It gave them time to get away, but it was more of an idle threat. They didn't come back.

"Not true," she told me.

The tone of her voice, the fear that I could pick up through the phone, suggested that she knew something more. I asked her what was happening.

"It's the dreams," she said. "I've begun to dream about them. Standing near my bed, watching me."

For me, this was something new. I'd never heard of a repeat abduction. It has always seemed that abduction was such a rare phenomenon that no one person would be abducted again. For there to be repeats, it would seem that the aliens would need some way to track the people: a banding and radio transmitter like those naturalists used to monitor the movements of wild animals.

I told her that I thought it was probably anxiety manifesting itself in the form of dreams about the aliens. She didn't think so, but if I wasn't interested she would try to find someone who was.

Because I knew her story and knew that she wasn't one to get hysterical over nothing, I suggested that we get together and talk about it. Saturday afternoon was set as the time.

In the intervening years, she and her husband had moved. From the looks of the house, and the section of town where it stood, it seemed that their careers had been more than successful and they had made a lot of money.

Almost before I was in the door, she asked me, "What about nose bleeds?"

"Nose bleeds?" I said, thinking that one of the signs of elevated blood pressure and high anxiety is nose bleeds.

"I woke up and my pillow and nightgown were covered in blood."

I suggested that we sit down and talk about what was going on. I still wasn't convinced that there were new UFO incidents involved. Maybe anxiety over the sighting and abduction of ten years earlier, but nothing new. It turned out that I was wrong.

Ramstead began describing the dreams she was having. The aliens were back, watching over her. She thought they had been in the house, thought they had been in her bedroom, and thought they had taken her out.

"Where was your husband all this time?" I asked.

"Sleeping right there. He never woke up."

"Then what happens?"

"They do it again. They take me away, examine me, and bring me back."

"How often?"

She shrugged and said, "Once a year."

"Vivid dreams," I said.

"No," she snapped. "Not dreams. That's what everyone would like to think, but they're not dreams. And how do you explain the blood on my pillow?"

I could think of a dozen mundane explanations, from dry air to some kind of nasal infection. I didn't say any of that. I wanted her to talk.

And talk she did. She told me of her dreams: phantoms in the night floating out of the house and into the open fields behind the house; the cold and brightness of the ship; more probing, but this time the needle, the instrument, coming down toward her nose. She talked about a flash of pain there and of a feeling of being stuffed up.

She was returned to the house and the next morning awakened to find blood on the pillow. It frightened her, but not enough for her to say anything other than to tell her husband he must have punched her in the night. They made a joke of the blood and the nose bleed.

But that wasn't all. She talked of another visit: the creatures floating both her and her unconscious husband out, to the ship hovering behind the field.

"Now wait a minute," he said, suddenly agitated. "I've nothing to do with this."

His response seemed to be wrong. He had lost the edge of his humor and seemed to be denying it with too much vigor. I had the impression that if his wife wanted to believe that aliens were coming to visit, that was fine with him. He just wanted to be left out of the story. Now he seemed to be frightened.

"Obviously," I said, "there is a simple solution to this whole thing. Hypnosis."

Susan Ramstead readily agreed, but her husband again said that he wanted no part of these ridiculous stories. She talked to him for ten or fifteen minutes and he reluctantly agreed. We would have another hypnosis session in about a week.

Unfortunately, hypnosis is not the pathway to the truth. It can open doors that have been locked, but too often the longer the session takes, or the more sessions there are, the witness begins to "perform" for the hypnotist. The subject can pick up subtle clues and is very susceptible to leading questions. A skilled interviewer can take the subject wherever he or she wants to go. It's a difficult thing to question a subject under hypnosis and not contaminate the session.

And, to make this worse, Susan Ramstead had been hypnotized before. We had questioned her at length. In the years since that first session, she had become interested in UFOs, reading books and magazine articles about them. She had become an expert on all their various facets, knowing more about some aspects of the field than I do. What had once been an uncontaminated source was now one that might have been badly damaged. Her knowledge of the subject would taint the sessions.

Her husband, on the other hand, showed no interest in UFOs. He thought there was something strange going on but would go no further. And even though he hadn't read the books that Susan brought home, she talked to him about what she had read. He, too, was a contaminated source.

With that in mind, I arranged for a hypnotic regression session. This time, I had to separate the Ramsteads because I didn't want John to hear what Susan told us, nor did I want her to hear him. Reluctantly they agreed to that condition.

We conducted several sessions learning more about what was going on. Ramstead said that she had been told that the aliens had selected certain people as guinea pigs. Their lives were going to be followed while the aliens stood off and patiently waited for time to pass. They couldn't maintain a daily surveillance, but they could, periodically, swoop in and scoop up those selected people. With hypnotic regression, along with memory-enhancing drugs, the subjects could be interviewed. Their lives could be reviewed during those session with a complete biography produced. Once the interview was completed, the physical exam was made and then the victim was returned to her home.

Listening to Susan Ramstead describe these things surprised me. I found it hard to believe what she was saying, even under hypnosis and even after I had watched her go from being frightened by the encounters to a resignation that suggested she could do nothing about it. The aliens were going to keep picking on her and she was powerless to stop it.

Then I remembered the history of the UFO phenomenon. First, people were willing to accept the idea of flying saucers, as long as they stayed in the sky. Landing reports were at first rejected. Then the occupant reports started and the Air Force labeled all reports of creatures as being "psychological." It was all right to report a craft but not the creature in it. Abduction reports were rejected at first. Those are now accepted as part of the phenomenon, so why not repeat abductions? Why not aliens who study the lives of certain people so that they can understand life on Earth?

With that in mind, we kept going. We interviewed John Ramstead. He told us that he awakened one night, saw the small creatures standing at the end of the bed: small gray men with big, dark eyes, no facial features, and pale skin.

He tried to move but found he was paralyzed. He wanted to get up but couldn't. Panic began to spread through him. One of the creatures moved to him, touched his shoulder, and he relaxed.

As he watched, his wife was taken from the room. One creature stayed with him and the others left. A long time later, Susan was returned and put in bed and the creatures left. As they went out the door, John went back to sleep. The next morning, he remembered nothing about the incident.

Under questioning, he told of another visit. This time he watched Susan taken from the room, but then the creatures returned. One of them stood near him and raised a hand. Ramstead reported that he was floated from the bed and then the house. He described the interior of the ship—a cold, bright environment. His body was probed, there were needles and cuts and tissue samples taken. They asked him no questions, and in fact, didn't communicate with him at all. They made their physical examination and returned him to the bed. A few minutes later Susan was brought back in. The next morning, there was blood on her pillow.

There were other visits by the gray men who came in the night. There was a period when Susan Ramstead reported that she was no longer interested in sex. She avoided contact with her husband, but he didn't care that much. As she began to wonder if she was pregnant, the aliens returned, and the feelings that she had complained about, the lack of desire for sex, her general feeling of not being well, evaporated.

We learned as much as we could from the various sessions. Susan Ramstead wanted to know if she had been pregnant during that two-month period. I told her that I didn't know, but that I found the thought frightening. Now the aliens were conducting experiments into the reproduction of humans. Speculation about that led into the realm of science fiction. I couldn't help remembering the case of Antonio Villas-Boas (*see October 1957: Antonio Villas-Boas*) who claimed, in 1957, that he was abducted and subjected to what for all intents and purposes seemed to be an experiment designed to test human reproduction. Betty Hill talked about a lot of little Betty Hills running around in space. Maybe it was no longer science fiction.

Under hypnosis, Susan talked about the last visit. A tiny metal object had been removed from her nose that had been there for a long time. Suddenly she felt better; her head was no longer stuffed. They took the sphere, dropped it into a metal tray, and then got her ready to return to the house.

It was after this last visit, where there had been so much blood on her pillow and her nightgown, that had triggered the call. She also told me that the periodic headaches she had experienced were gone. It was as if the metal object in her nose had caused her headaches. The feeling of having a stuffed nose went away with the sphere.

Under hypnosis, she told me that she had gotten the impression that there would be no more nocturnal visits. She and her husband had seen the last of them. The experiment was over, they had removed their tracking device, or whatever the sphere was, and moved onto others.

We completed the sessions and again I thanked them, not

sure of what to make of their report. It seemed so bizarre, but then, twenty years ago, Barney and Betty Hill's report that they had been taken into a spaceship had seemed bizarre. And, compared to them, Antonio Villas-Boas's story of sex on a flying saucer was the stuff of tabloids.

Since then I have learned that repeat abductions are not that unusual. Many have reported that the aliens put something up their noses. A naval officer claimed that a small metal sphere was removed from his leg and taken away by Navy doctors. People have come forward talking of a lifetime of abduction and contact with the aliens.

This is one area of UFO investigation that needs more research. There is something going on and we don't have much of a clue as to what it is. At some point, someone is going to provide us with the answers, but until that happens, we're stuck with interviewing the victims and trying to make some sense of it.

June 12, 1988: Don Schmitt

On June 12, 1988, I caught up with Don Schmitt in Milwaukee, Wisconsin, where we both had gone to attend the X-Con science fiction convention. Knowing that I was preparing the manuscript for this book, I asked if he'd like to talk about the current state of UFO research, what was happening at the moment, and where he thought we'd be going in the future. He agreed and the following is that interview.

(Q) First I'd like to know a little about your work at the Center for UFO Studies. Just exactly what do you do?

(A) Well, I had been working as an investigator for the Center, especially requested by Allen [Dr. J. Allen Hynek]. I'd been an investigator for APRO prior to that and we'd set up an investigative network around the state [Wisconsin]. We concerned ourselves mainly with recruiting the cooperation of law enforcement agencies.

Using my background as a technical illustrator, I was sending illustrations of sightings down to the Center and Allen saw this was something that they had not attempted. It was almost like having a police artist working for the Center who could re-create witness testimony. He was pleased with my work. It was in the late 1970s that he began to refer cases from Wisconsin and the surrounding states to me.

Unfortunately, many of them were nothing noteworthy. Most of them I explained. I can recall up in Rhinelander [Wisconsin] in 1985 there was a rash of sightings around the airport. The United County police, the sheriff's department, and the Rhinelander police were all involved. They were staking out the airport each night. There was an astronomer who was on the Center board at that time who was involved. Allen asked if I would look into it and see if there was anything going on.

My conclusion was—and we pretty much established it by staking out the airport—that it was just military aircraft coming in after hours. They would come down low, between the trees, with their landing lights on, and because of the unusual lighting configurations of some of the aircraft, the local law enforcement men and the astronomer were unfamiliar with them.

We were all down at Allen's residence in Evanston, and he [the astronomer] was arguing right and left we had to be wrong. No matter how we presented our data, it had to be legitimate UFO activity. Allen took me aside and said, ''That's why I'm going to keep giving you cases.'' We had it right.

(Q) Is this a paid occupation for you?

(A) It's strictly voluntary. As it is for all the UFO organizations throughout the country. It's generally part time, though there are times when it could become full time, especially during heavy activity.

(Q) The UFO phenomenon is pretty much cyclic. Are we at a point where it is coming around in the cycle again?

(A) There is no question there is an increase in activity as of 1988. We are receiving a continuous flow of reports that are coming, essentially, from all corners of the country. That is something we have not had recently.

As far as the Midwest is concerned, we had a slight flap late in 1979 and early 1980. That was in Minnesota, Wisconsin, Illinois, and Michigan. We had a flurry of activity in the south central area of Wisconsin in the early part of 1987 which received international coverage. We had the big sighting in Australia [January 1988] involving the Noll family in the outback. It [the UFO] lifted the car up, put it back down, and blew a tire out. There were other witnesses to the UFO. There was a tuna fishing boat that had a separate incident.

(Q) I understood that it had been described as a hoax.

(A) There was an interview in the "UFO Update" section of OMNI and the explanation is that the Noll family had been sleeping. That it was 1:30 in the morning, out in the middle of the desert and that it was, essentially, white line fever. When they hit something, they panicked and the driver slammed on the brakes and blew a tire. Prior to this they had been watching a bright star, which was something that appeared unusual to them at that time. Putting this whole thing together, they concocted this UFO incident.

One thing the OMNI interview does not do at all is acknowledge all the witnesses. It mentions nothing at all of the tuna fishing boat. The likelihood that both groups [the Noll family and the tuna boat crew] would describe the same experience where their voices were distorted is highly remote. I've never heard about this in any type of UFO situation. It's interesting that they both would describe the same thing fifteen minutes apart without either party knowing of the other experience. (That is, after the sighting, the voices of all the parties were distorted, sounding as if they had been breathing helium.) The article doesn't concern itself with that.

(Q) The trend is toward more sightings. Are we getting more occupant sightings, abductions—where is the phenomenon going?

(A) There has been more interaction as far as an open approach. Not that we're getting more reports of lights in the sky or daylight discs. In fact, close encounters of any kind are way down. We're not getting the occupant cases as we

used to through the mid-1950s and especially in 1973. We
certainly are getting more abduction cases, however. So it's
a situation where the phenomenon is showing more of a direct
approach, more motive, and more purpose. But yet, it's more
secretive. That's where we're concerned. That these are legitimate experiences and that it's gone underground. And,
they're now picking people at will.

(Q) I noticed in 1954 we had one kind of occupant—the
short humanoid in the space suit—and in 1973 they didn't
wear suits. Are there any indications that there is more than
one group?

(A) Once again, if we would use the abduction account
descriptions as far as they are actual occupant cases, it's very
similar to the mid-1950s descriptions. Humanoid, the dis-
proportionate head, and large, almond-shaped, and very dark
eyes.

(Q) This is opposed to the occupant descriptions in 1973.
The 1954 group is back.

(A) We still get a smattering of the other type described.
What's interesting to us is as little as certain cases have been
publicized, we are getting confirmation of some of them. In
the 1950s we had the human "occupant" appearing and even
if we dismiss them all as being contactee-oriented, there occasionally were a number of human occupant cases that stand
as being some of the better cases.

(Q) In the Pat Roach case in 1973 she claimed to have
seen a human on the craft working with the aliens . . .

(A) We are getting an increasing number of cases where
they describe the two as working together. The humanoid
with the human-appearing entities during the course of an
abduction. Now what this indicates we can only speculate.
But as you know, these are not the norm. You would not
expect everyone to be aware of these cases.

(Q) So you're saying we're back to the 1954-type occupant.

(A) If they ever left. But let's just say that even if we take
the 1954 cases and go up to the Betty and Barney Hill incident
in 1961, and even into the abduction accounts beyond that,
the abduction accounts generally have all represented the
same type of occupant. Once again, there are a select few
that have described other types of beings. Pascagoula is cer-

tainly an example. Granted, we do occasionally get those where they feel there is nothing biological about the particular beings involved.

(Q) Now you say the abductions are still going on. Do you have a case of someone being abducted in 1988?

(A) I was just reading of a case that happened in Great Britain from December 1987. It involves an ex-policeman and it involves some photography. It reads again as a typical abduction account.

(Q) Can you give us a little more detail about it?

(A) In this particular case the occupant is described almost on the order of the Kelly-Hopkinville entities. The actual shape of the entity is described with the elephantine ears, the long arms almost dragging on the ground, and the almost clublike feet, which once again is almost unique in the Sutton case.

(Author's note: The Sutton family in the Hopkinville, Kentucky, area is one of the few occupant cases reported to the Air Force. On August 22, 1955, Bill Taylor went out to the well for a drink and came back with the tale of a spaceship that had landed in a nearby field. The creatures seemed to attack the farmhouse of the Sutton family and to roam all over the adjacent area. They fired at the creatures, the shotgun blasts knocking them from their feet but apparently not hurting them. Finally the Suttons ran to their car and fled. The next day, deputies could find no evidence of the creatures or the ships, though they did say something had scared the Suttons.)

The abduction itself was early morning and there was an occupant sighting involved. There was complete recall of the UFO, which is described as classic saucer-shaped. The abduction is completely typical as far as most go.

(Q) Was he in his car when he saw the object?

(A) No, he was out shooting some photographs of the early morning moor areas. It was about twenty minutes before sunrise so he was hoping to get into the area for some sunrise shots.

(Q) Did he see it land?

(A) He didn't see it land. He confronted the occupant.

(Q) Not unlike several cases from 1954.

(A) Right.

(Q) Did the occupant respond to him in any way?

(A) Well, he was running off as far as the witness could tell. In a somewhat open area—down a trail and much to the witness's disbelief, he started to pursue it. When he mentioned it, he said, "I took off hell-bent to catch it."

It's like so many of the abductee reports. They are driving down the road and suddenly pull off to the side and wonder why they are doing it. It's as if they've lost control of their own senses. So the occupant turned and sort of waved him off. Then he stopped and it just took off running up a slight incline. The object rose up from behind the trees and it was gone.

He immediately got in contact with someone in the area who was involved with the local UFO group who contacted Jenny Randles.

There were actually four people then who knew of the case. Two days after the incident the witness was paid a visit by two people that showed him British Air Ministry Intelligence badges, complete with photographs, their names and everything. They wanted to know about the UFO sighting. They asked him about the photograph and he mentioned he had turned it over to a friend who was going to check it out. They said, "Okay. Fine," and left.

He immediately got on the phone with Jenny and asked her why she had let this out. She said she hadn't told anybody. We promised complete confidentiality. Right away the suspicion is whose phone is tapped.

(Q) Now subsequently he was abducted?

(A) No. As they were working with him and the abduction came out afterwards, in regression.

(Q) So he didn't remember being abducted?

(A) No. Not at that time.

(Q) Did he describe the interior of the ship?

(A) Once again, as they generally described it. Highly illuminated without having any direct light source, very cold, and a hospitallike environment.

(Q) Did he describe the examination?

(A) Not as yet. So it's not even to say there was an examination involved.

(Q) Other than the abductions, such as this case from England, are we getting occupant reports?

(A) No.

(Q) Not a trend toward gathering samples or anything like that?

(A) No. I'm becoming a little concerned because you have certain researchers who are now going back and taking every occupant case and automatically questioning whether it was an abduction or not. They've been taking it a step further and questioning whether each close encounter was an abduction as well. Now granted there is that possibility but to start actually grabbing at straws and trying to play up experiences that the witnesses feel were nothing more than a sighting isn't right. They don't describe any time loss. Why place that burden on the witness and have them believe it's possible?

Where we have to be careful is with people who aren't looking for that release. This feeling that something else might have happened. But we cannot create an entire scenario that only accentuates their difficulty, their whole problem, making it all the more difficult for them and making it all that much more difficult for their spouses.

One of the abductions we've been working on turns out to be more difficult for the husband because he has to sit there and watch his wife relive this experience. It was very demeaning, very dehumanizing.

(Q) Can you tell us a little bit more about this?

(A) It's a daytime experience, involving a teenage girl at that time. It happened twenty years ago. The fact it was daytime, which is seldom reported, makes it interesting.

She was driving down a road to meet with a girlfriend to go shopping. Up ahead, in the road, she saw what appeared to be a work crew, a number of men working on both sides of the road and a couple of men standing in the middle of the road, but no warning sign, no flagmen, and no vehicles. As she comes to the crest of the hill, the first thing that strikes her is that they're all very short and almost all identical in stature. They all are dressed in blue-gray coveralls.

So, as she approached, her car engine stalled, which also is commonly described. The two men standing in the road turned and for the first time she saw the eyes. She said they looked hypnotic.

(Q) Facial features?

(A) Rather diminutive in that the heads either had on a type of headpiece that covered the hair or they had no hair. She couldn't see any hair on any of them. The eyes were very dark and as the one got closer she saw that the eyes were solid in color and there was no pupil.

That was essentially all she remembered at that point until she was driving and feeling compelled to turn to look back and being told not to. She continued on to her girlfriend's house. She thought she arrived on time and was annoyed with the fact that her girlfriend was in her house clothes. They got into an argument until the girlfriend pointed out she was two hours late. She was surprised to learn it was two in the afternoon and not noon as she had thought.

(Q) Obviously she was abducted . . .

(A) Under regression she described where they came to the sides of the car and that telepathically she was hearing that they wanted her to get out of the car. The fear that came out at that time, which is very typical of that.

She was led across the road and walked across the field. What's interesting about this is that she paused and she started to question how they got over the fence. That's a unique feature—that she was actually questioning things that were happening at that time.

One thing we always look for, too, is whether or not they describe things in the first person. She was describing things as they happened. She was reliving the experience. When they look back and describe it almost as a story, I'm a leery of the fact that they're trying to tell you essentially nothing more than a story. But she was describing, in great detail, seeing the ship.

(Q) And the ship was . . .

(A) Resting in a cornfield as far as she could tell. A dome-shaped saucer, flat on the bottom, a type of tripod landing gear, with a hinged ramp that was resting on the ground.

Usually the people in an abduction account don't describe being taken up the ramp or remember going into the ship. Very often they describe all of a sudden they're in this room.

That's where the accounts generally pick up. She described actually being led up the ramp and being taken into the object itself. All at once she has the feeling she was inside a refrigerator. Very cold. Uncomfortably cold. Very bright.

It is interesting to watch that through the regression that she turned white, the goose bumps just flared up on her arms and neck. She was subjected to a typical examination. Her apprehension, her fear, and her outcry at seeing them appear with the needle was all very real. She described the needle being inserted into the abdomen.

(Q) Did she describe the interior of the ship at all?

(A) Just yesterday [June 11, 1988] we had her make some drawings of the interior of the ship. Once again it was very typical. Overhead, suspended above them, were instruments where they could reach up and take things down. The monitors were all there. There were two monitors, one on each side of the table. There was a counter that wrapped around the outer circumference of the room. A doorway . . .

(Q) A regular doorway?

(A) Well, just that it led into another compartment which she was taken into.

(Q) I mean a regular door with a knob?

(A) When they did take her into the other room it just happened to be open. It appeared as a doorway. As for the materials involved, it was like a metal but it wasn't metal, almost like a plastic-type metal. Once again, a gray, a very bland type of material. No colors.

(Q) Then the abduction took about two hours?

(A) If we go by the time loss involved, then yes.

(Q) This was 1968, 1969?

(A) 1968.

(Q) That's pretty much a typical abduction case?

(A) Yes. The problem we're having is that we have to always consider the fact that we're dealing with hypnosis, drawing into the subconscious as far as you're just drawing on the past memories of the experiences. That's open to a lot of different interpretations.

(Q) Coral Lorenzen made a big deal out of the hands. Did she describe the hands?

(A) Yes. Well, she had some problem describing the hands

because you don't want to ask anything that could be leading. She did mention hands so we could mention hands. She described when they were doing things and they took a blood sample from her finger, if it was a blood sample. They had long, slender fingers without fingernails. There were five fingers. Four fingers and a thumb. But it was not an opposing thumb. It was just a fifth finger, which has been described before.

(Q) Did she describe any humans with them?

(A) Not immediately and not specifically. She described the one that came in and did some scraping on her arm. She said that it was a female. We asked her why she thought it was a female. She said it has hair. Once again the others had hair. But why do you think it's a female? Because it looks different. Describe the hair. It's dark, very dark. It's long, straight hair. How is she different? Her eyes are different. Her face is different. She almost looks human. How else is she different? Well, she's taller. So, if you want, you can get to a human-appearing individual associated with them. That was a little promising because she would have had to have done some very specific reading or research into the subject to learn that.

(Q) One of the things people really get into are the crashed saucer stories. I know Frank Scully was responsible for some of them and there was the Spitzbergen Island crash and Dorothy Kilgallen talked about a crash in England. Now Roswell, New Mexico, is the latest . . .

(A) I wouldn't say that it's the latest; I would say that by far, the most evidence that a crash might have occurred is in Roswell.

(Q) What about Ubatuba? [*See September 12, 1957: Ubatuba Brazil*]. The one that was seen to explode in midair?

(A) As far as Dr. Fontes, I think he did an excellent investigation in trying to secure the cooperation of different laboratories and people who could do the metal analysis and following through on it. The problem is that the debris has finally disappeared. As it turns out the case ran up to the roadblock and then they never did complete it. The one analysis they did get showed the metal as being pure magnesium, that it was 99.9 percent pure and that it could have been made at that time [1957] is very unusual.

(Q) What is the feeling now, granted the sample is missing, what is the feeling now about it?

(A) I don't think that even if it would have been considered as highly unusual as some of the preliminary tests suggested, it would have been enough to present it as evidence that it was something manufactured off the Earth. If anything, it would be classified as something so highly unusual but that there must have been some type of special refinement used. It, by itself, would be enough.

(Q) So the Ubatuba sample is still considered as a good piece of evidence.

(A) It's still cited as something highly unusual and that it could have been part of a legitimate UFO.

(Q) So now we've come to the best of the UFO crash cases, to Roswell and the MJ-12 . . . [see July 2, 1947: Roswell, New Mexico and September, 1947: The Majestic Twelve].

(A) I think even aside from the MJ-12, Roswell stands an authenticated experience. To date Bill Moore and Stan Friedman have tracked down and talked to more than ninety-two first-, second-, and third-hand witnesses—eight witnesses alone who handled the debris. They could describe the structure of the cylinders that were present at the site. They describe the hieroglyphic symbols that were on the cylinders.

(Q) This is the only crash site?

(A) Leonard Stringfield, who has done quite an amount of work, especially in crash retrieval cases . . . these go up into the mid-1970s, but mainly in the later 1940s and early 1950s, has listed several. In many cases he's dealing with first-hand witnesses. Ray Fowler's Fritz Weaver [Werner?], which is a pseudonym he had for a contact involving the retrieval of an object. Colonel Willingham, and the Aztec, New Mexico, crash incident. The Socorro crash. Essentially all down in the southwest and all at a time when there was a heavy concentration of UFO activity around that area.

I don't place any credence in Scully's account. That's been thoroughly discredited. Spitzbergen has been eliminated. But Hynek even admitted in his later years that something crashed in Roswell. The question about it comes from what it was and the fact that so many witnesses feel that something had happened and the way the press was silenced . . .

(Q) Today you wouldn't have had the press so easily silenced . . .

(A) When Brazel was finally released to go back to his family in 1947, he spoke to one of the reporters at the local radio station. All Brazel would say is, "They scared the hell out of me. I can't say a word about it." And that was consistent with some of the other accounts when they were swearing people to secrecy. They were so concerned that this would get out . . .

(Q) So right now we're still searching for the answers about Roswell?

(A) And since then there have been rumors concerning some special UFO project that was set up at that time in 1948.

(Q) Which would be the Majestic Twelve.

(A) In 1948, for example, Wilbert Smith, who worked for the Canadian Department of Transportation, was working on an electro-geomagnetic propulsion system. Having heard rumors of the retrieval of this object at Roswell, he was concerned whether we had any information we could share with them concerning this type of propulsion system. They received a report that has been publicized . . . it's mentioned in *Clear Intent*, Bob Hastings has it in his UFO cover-up lecture, Stan Friedman is using it, and it's in Timothy Good's *Above Top Secret* . . . in the document, if legitimate, it states, first of all, flying saucers exist. Their modus operandi is unknown and a small group of scientists under Vannevar Bush is working on the project at this time and it is the most highly classified subject in the United States government.

Now this was before we knew anything about MJ-12. It was since then that Robert Sarbacher, who worked on many secret government projects, was contacted after he completed his government service by William Steinman. Steinman had heard rumors to the effect that Sarbacher knew something about the retrieval of a crashed UFO and bodies.

Sarbacher wrote him that he was contacted specifically in 1950 to go to a secret meeting where they were going to be shown the recovered UFO and dead alien bodies. He said because he had a commitment overseas as assigned by his higher officers at that time he could not make it, but he was briefed on the situation afterwards. He was told that the United States did have crashed UFOs and they did have dead alien bodies. He did have them described to him, which, once again, is the standard humanoid. A small group was working on it as appointed by President Truman.

Since then Stan Friedman has talked to Sarbacher, Jerry Clark has talked to Sarbacher. Sarbacher passed away in 1986, but in every case he repeated the exact same story.

Now the fact that it mentions this secret group and there were more and more rumors out about the fact there was some special group that was involved in the actual recovery of a crashed UFO is important. Currently its code name is Project Aquarius. There is mention of Project Aquarius in some of the recently declassified documents. We are drawing the assumption that because it is mentioned in UFO-related cases that it may have been the project set up after the shutdown of Bluebook. Or it may have been the actual UFO project that was going on at higher levels over Bluebook.

(Q) Just for clarification, your assumption is that Bluebook, even back in 1952 when it was a fairly legitimate UFO investigative . . .

(A) I don't know that it was ever a legitimate investigation.

(Q) But you're saying that Bluebook was a cover for the true project.

(A) Hynek had often stated to me that he realized from early on that Bluebook was little more than a front. They were not getting any of the good cases. Once in a while when they did get a good case they, as he put it, would turn handsprings to get it away from him. He said that he knew all the hardcore cases were going over Bluebook. He was assuming they were going to NSA or Air Force Intelligence.

(Q) So they, the Majestic Twelve, may have been the committee who ran Project Aquarius?

(A) It was a separate entity in that it was after the Roswell incident came out, that Bill Moore received a phone call from someone who identified himself as someone in Air Force Intelligence. He told Moore he was on the right track and that he, the caller, would like to give Moore additional information. It has since snowballed into a dozen sources telling essentially the same story. The government knows fully well, has known since 1947, about the reality of the phenomenon, that it is extraterrestrial. There was a crash in Roswell.

(Q) What is the current state of knowledge? What are the trends?

(A) As you yourself saw in the Pat Roach case, for example, that if we accept it as a legitimate, physical experience, if there is anything true in the incident at all, you can't help feel but one step away from the phenomenon. That is, this individual is your link to the actual origin of the UFO phenomenon.

(Q) You obviously accept UFOs as extraterrestrial spacecraft . . .

(A) Not immediately. I see it as being the strongest possibility. I see the evidence pointing more to something off Earth, an intelligence off the Earth. Whether it is something right here or originating off Earth, I really can't say.

(Q) Where do they come from? Can you speculate in that direction?

(A) No. We have no information other than Betty Hill's star map suggesting Zeta 1 and Zeta 2 Reticuli. At the Center we're in the process of setting up a research project dealing with the abduction cases that might give us a clue.

(Q) Where we've gone in UFO research is we started out with Kenneth Arnold's daylight disc, we've gone through the landings, the occupants, and the abductions. We're looking away from the discs, the landings, and looking to the abductions. Is that where UFO research is headed?

(A) Yes. The likes of Dr. Dick Haimes, Dr. David Jacobs, and certainly Budd Hopkins . . .

(Q) Dr. Leo Sprinkle . . .

(A) Sprinkle since APRO; in fact, APRO was the first UFO organization that took any of the abduction accounts, for that matter any of the occupant reports, seriously. So, we are once again to assume that we're dealing with some type of stimuli, that something is interacting with these people, something is causing these people to show all the symptoms of being victims of something. That whatever this is, if it is psychological or not, we first have to address the possibility that it is psychological. Either we substantiate it or we eliminate it. We aren't going to go into this accepting the physical reality of the abduction accounts until we can eliminate the psychological.

(Q) We've moved away from the days of the college student field investigator . . .

(A) Or as Hynek used to put it, little old ladies in tennis shoes.

(Q) We've moved away from those people and to people who are highly trained, with specific equipment and with specific questions in mind. We've moved away from the hobbiest, to the professional . . .

(A) And I resent anyone referring to it as my hobby. I don't see it as a hobby at all because once again, and not for selfish motives, but we are possibly dealing with, potentially, one of the biggest stories of all time. But beyond all that, if the abductions are happening as described, my God, shouldn't we all be concerned? Shouldn't we all be at least interested?

October 1988: The Montana Crash

The search for UFOs has moved from the field and into the archives. It has become a paper chase. The Roswell incident has shown that. It wasn't the sighting that got attention because the Air Force and the government were fairly successful in hiding the data. It was clues scattered through various files and newspapers, and the discovery of a briefing document that led to Roswell. Although the Roswell case file in this work was dated July 2, 1947, for me, it could have been dated August 1986 because that was when I first learned of the significance of Roswell. Because of that, and to demonstrate where UFO research is today, I've dated this one with the time I learned of it.

According to a very short piece that appeared in the *Cedar*

Rapids Gazette on July 7, 1947, a pilot reported that he downed one of the flying discs. The short story, datelined Bozeman, Montana, claimed that a pilot had knocked down a "pearl gray, clam-shaped airplane with a Plexiglas dome on top." That was all I knew, but the suggestion of another crash just days after Roswell intrigued me.

By way of contrast, it was on July 9 that the *Gazette* reported that the Roswell incident was nothing more than a weather balloon. Remembering that information about Roswell (namely that *Gazette* article had been in my files for over fifteen years), I decided that it was time to pursue the Montana crash.

My first act was to call Bozeman, Montana, and get the number of the local newspaper. With a date, they might have something more on the sighting. It might provide me with a clue about where to take the search. I managed to get someone on the phone at the *Bozeman Daily Chronicle*, but she was no help. She kept insisting that I call the United Press since it was their story. When I asked if there were any military bases around Bozeman, she snapped, "You'll have to call the UP," and then hung up.

That, of course, wasn't any help at all. During my years of research, I had often called newspapers looking for leads and had received good cooperation from some of the largest in the country. The Bozeman paper, one of the smallest, didn't have time to help.

Failing there, I called Warren Smith. He canceled a dinner date and headed to the local library. A couple of hours later, he called back saying that he had learned more about the crash. According the the information he had, the plane, a P-38, was flying over Montana when the pilot turned and saw a formation of objects following along behind him. He described them as fifteen feet in diameter and four feet thick. One of them broke away from the formation and buzzed the plane. It caught the P-38 from behind, flew close to it, and then seemed to break apart, the pieces tumbling into the Tobacco Root Mountains due west of Bozeman and south of Butte.

There wasn't much other information. The description that Smith found matched the one I had, though it was described as a yo-yo instead of a clam. The pilot and his photographer were from Los Angeles.

Smith and I discussed the next move. I figured on calling the papers in Los Angeles to see if there was anything in them because the pilot was from there. Smith looked through the *Time* magazines, and found a veiled reference to the crash and reports of an aircraft accident in which the pilot seemed to be a ten-year-old boy. Walter Winchell claimed that he knew all about the Montana crash and he included the cryptic note that a body had been pulled from the wreckage.

Now, we had a possible crash with a dead pilot. The description, of a child, meant the pilot was three and a half to four feet tall and that he was slender. The descriptions of the aliens that we've got from abductees, saucer sighters, and from the Roswell information talked of small, slender creatures that could be described as boys.

As I had done with the Roswell information, I decided to see if the Air Force Bluebook files had anything on it. I studied the July 1947 index and then the cases, and found no reference to a crash in Montana. Unlike Roswell, I wasn't sure it was as significant. In Roswell we knew the Air Force Intelligence had been involved. In Montana there was no such knowledge. In those days of everyone seeing everything and no one sure of what was going on, it wouldn't be surprising if this case somehow got overlooked.

Still . . .

The real problem was a lack of hard information. Other than knowing something had happened in Montana and that it involved a P-38, I didn't know much. Bozeman had been no help and I had been unable to get through to the libraries at either the *Los Angeles Times* or the *Herald-Examiner*. Because the University of Iowa's main library had microfilm copies of several newspapers including the *Des Moines Register* and *The New York Times*, that seemed to be the next stop.

The New York Times had nothing about Montana. They carried, on the front page, the story that claimed Roswell was a weather balloon, but nothing about Montana.

The *Des Moines Register* was more helpful. Though there was nothing on July 7 about the crash, the next day the headline read, " 'Flying Saucer' Hoax Is Told." This was the first time that I had found a long story about the Montana crash.

According to the article, the pilot claimed his plane had knocked down a flying disc, but his boss, J.J. Archer of Los Angeles, branded the story a hoax.

Vernon Baird, a pilot of a commercial photographic plane, was at 32,000 feet and flying at 360 miles an hour when one of the discs appeared behind it. It got caught in the prop wash and came apart like a clamshell, spiraling to the ground. Archer said that Baird later admitted to him that he had made up the story.

So now we had the boss of the man claiming it was a hoax, but nothing from the witness himself. And, no reference to it in the Bluebook files, though many of the hoaxes perpetrated at that time had found their way into the files. Roswell had been labeled as a balloon in the newspapers and there was no reference to it either. That could mean something.

If it hadn't been for Roswell, I would have let the investigation stop right there. An admission of a hoax should have ended it, but Roswell showed just how quickly the Air Force could swing into action plugging the leaks. Within hours, the vast public relations machinery had been started and newspapers that hadn't carried a thing about the Roswell crash were telling readers that the crash was not a flying disc but a weather balloon.

It seemed to be time to see if any of the major UFO investigative centers, The UFO Archives, or the Center for UFO Studies had any idea about the Montana crash. It could be that other researchers, seeing the July 8 story, had stopped looking at that point.

I made calls to various contacts and had little luck tracking them down. Don Schmitt was the first to call me back. We talked about many things. Finally I asked him if he'd heard anything about a crash in Montana in 1947.

"No. Not in Montana. Rumors of one in a western state, it might have been Montana, but nothing specific."

I told him a little more and he said that he hadn't heard of it. I pointed out that one of the articles claimed that the case was a hoax, but given the way the Air Force had moved to

hide the Roswell story, anything was possible. The fact that
neither Roswell nor Montana had a mention in the Bluebook
files was important. Schmitt suggested that I contact Len
Stringfield, who had put together a comprehensive list of
possible crashes and retrievals. He might have something.

Stringfield was unaware of a crash in Montana. I gave him
the details and it rang no bells. He did mention that he had
once talked to an Air Force officer who said that he had been
involved in a retrieval in a western state.

"As opposed to southwestern?" I asked.

"He said western. It might have been Montana."

We talked about the Montana case, but he knew nothing
about it. Not that he thought it strange. Given the time and
what was happening, it made sense they could bury it. I told
him that given the descriptions I had heard and that the article
found by Warren Smith said it came apart in the prop wash
of the plane, I thought it was probably a hoax. That was
reinforced by Archer's statement the next day.

After I hung up, I read through the article again. Baird,
flying the plane, was on a photographic mission for a government agency. I looked at that and said, "Oops." I hadn't
noticed the comment that Baird had been working for a government agency.

I remembered that the government had moved within hours
to bury the Roswell story. Now I had a statement from Baird's
boss saying that it was a hoax. I had a statement that Baird
was in the area working for a government agency. And I
knew, from reading the papers around July 7, that ground
and air searches were being conducted to search for and to
photograph the discs. *The New York Times* talked about five
planes from the Oregon National Guard cruising over the
Cascade Mountains. Other planes were standing by, as far
south as Muroc Army Air Field in California.

And I had the story of a P-38 working for a government
agency, filled with photographic equipment, cruising over the
Tobacco Root Mountains in Montana. I had air searches in-
stituted to look for the discs. But I also had a boss telling
reporters that it was all a hoax. Not Baird himself, but the
boss.

The next move was to find Baird or Archer. With only

their names to go on, it seemed to be a task that would be next to impossible, especially because I was assuming they were from L.A. and the information was forty years old. But given the fact that there was a government agency involved, it was important to pursue it further. Directory assistance couldn't help. Too much time had passed, and there was no reason to assume that either man still lived in L.A.

I went back to the phone and tried the newspaper libraries again. I finally managed to get through to the *Los Angeles Herald-Examiner*, told them what I wanted, and Jamie McInnis asked me to call back in an hour so that she would have some time to make a search. When I did, she said she had been busy, but if I would give her my address, she would send along anything she found. That seemed to be the way to go, so I agreed.

While I waited for that, I made another trip to the University of Iowa to search for more on the Montana crash. I took the *Time* article, which referred to a story in *The Saturday Evening Post*, and went to work. In minutes I learned that Walter Winchell, who was the source of the quote, was talking about a short story that appeared on April 5, 1947. "Note on Danger B" was written by Gerald Kersh. Winchell had been quoting the last paragraph of the story, a work of fiction, that contained the mention of the crash. It was a coincidence that the crash took place in Montana and that was all. It had nothing to do with Baird's story of the flying discs.

I learned one other interesting fact. Searching through the *Guide to Periodic Literature*, I found that they didn't put the references to UFOs under flying discs or flying saucers, but under illusions and hallucinations. Some unidentified editor had decided that the stories were nothing more than that. It is no wonder that half the public laughs when you mention flying saucers to them.

The *Herald-Examiner* material arrived a couple of days after I talked to McInnis and the article there did contain more information. Baird was accompanied on the photographic mission by George Suttin. Suttin claimed that he didn't think of his camera until after the objects had disappeared. That bothered me. I could see a normal person, driving along and confronted by spacecraft from another world, being so excited and so stunned that the camera would be forgotten. But Suttin was a professional photographer and it seemed hard to believe that a man on a photographic mission would forget to take pictures.

The *Herald-Examiner* provided one other clue. Both men worked for Fairchild Photogrammetrics Engineers Company. With all that information, I should be able to learn a little more about it.

Directory assistance in L.A. had a listing for Fairchild Publications but nothing for Fairchild Photogrammetrics Engineers Company. I hoped the publisher was the company I wanted with a new name. No such luck. I was running into dead end after dead end.

The thing was, I felt that the case, given what I knew about it now, would turn out to be a hoax. The description of the prop wash tearing apart the disc worried me. Something that could be ripped apart by the prop wash of an aircraft, no matter how turbulent that prop wash might be, certainly wouldn't be able to withstand the rigors of spaceflight. And even if it was only a scout ship, sent out into the atmosphere but not traveling through space, it still didn't help. It was still too flimsy.

Glen Boettcher, a friend, made a recent trip to L.A. While there, he did some research for me. Like me, he was unable to find any of the men listed in the news story, but that wasn't surprising. Our best hope was for him to find the Fairchild Photogrammetrics Engineers Company. Using old phone books, he located them in one year, but the next they were gone, either bankrupt or sold to another firm. Tax records might have told us something, but Glen didn't have time to search through the thousands of documents necessary to learn the answer. He did what he could and called the old number for Fairchild. It was now a McDonald's.

Still, I had three names and I might be able to do something with them. However, the deadline for this was pressing. As it stands now, I have to assume that the case is a hoax, started by a bored pilot on a long flight and suggested by the stories of flying discs that had filled the papers for the days that preceded his report. The reasons for believing this are the admission of a hoax, the suggested flimsy nature of the craft, and the fact that no one had written much about this case after the admission of a hoax. But with Roswell in the back of my mind, I'll continue the search. Maybe we'll find a way of tracing the men or the company and learning something about it. That worked recently in Las Vegas. Until then, the case remains open.

October 27, 1988: Warren Smith

Warren Smith is a researcher and a writer who has been chasing the UFO phenomenon for over twenty years. He was the first researcher on several major cases, and has had his work published in all the magazines devoted to UFOs over the years. He has written books on the subject, and as Eric Norman, wrote about the hollow Earth theory. He is always interesting, and his knowledge of the subject is, at times, astounding.

(Q) What have you done in relation to your own personal investigations of UFOs?

(A) Well, I used to chase the things for various magazines, newspapers, and did several books on the subject. I was always fascinated by the entire field of UFOs. I believe in UFOs. I don't know where they come from so I keep an open mind on that at all times. I really don't have all the answers because there have been so many cover-ups and things of that nature that I think . . . we don't know what is right on these objects, which story to believe and that sort of thing. There could, for example, be abductions and abduction stories set up to provide a cover-up of something else.

(Q) Okay, you've talked about cover-ups. Could you elaborate on that? Was Project Bluebook a cover-up?

(A) I think Project Bluebook was probably a cover-up of sorts. I don't see it as an absolute cover-up. I think it was a place where it defused the situation and sort of allowed the Air Force, the government, or whatever it was, to kind of get these reports in, and just sort of hold these people down. It was sort of a reporting center.

Yeah, it was a cover-up to a certain extent, I think. They sure as hell weren't telling everything they know back then.

(Q) If I wanted to prove cover-ups took place, where would I look for the information?

(A) Probably the report of the Condon Committee would be a good starting point [see 1969: The Condon Committee]. And the article John Fuller did in Look magazine [1968]. That's, I guess, the biggest cover-up we've had in the field.

(Q) The article suggests the Condon Committee was a cover-up?

(A) Yes. Absolutely. In fact, I had that damn story before anyone and I wanted to write it. Brad [Steiger] and I discussed it and he decided I should hold off on it and then John Fuller came out with it.

(Q) What did you have?

(A) A weird thing. A radio reporter here in town [Clinton, Iowa] had interviewed a fellow who was with the government and who had just come from Colorado. During the course of the conversation that night, the guy starts talking about what a cover-up it is. He was willing to go on the record and I didn't follow through on the story.

I had seen Condon at a UFO meeting in New York City. This was when the committee was there. The guy [Condon] was getting a real charge out of it because he would associate with what I call the weirdos. The people with absolutely weird stories. The lady with the hat from Venus, that type of thing. Condon was always happy to pose with her. He didn't seem to be interested in anything but to be photographed with the weirdest people. Those are the pictures that showed up in the New York papers.

(Q) You say it was a cover-up. Do you know why?

(A) One theory of mine has always been that these are vehicles that are interconnected to the U.S. Government. They'd be a good secret weapon.

The second reason is that the government knows what they are and they're scared to death to tell us.

Or, maybe they don't know and they don't want the general public to know that they don't know.

(Q) We've been talking about cover-ups. Have you run across any in your research?

(A) Not too often. With the Schirmer case—that's the patrolman from Nebraska who was involved with UFOs—I came very close, I guess. I did the book on that. I had everything—photographs, drawings, and interviews—finished the manuscript and it never got published.

I don't know if that was a cover-up because that was about the time sales of UFO books had begun to slacken off. Economics might have killed it.

But Schirmer, he had some experiences with cover-ups. People following him, things of that nature.

(Q) Was there anything real unusual about his case?

(A) Well, he was one of the first to talk about being aboard a UFO that landed in Ashland, Nebraska.

(Q) So he had total recall without hypnotic regression?

(A) Pretty much at first. But there was missing time. So Bill Williams, a hypnotist from New Hampshire, came out and we met in Des Moines. One of the suggestions he gave Herb [Schirmer] under hypnosis was that he could talk about this in the future.

So, there is a cover-up on these abduction stories from the other side. You might see the creatures have their own cover-up going.

And they left the feeling with him that they would all meet again. In fact, he said when he was moving off the ship that one of them reached up and put his hand on Herb's shoulder and said something in his language that Herb didn't understand. He gripped Herb on the shoulder as if to say we will meet again.

Virtually all Herb knew up until hypnosis was that he'd seen a UFO. He reported it in his police logbook.

(Q) Was he examined while on the craft?

(A) No. But the thing with Herb that was kind of fascinating was that after this happened in Ashland . . . It was late at night. It happened in a field up off the highway and he'd shot [driven] up into that field before he really realized what he was doing. He saw lights up there and being a good Nebraska farm boy, knew something was going on up there that shouldn't be.

So he shot up in there and the car engine died and the lights went dead. He saw these two guys walking toward the cruiser. He was getting panicked. They placed a little device right behind his ear. He became very docile after that. They said they were not there to harm him. They invited him on board.

But the thing that fascinated me was the religious zeal that came about after this experience. And it always left me wondering what they were doing in that field and why they picked him.

(Q) You said that he had some additional problems with government people.

(A) They were government people. At least Herb thought they were government people. He lost a couple of jobs. For one thing, after you've seen a UFO you really don't have the credibility to be a police officer.

He went to work for a packing company and some people came around. He didn't know who they were but figured they were government. They said to his employer, "Say you know this was the guy who saw the UFO. He's really not very stable. Do you really think you should have him working around here?"

So he wasn't working there very long. And he lost a couple of other jobs like that.

Now what was fascinating, as I said—and I got on the case early—was the missionary zeal that he got when he figured out this is what happened—he wanted to get out on the lecture circuit. He wanted to get out and tell everyone about this. To watch that—watch that evolution and see how it all came about was fascinating.

(Q) Didn't you have some trouble with the CIA at one time?

(A) I don't know who it was. It was up in Madison, Wisconsin. I was investigating a sighting and a farmer gave me a piece of metal from a UFO. Like a damn fool, I went about town asking people if they'd ever seen anything like it.

(Q) Let's back up for a moment. He gave you a piece of metal? Where did he get it?

(A) Supposedly this thing, this UFO had been spotted, hovering about an interstate interchange and had shot off some sparks. And what some call slag. He'd picked it up after seeing the UFO.

Let's see. Mrs. Marie Knipper, a lady in her late fifties, her friend, and two teenage girls were driving from Janesville [Wisconsin] to Stoughton and the UFO appeared over the interstate highway. It buzzed their car and followed them all the way to Stoughton and left the interstate when they turned off it. This thing kind of stopped and hung above the interchange. That's where the sparks and the slag supposedly came from. The thing knocked off the slag and followed them some more. She had to go in a roundabout way to get to her house. Her route looked like a giant "C" so that she could catch the bridges. This thing went straight ahead and just kind of hovered over her house.

One of the things I could never figure out was on the night of the sighting, a fellow who lived fifty miles away had driven over and saw the UFO. He considered himself to be a master mentalist and he'd "known" there was going to be something exciting going on at her house that night. He knew her slightly . . .

(Q) He just showed up.

(A) He just showed up.

(Q) So you got there and you picked up the metal, or the farmer picked up the metal . . .

(A) And he gave me a piece of it and I wandered around like a damned fool with it. This area was a hotbed of UFO activity at the time. I had talked with lots of people who'd seen all kinds of things.

I wasn't even thinking that anyone was on my tail. I asked around, showed the metal to several people, and asked if they knew what it was. It looked like part of an aluminum beer can or pop can that had been melted down. To this day I can't tell you what it might have been or what it was.

But in the process of following this case, I started being followed. How that came about, how I learned about it, is unusual. I was staying at the Holiday Inn there in Madison.

One of the maintenance men stopped by my room one morning and says, "You know there are some guys following you?"

I asked, "What are you talking about?"

He says, "They're over in the service station and when you go they go."

That was the tip that got me off on that thing. Later I began to get paranoid as people will do when they're out on these cases. So, I took this piece of metal, tied it to a piece of string, took the back off the television set, and hung it up there.

The maintenance men there were pretty good and they were alerting me that my room was being searched whenever I was gone. And then I began to play cat and mouse with these people. But then, one night I came back and two guys were sitting in my room. They wanted the piece of metal and didn't identify themselves. Whatever I wanted to say they were, that's what they were.

(Q) If you said they were CIA, they were CIA . . .

(A) They were CIA or if it would make me happier if they were FBI, then they were FBI. Anything that I wanted.

(Q) Did you surrender the metal to them?

(A) I sure as hell did. They told me to remember who I was and remember my family and I could consider that to be a threat. I thought about it and I gave them the metal.

(Q) And you have no idea who these guys were?

(A) Well, I got a license plate number off their car. That much I did get. But then you run into the fact that the number has not been issued. Of course a little further investigation in Illinois and you discover that was one of the numbers issued to government agencies.

(Q) So it was a government agency of some kind?

(A) Of some kind. They just block off a certain number of license plates for the use of the FBI in stakeouts and stuff like that.

(Q) Is that your only run-in like that?

(A) Primarily. I never felt as threatened as I did up there. That was really a scary situation. To this day I don't have a hell of a lot of answers about it.

(Q) Any evidence that cases didn't go to Bluebook?

(A) All I know for sure is that the CIA kept damned good track of foreign sightings because at one time I was getting most of their foreign sightings. They were using an English language translation firm up in Massachusetts. I had been told back then that they had computers to do that. But any little incident about a UFO in a foreign language newspaper was then translated for the CIA.

(Q) They were looking specifically for UFO items?

(A) This is all they did.

(Q) Did you ever come up with a code name for a secret project?

(A) No, not really. Now I started out with NICAP. Now there was a cover-up if I ever saw one.

(Q) Are you suggesting that NICAP was a conduit into the CIA or something like that?

(A) Yeah, yeah. I had tried to get along with NICAP. When I first started writing I needed help and thought there's a great source of sightings. And these people turned me off.

(Q) So you're suggesting that NICAP may have been a conduit into the government . . .

(A) Oh yes.

(Q) Is there a reason you believe this?

(A) Admiral Hillenkoetter for one. The fact that Major Donald Keyhoe was their main man.

(Q) Wasn't he kind of at war with the Pentagon?

(A) I think that was a put-up. I don't think a retired major is ever going to get into a war with the Pentagon. It was a beautiful little thing they did. All the sightings ended up with NICAP.

(Q) You suspect a cover-up. You're familiar with the Roswell case. Did you ever get any rumblings of something like that?

(A) This was after that. This was 1950 and I was working on the Lorain [Ohio] *Journal*. There was a fellow employee there whose wife was spending some time at a dude ranch or something down in Texas because she had some kind of illness. I didn't pay too much attention but every day at noon this fellow would read me the letter from his wife.

One day it got interesting. She was talking about "last

night, everyone was excited here at the ranch.'' There was a light in the sky. I don't remember if she said fire or not. It was like an object coming down. It could have been an airliner or an airplane or shooting star or something like that.

She said, ''Tomorrow morning the ranch boss and some of the hands are going out there. They think it landed over there in Mexico. They're going to go down and check it out.''

The next day the letter said they'd gone out and they'd come back and it was, she called it, a flying disc. It had crashed and there were some smaller than normal ''men'' in spacesuits. They apparently were not from this planet.

After that the letters got back to normal. About that time I got a job on the Las Vegas *Review-Journal* and I left Ohio and never thought much about it.

(Q) The obvious question is, do we have a name?

(A) No. I can't remember the man's name. I've thought about calling the paper to see if there is an old-timer there who might remember the man's name.

(Q) Is that the only story you've come across that suggests a crashed disc?

(A) I've talked to people who've been out to Wright Field and they've got great stories about those hangars out there. All kinds of good stories that we can't verify.

(Q) Can we name names? (Author's note: He did, but then decided that the witnesses, at least one of whom still worked for the government, might lose their jobs. The names have been deleted at Smith's request.)

(Q) To sum up then, in your opinion, the government has known, virtually from the beginning, what was going on— they have participated, and this is documented through the Robertson Panel and everything else, in a cover-up, they have actively debunked, ridiculed sightings . . .

(A) Yes, I think that's all fair and accurate. I ran into it myself in Madison. Herb Schirmer was harassed and lost his jobs, witnesses have been intimidated, and evidence has been stolen. Herb showed what happened to people who report UFOs. I think that we've seen enough over the years to prove the government is hiding something from us. Roswell is documented. Something came down there. It went into the intelligence system and the case disappeared then for forty years. I don't think we're going to get all the answers until the government decides it's time for us to have them.

(Q) Thank you.

November 19, 1988: The Last Chapter

In the years that the research took to complete this work, I changed my mind about the reality of the phenomenon several times. There were people who told me that I would eventually reject the extraterrestrial hypothesis and that I would move to a psyshic solution or a time travel solution or one of the others that have been offered. Instead, I rejected the idea that UFOs were spacecraft in favor of the idea that UFOs were no more than misidentifications.

Now, after years of studying the whole field, I've come back to the extraterrestrial hypothesis. The reasons are many and varied, but they are reasons developed through my own research and not that of others.

Take, for example, Project Bluebook. Looked at as a whole, one where no proof positive ever showed up, the suggestion would be that there are no flying saucers. If the Air Force, in over twenty years of investigation, couldn't find the evidence, then it probably just didn't exist.

But my investigations showed me that there was another, secret investigation—one classified higher than Bluebook. That's no longer speculation. It's fact.

The first evidence of it is the lack of a report about Roswell in the Bluebook files. An extremely clever move would have been to leave the balloon answer in the files, but someone removed all references to Roswell. There are dozens of cases from June to July 1947 in the files, and we know that Air Force (Army) Intelligence had the case. Marcel was from the intelligence section and the debris was sent to Wright Field. It was in the system, but it fell out. No references at all.

The second evidence is the Kinross case. From talking to Air Force officers, I know reports were filed from that time frame. I even know the details of some of them, but they never got to Bluebook. The reports were filed, they could have been classified in accordance to AFR (Air Force Regulation) 200–2, and they would have been safeguarded. The loss of a classified document, regardless of the subject, is not something that would have been taken lightly. Even with that, those reports and all references to them are missing.

The third evidence is the gun camera films. We know they were taken. Don Schmitt told me he knew of sixteen, I know of nineteen. There were references to them in Bluebook, but the files were not there. The references were veiled, mere mentions of gun camera footage inside of reports and other documents, but no case files and no analysis of them. More evidence that went somewhere but not to Bluebook.

The question becomes, then, why would the Air force cover it all up? People have suggested they were trying to avoid a panic. If the people knew what was in the files, there would be chaos.

I was never happy with that answer. Too much had happened in the years after the first sightings in 1947. People were used to the idea and there were, literally, dozens of movies from Hollywood that dealt with the subject. Panic was not a satisfactory answer.

Then came the story of the Roswell crash.

For years I rejected the idea of crashed saucers and dead aliens. The main reason was a lack of proof, but there was also the Scully book that seemed to underscore the ridiculous nature of the belief. Besides, we were talking about a technology that had built craft to cross interstellar space. It didn't seem likely they would screw up and crash.

There had been Robert Carr, but he had talked of sources he couldn't name. His accounts seemed to be a rehash of the Scully report that almost everyone accepted as a hoax. Without more and better proof there was no reason to accept any of the reports. And then came Roswell.

The reasons for accepting it are many and varied. First and foremost is the fact that the names are named. There is Jesse Marcel, William Brazel, his son, and a dozen others with firsthand knowledge. It is not another Robert Carr with unknown sources and possible locations. We know it was Roswell and we know the names of the participants.

And, of course, there is the confirmation from a source I can't impeach. In 1976, while researching UFO landing trace cases, I talked to an Air Force NCO who had told me he had faked UFO sighting solutions on orders that came from the Pentagon. This was done so that everyone would believe that the sighting was of a weather balloon.

I asked if he did it often and he said that he'd only done it once. I asked him where he'd taken it and he said, "Roswell."

In 1976, when I heard the story, I didn't think much of it. It was just another example of the Air Force and the government trying to hide the truth from the public. But then the Roswell story came out and I realized that the NCO was talking about taking his balloon to Roswell to explain the wreckage found there.

He only did it once, but then, he only had to do it once.

And now the answer for why they would want to cover it up becomes obvious. In July 1947, they had the answer. They knew exactly what the UFOs were and they didn't want anyone to even suspect they had wreckage. The cover-up was designed to protect that knowledge.

If I was to accept one crash, why not others. There was the Majestic Twelve paper that talked of a second crash on the Texas-Mexican border. That document is questioned, and rightly so. But if it is authentic, it is dynamite.

But there is no proof that it is authentic.

Again, talking to Warren Smith, he told me of a fellow in Lorain, Ohio, whose wife was writing him letters. Smith was there, as a young man, and the older gentleman insisted on reading the letters to him. Smith listened but didn't think anything of them. In 1950 he wasn't interested in UFOs, and didn't care about a possible crash.

But he did remember some of the details. He remembered

about the crash, the little, charred bodies, and the location —somewhere to the west of Laredo. An interesting story until the briefing paper surfaces and suddenly that story becomes more important. Smith and I begin the search for the man and his wife to interview them again.

So, we have a briefing paper that might be a hoax. We have letters that might be a hoax. We have two groups of people who don't know each other talking about the same incident. Could two separate groups invent the same story? Sure. Is it likely? Not really. The conclusion? The briefing paper is probably authentic and in that case, the United States has, at least, two alien spacecraft.

Now I take a look at some of the other reports: films of UFOs that the government labeled as birds—not because the film looked like it was of birds, but because an answer had to be found and found quickly—more evidence of the cover-up.

I look at the Brooksville, Florida, case. The Air Force took the evidence but didn't return the same sheets of paper that they took away. More proof there was a cover-up.

So, now I accept the idea that there are alien spacecraft flying through our atmosphere. I accept the nuts-and-bolts answer because it was nuts and bolts that were discovered at Roswell. I think that the Air Force, the government, the Majestic Twelve or whatever the committee name was knew from July 7, 1947, knew what was going on and conspired to keep the general public from learning the truth. I think the evidence shows this. I think it proves it.

And, if you look at the history of the UFO investigations, by adding Roswell to the equation, the whole thing makes sense. The slipshod investigations, the answers that were ridiculous, the denial, and the lies, all make sense. They knew. They knew all along.

UFO research has now moved out of the field. Another story of a daylight disc is not going to help us. Another report of nocturnal lights means nothing. Even the hardcore skeptic has to admit that something is going on. It's the interpretation of the facts that is open to question. Philip Klass will admit there is something going on, but he believes it's a result of hoaxes and misidentifications. I now believe that Phil Klass, who honestly believes he knows the truth, is wrong. UFOs, meaning spacecraft, do exist.

So, now we're out of the field and we're into the archives. We're in a paper chase to learn what the government has known since 1947. We file Freedom of Information requests, we chase documents, and we fight over authenticity. The Majestic Twelve briefing paper is being examined and compared with other documents of the time. The typeface of the typewriter is being researched. Experts are comparing it to other documents written by Admiral Hillenkoetter. The fight there continues.

And we're in darkened rooms while men and women recount their experiences on board alien craft—not the friendly aliens of *Close Encounters of the Third Kind*, but not the hostile aliens of *Earth vs. the Flying Saucers* either. We're learning of alien scientists who treat people like our scientists treat laboratory animals. They don't seem to recognize our intelligence. They're gathering their information and anything they have to do to gather it is fine.

The new trend seems to be repeat abductions, as if our people have been banded in the same way that we band animals. The progress is monitored, the people periodically taken out of the environment to be examined again, and then sent back again.

Our job is to talk to these people and gather information about their experiences. How unfair that sounds. First they have to put up with the aliens intruding in their lives and then have to put up with researchers trying to learn everything they can about the experience.

But that is where the research is—in the homes of victims and in the libraries where the documents lie. No longer are we chasing the lights in the skies, talking to the witnesses of those lights. We're chasing the men and women who have the inside knowledge. We're chasing the reports and memos and documents and testimony from those people. Ten years ago, if you had suggested that the answers to the questions would be found inside, in libraries and archives and darkened rooms, I would have laughed at you, sure that the answers would be found in the burned areas on the ground, or the films being taken. Now, today, I'm convinced that the answers have already been learned by a select group of people. The answers to the puzzle exist, here on Earth, and it's going to be someone in an archive who's going to find them.

That's an ironic thing. The answers to whether there is life on other planets is not going to be found in the field or by studying astronomy. The answer is going to be found in a library—just where you've always been told to go to find the answers to the difficult questions.

What to Do if You Sight an Unidentified Flying Object

One of the most-asked questions is where can I report my UFO sighting? The U.S. Air Force recommends calling a local university. The local police will sometimes investigate, but then the information is filed and forgotten. If there is a local UFO organization, they might offer a few suggestions. The problem with all this is that your sighting is lost in the shuffle of paperwork. Ironically, it could be the one sighting that all researchers are waiting for.

So, if you see an unidentified flying object, the best way to report it is:

The J. Allen Hynek Center for UFO Studies
2457 West Peterson Avenue
Chicago, IL 60659

Or phone twenty-four hours a day

(312) 271-3611

The repository for much of the information used in the completion of this work was:

THE UFO ARCHIVES
P.O. Box 264
Marion, IA 52302

A wide variety of Special Reports are available from The UFO Archives for a small fee.

Sources

The following is a partial list of the sources used in the preparation of *The UFO Casebook*:

June 24, 1947: Kenneth Arnold:

Various accounts including CEDAR RAPIDS GAZETTE in June 1947, THE REPORT ON UNIDENTIFIED FLYING OBJECTS by Edward Ruppelt, and the Project Bluebook files.

July 2, 1947: Roswell, New Mexico

Personal interviews with Bill Brazel, Don Schmitt, Ralph Heick, and other local residents, Len Stringfield, Frank Joyce, THE ROSWELL INCIDENT by Charles Berlitz and Bill Moore, and various newspaper accounts including THE RO-SWELL RECORD, LA HERALD-EXPRESS, DES MOINES REGISTER, FORT WORTH STAR-TELE-GRAPH, CEDAR RAPIDS GAZETTE, LAS VEGAS RE-VIEW JOURNAL, ALBUQUERQUE JOURNAL

July 31, 1947: Maury Island

Official Project Bluebook Files, Kenneth Arnold, and various newspapers from the period.

September 24, 1947: The Majestic Twelve

Interviews with Don Schmitt, the MUFON Symposium, and Philip Klass.

January 1948: The Mantell Case

Official Project Bluebook Files.

September 1948: Estimate of the Situation

THE REPORT ON UNIDENTIFIED FLYING OBJECTS, Donald E. Keyhoe, and a personal interview conducted with an Air Force colonel.

November 1948: Project Twinkle

C. C. Wylie, University of Iowa, James A. van Allen, Official Project Bluebook files, Institute of Meteoritics, University of New Mexico.

1948: The UFO Crashes Begin

The DENVER POST, TRUE magazine, Frank Edwards, Donald E. Keyhoe, Jim Lorenzen, Coral Lorenzen, Bill Brazel, OFFICIAL UFO, the UFO REPORT, Len Stringfield, the ROCKY MOUNTAIN NEWS, the APRO BULLETIN, the UFO ENCYCLOPEDIA, and Status Report No. 3.

August 1950: The Great Falls Movie

Official Project Bluebook Files, the Condon Committee Report, RML Baker, and APRO.

December 6, 1950: El Indio, Mexico

Warren Smith, the MJ-12 report, and Richard Henry, and personal interviews conducted with two sources.

August 1951: The Lubbock Lights

Official Project Bluebook Files and interviews conducted with a number of witnesses.

July 2, 1952: The Tremonton Movie

Delbert C. Newhouse, official Project Bluebook Files, the Condon Committee Report, RML Baker, and APRO.

July 1952: The Washington Nationals

Official Project Bluebook Files, CEDAR RAPIDS GAZETTE, WASHINGTON POST, and various Air Force officers including Captains David Johnson and William Jones, and personal interviews with seven others.

January 1953: The Robertson Panel

Official Project Bluebook Files, the Condon Committee report, and J. Allen Hynek.

November 23, 1953: The Kinross Case

Donald E. Keyhoe, the Project Bluebook Files, Lieutenant Colonel Robert Towns.

July 4, 1953: Walesville, New York

Donald E. Keyhoe, Coral Lorenzen, J. Allen Hynek, and *The* NEW YORK TIMES.

1955: The Gun Camera Films

ABOVE TOP SECRET by Tim Good, J. Allen Hynek, Chester Lytle, official Project Bluebook Files, and four Air Force officers who requested their names be withheld.

April 1956: The Allende Letters

Sidney Sherby, Carlos Allende, Jim Lorenzen, Donald E. Keyhoe, Brad Steiger, Joan Whitenhour, OFFICIAL UFO, Dade County Coroner, correspondance of Morris K. Jessup, and Bernard O'Connor.

September 12, 1957: Ubatuba, Brazil

Jim and Coral Lorenzen, Olavo Fontes, Condon Committee report, the APRO BULLETIN, and official Air Force records including the Project Bluebook Files.

October 1957: Antonio Villas-Boas

Coral Lorenzen, Olavo Fontes, and the APRO BULLETIN.

November 1957: Levelland, Texas

Official Project Bluebook Files, Coral Lorenzen, various newspapers from the period, and personal interviews conducted with a number of the witnesses.

April 24, 1964: Socorro, New Mexico

Official Project Bluebook Files, J. Allen Hynek, Don Schmitt, and Philip Klass.

September 4, 1964: Glassboro, New Jersey

Official Project Bluebook Files, Donald E. Keyhoe, and Coral Lorenzen.

March 2, 1965: Brooksville, Florida

Coral Lorenzen, John Reeves, and the local sheriff's department.

June 24, 1967: Austin, Texas

Official Project Bluebook Files.

July 10, 1967: Meridian, Mississippi

Official Project Bluebook Files.

January 17, 1969: Crittenden, Virginia

Official Project Bluebook Files.

1969: The Condon Committee

Warren Smith, Edward U. Condon, J. Allen Hynek, Project
Bluebook Files, and the final report from the Condon Committee.

October 1973: The UFO Occupants

Charles Hickson, Pat Roach, James Harder, Susan Ramstead,
Leigh Proctor, Coral Lorenzen, the APRO BULLETIN, various newspapers from October 1957, and a number of witnesses who asked their names be withheld.

February 1975: The Minnesota Mutilations

Michael J. Douglas, Bill Pitts, Mike Rogers, Philip Klass,
Coral Lorenzen, APRO BULLETIN, Daryl Evans, George
A. Yarnell, Colorado Bureau of Investigation, DENVER
POST, CEDAR RAPIDS GAZETTE, Don Stickle, Jeff
Davis, Percy Stitch, and the ROCKY MOUNTAIN NEWS.

January 1976: Maxwell Air Force Base

Official Project Bluebook Files.

February 1977: Pineville, Missouri

Monty Skelton, Carl Armstrong, Lawrence McCool, Ivan
Kanable, Evelyn and Virgil Hottenger, Ron Cargile, Carl
Smith, Edward Fletcher, June Hilton, and Kansas City Center
(FAA radar facility).

April 1981: Van Allen on Tunguska

James A. Van Allen.

June 1983: Susan Ramstead

Susan Ramstead.

June 12, 1988: Don Schmitt

Don Schmitt.

October 1988: The Montana Crash

Warren Smith, Jamie McInnes, *Los Angeles Herald-Examiner*, CEDAR RAPIDS GAZETTE, DES MOINES REGISTER, Glen Boettcher, TIME, and Len Stringfield.

October 27, 1988: Warren Smith

Warren Smith.

Note: In many cases the witnesses asked that their names not be used in conjunction with UFO stories. Some of them feared ridicule, some of them wanted to tell their stories and not be deluged with inquiries about the subject, and others feared losing military and government pensions. It must be noted that Bill Brazel, for example, told me that people from all over the country have called him, told him what he had seen, what he hadn't seen, or called him a liar. Some witnesses, fearing, with justification, this kind of harassment, asked that I withhold their names. Reluctantly, I agreed, feeling the information was important no matter what the restrictions on it.

Index

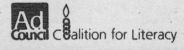